THE ROOKIE AGENT

A Di9 Novel

M.K. Burns

For my wife and son.

CHAPTER 1

Saturday, July 4th, 2026

Philadelphia

Today is supposed to be a hot one. At 8:00 in the morning it is already seventy-eight degrees and muggy. For most people in the United States that sounds like an amazing day for a barbecue to celebrate the holiday. For Bryce Stone it is just hot and he won't need any extra help sweating.

He paces anxiously inside his room at the Ritz-Carlton while waiting for his brother. It has been one week since he started working at Di9 and he has already been chosen to go on assignment. Nobody wants to fail, but his level of uncertainty after just one week on the job makes the mind wander.

He goes over the details of the assignment in his head while he's waiting. The mental checklist he has would be too much for almost anyone else, but his mind is not like most. His photographic memory helps him remember things that others would forget.

It's 8:05, already five minutes past the time he was supposed to leave. Being late on your first assignment is not a good look for anyone, let alone someone who's only been there for a week.

Sitting on the bed he takes out his phone to look at its background photo. In the picture his wife, Kayla, is holding their son on her lap as they sit on the couch. She is smiling and looking at their son, Michael, as he laughs hysterically. The picture is from almost a year ago when he was still five years old, and Bryce can't remember for the life of him what Michael was laughing at, but it always calms his nerves and makes him smile.

Suddenly he remembers the cheese danish he bought from the restaurant last night. He walks over, grabs it out of the fridge, and brings it back to the bed.

Knock Knock Knock

Bryce walks over and opens the door still holding his danish in his hand. Confused, the first thing he sees after opening the door is himself.

"I got you this, I just wanted to let you see how bad you look with that beard. You need to shave; you look homeless. At least trim it and keep it nice." The man says, holding a mirror up in his face.

Refusing to look away, he reaches down to take his watch off and holds it up, "I got you something too, Travis. It's called a watch. Do you want me to teach you how to read one?" He responds.

Travis slowly lowers the mirror to look at his brother, then down, and back up at him. Then like a flash he smacks the danish right out of Bryce's hand. It thuds against the wall and falls face down on the floor.

"Really?" He asks with his hands out in disbelief.

"What, I thought I was doing you a favor." Travis says, patting him on the stomach.

"I was just about to eat that."

"You still can."

They stand still and silent for a few seconds as they stare at each other.

"You know, you're lucky you're my brother. I'm still bigger than you even though you're older. I love my danishes and pastries, if anyone else did that they would be lying on the floor next to it." Bryce says, peeved.

"Sounds like you need a drink to take the edge off, want me to buy you a shot at the bar before we go?"

"No thanks, I don't drink."

"Still? Is that because of Dad?"

"Yup, I saw what the drinking did to him. I'm not going to let the same thing happen to me."

"Let's go, we're running late." Travis says, changing the subject.

"Do you think? You couldn't even be on

time for my first assignment? You know I'm nervous; I threw up right before you got here." Bryce says, reaching down to grab his bag before making his way out of his room.

"Oh, by the way, you're only a half inch taller than me." Travis states.

"Yeah, but standing six feet tall sounds so much bigger than five feet, eleven and a half inches, don't you think?"

They walk in silence down the hall towards the elevator. In a matter of seconds their mood changes from brotherly banter to unprecedented focus thinking of the tasks they need to complete.

It isn't very often the President of the United States makes a speech out in the open with mass crowds around him, but today is different. Today is the 250th birthday of the United States of America. And what better place to give a speech than the City of Brotherly Love where the Declaration of Independence was signed?

It takes months to plan something like this. Streets need to be closed down, there has to be a plan for public transportation, and requires the collaboration of protective agencies to keep people safe.

As prepared as Di9 might think they are, there is always a lingering thought that something could still happen. Which is why they want their Agents on the scene.

Seven hours and forty-five minutes remain until the President speaks when Bryce and Travis get in their car. The engine idles while both men buckle up before putting the car in gear and heading on their way.

"Great, it's already 8:15. We were supposed to leave fifteen minutes ago." Bryce says.

"Take it easy, we'll have plenty of time to get ready. I'm telling you the last two hours before the speech are always so boring. You'll wish we would've gotten to work even later."

"That's easy for you to say, you're the top Agent. I'm just a new analyst."

"To be honest with you, I have no idea why any of us are here."

"What do you mean?" Bryce asks.

"I just think it's a waste of time for us. The Secret Service and the FBI are both going to be there."

"Why do you think we are here then? There haven't been any threats to the President that I'm aware of."

"That's the thing that makes it weird. Anywhere the President goes there are always multiple threats. Usually it is nothing more than someone just running their mouth. But for today's speech there was nothing, not one threat."

"Well that's a good thing, isn't it?"

"Maybe, maybe not. 99.9 percent of the

time a threat never comes to fruition. It's the time when there is no threat that is most dangerous. I mean what kind of threat is it if you tell the opposition you're coming?" Travis asks.

"Do you think something is going to happen?" Bryce asks curiously, seeing a look on Travis's face that he hasn't seen in a long time.

"I couldn't tell you, Washington is playing a hunch. He's very good at listening to the data we bring in and the information we receive from the dark web, but he's excellent in listening to his gut."

"Which is why you think we're here today?"

"Yup. Like I said, you have two agencies already here with the President. This isn't something we normally do either, but Washington wanted six Agents there today along with a bunch of you desk sitters."

"Should we be scared? Are you scared?"

"I'm never scared, but I am a bit nervous to be honest and I never feel that way. I wouldn't worry though, I'm sure everything will go exactly as planned." Travis says with a wink.

"Well let's hope so. I'd hate for something to happen at all let alone when we are on watch."

Bryce and Travis sit in silence for the next ten minutes until they finally get to their destination. As they make their way towards the building, both brothers have the same exact focused look on their face. The only difference is that Travis has confidence behind his focus. Bryce looks calm on the outside, which only hides his insecurity and nervousness inside. Just like a duck sitting on the water looks calm but what you can't see underneath is it's legs kicking frantically trying to stay afloat.

Approaching the door he grabs the handle and opens it for his brother. "After you, Agent Maine." He says to Travis.

Travis walks in, followed closely by Bryce and Before the door can even close Agent Washington briskly walks up to them, "Well look who it is, Travis Wolf and Bryce Stone. It's nice of you two to join us." He says sarcastically.

"Sorry, sir, but you know Bryce, he's always running late." Travis replies.

Bryce looks at his brother and just shakes his head.

"You mean the guy who has showed up to work at least an hour early every day so far? Yes, I'm sure it was Bryce's fault." Washington responds.

"You show up to work an hour early?" Travis asks, looking at his brother in disbelief.

Bryce stays silent and shrugs his shoulders. The look of disapproval he gives his brother for giving him a hard time is just laughed off by Travis.

"What are you two doing just standing there, get to work." Washington barks.

Bryce and Travis give a head nod and a fist

bump. "Be safe, I don't want you to die out there today." Bryce says.

"Every man dies, not every man really lives." Travis says in a very bad Scottish accent to lighten the mood.

"That's *Braveheart.* At least make them a little harder from now on." Bryce responds.

"Yeah, I know. I just couldn't help myself with that one. You kind of set me up there. I'll see you soon, brother."

Bryce watches Travis walk away until he is out of sight and shakes his head turning towards Washington.

"What's wrong, son?" Washington asks.

"I don't know how he does it."

"What do you mean?"

"How does he stay so calm? I'm going to be here behind a desk, and I can barely keep from shaking I'm so nervous. He's going out there in the field where the action is."

"You'll get there. It comes with experience. He was just like you when he first started. In fact it actually looks like he's a little nervous today too. I haven't seen him like that in a long time."

"Do you think everything will be okay?"

"You can never know for sure. All you can do is prepare the best you can and things more often than not will work out."

"You don't seem nervous at all, sir."

"Like I said, we can't be any more

prepared. I have five other very good Agents out there along with your brother, and he's the best there is."

CHAPTER 2

Saturday, July 4th, 2026

3:45 P.M.

The streets are filled with people and they push to get as close as they can to where the President will be speaking. The stage is set in front of city hall surrounded by barriers and special Agents, each one is alert and ready to act at a moments notice.

The President is sitting on the stage between two of his Secret Service members listening to the Governor of Philadelphia speak. Collaboration between the Secret Service, FBI, and Di9 hadn't been done since Di9 formed after the attacks on September 11th, 2001. Di9, just like the FBI, has their Agents spread out around the area. Agent Maine stands behind the President, scanning the crowd while Agent Florida stands on ground level in front of the stage along with a few members of the FBI.

Agents Montana and Oregon are fifty yards from the stage making their way through the crowd. They are on opposite sides of the street looking for anything suspicious. Agents Dakota and Michigan, Di9's best snipers, are on the rooftops keeping a close watch. Agent Michigan is two hundred and fifty yards away from the President on one side of the street while Agent Dakota is five hundred yards away on the other.

"All Agents check in." Washington says through the secure Di9 channel.

"Agent Maine, all clear."

"Agent Florida, all clear."

"Agent Dakota, all clear."

"Agent Michigan, all clear."

"Agent Montana, all clear."

Washington waits for the last Agent to check in but all he hears is silence. "Agent Oregon, check in." He says again.

Still there is no answer. Washington, now shaken, looks to the other members of the field operations team. All he sees staring back are looks of confusion and uncertainty.

"Does anyone have eyes on Oregon?" He asks the other Agents.

"Sir, I just saw him a few seconds ago but now he's not there." Agent Montana says.

"Go check it out. Everyone else be on high alert."

Immediately Montana walks towards where Oregon was located as the other Agents place their hands on their weapons ready to pull them from their holsters. Navigating a crowd this size is always difficult, but being on high alert makes it almost impossible.

He makes it across the street and steps up on the sidewalk and there is still no sight of Oregon. Scanning the area up and down both sides of the street gives him no information. Then, for no reason, he has a feeling that someone is watching him.

Slowly he turns his head and looks down a blocked off alley validating his feeling. At the far end of the alley he sees a man dressed in all black staring at him.

"Sir, I think I may have something." he tells Washington.

"What is it? Did you find Oregon?"

Before Montana can answer he sees the man in black tap his wrist before walking around the corner in the alley and out of sight.

"Montana." Washington says, sternly.

"It's not Oregon, but there is someone suspicious in the alley and I need to check it out."

"Who is it?"

"I'm not sure, sir."

"What did he look like?"

"He's dressed in all black from head to toe. Even his face was covered."

"Stand down and wait for backup. I'll send Agent Florida your way."

"Negative, sir. Leave Florida with the President. I'll handle it."

Without hesitating he jogs down the alley

towards the man in black. Pulling his weapon as he approaches the corner he slowly peeks his head around to see a dead end. The man in black is nowhere to be seen.

All that is there are three doors. One on the left, one on the right, and the last is right in front of him. Not knowing which door the man went into he decides to check one at a time starting from left to right.

He grabs the handle of the first door and realizes it is unlocked. Slowly he opens the door as quietly as he can. The room is lit well enough to see that the man in black is not there, but he can hear what sounds like someone gasping for air around the corner. Swiftly he moves toward the noise with his gun drawn until he sees a body lying on the ground. He does a quick double check of the area before approaching the body. His eyes widen with fear and disbelief.

"Oregon!" He shouts, quickly getting down on one knee to help his fellow Agent.

Before he can say anything else he notices the puddle of blood under Oregon oozing out of the side of his neck just above the shoulder. He sees the bleeding is caused by a knife and grabs a towel from the table to try to stop the loss of blood.

"Stay with me." Montana says to his fellow Agent, before calling in to Washington. "Sir, Oregon is down. He's been stabbed in the neck."

"Hang tight, I'm sending help right away.

Where are you located?" Washington says, in a panic.

"I'm in a building in the alley off Cuthbert Street across from the Masonic Library and Museum."

Montana glances down at Oregon and realizes his eyes are closed and he has stopped breathing. He checks the vitals of his fellow Agent and then slams the towel down in frustration.

"Sir, Oregon is dead." He says, deflated.

Washington is silent and drops his head. The rest of the room doesn't know what to do or say either. Something like this has never happened before and the only thing they know to follow up on is a man dressed in black in the middle of an overly crowded street in a major city.

"Montana, get out of there and make your way to the President." Washington orders. As much as he hates that he lost an Agent, he hopes that it was just an isolated incident with a crazy person. But what happens next brings his greatest fear to reality "Montana, do you copy?" He asks when he doesn't hear his order acknowledged. Then his eyes widen when he hears Montana gasping for air before choking. The horror of listening to one of his Agent's neck snapping followed by a thud on the ground leaves him devastated and terrified. "Montana!" He screams.

The sound of silence turns to static knowing exactly what happened. He's just lost his second Agent in the matter of seconds, this time by strangulation. An act of terror has just occurred and there is only one thing on his mind. Find the man in black.

CHAPTER 3

Saturday, July 4th, 2026

3:57 P.M.

"Code black. I repeat, we have a code black." Washington says, worried.

"Say again, sir?" Agent Maine asks.

"Two Agents are down. We are under attack."

Those words have never been spoken to any Di9 member in the field before. Each Agent appears calm and focused on the outside but inside they are rattled.

"Stay at your post and remain focused. We came here to do a job and we are going to finish it. The President is our main objective." Washington says, reminding his Agents.

Just then Agent Dakota is startled by the door on the roof swinging open. Quickly he whips his head around and pulls his sidearm, but to his dismay he realizes he is still all alone.

There aren't many places to hide on the roof of a building. He also knows that he had made sure the door was latched after he closed it, so it couldn't be a gust of wind that made it open. The only thing that could have opened that door was someone from the inside. With his gun drawn and pointed Dakota slowly walks towards the door.

"Come out with your hands up!" He yells, not hearing a response or seeing any movement. Now irritated, Dakota yells out again. "Come out slowly with your hands up!"

Again, nothing but silence.

"Michigan, can you see anything on my roof?" Dakota asks.

Michigan takes his eyes off of the President and swings his rifle around to take a look at the roof with the view finder. "The roof is clear but I can't see down the stairwell. I can only see the door."

The door creaks as it slightly swings from the breeze. Dakota approaches the side of the doorway and pulls a mirror from his pocket. He crouches to stay low and out of sight and leans around the corner using the mirror to look into the stairwell.

"There is nobody here." He says with a huge relief.

He walks towards the door to shut it and make sure it doesn't swing open again. Now standing in the doorway he looks down the empty stairwell and wonders what happened.

"I don't know what's going on. Someone had to open the door, but there is nobody here.

There isn't even....."

Michigan watches through his view finder as Dakota drops to his knees. He stays in that position for a couple seconds and then collapses to the ground.

"Dakota!" Michigan yells as he watches his fellow Agent bleed out. He is stunned and perplexed, there wasn't anyone in the stairwell or on the roof.

"Michigan, what happened?" Washington asks.

"I'm not sure, sir. Dakota said the area was clear. Now he's laying in a pool of his own blood."

"Do a quick check on the President and scan the crowd. Tell me what you see."

Michigan does as he's told and whips his rifle around to look at the President and then the crowd. "The President is all good. There are no immediate threats around him that I see. Nothing suspicious in the crowd either."

He looks back at the rooftop where Dakota is laying and is shocked to find the roof empty. "Sir, have you heard from Dakota?"

"No, I thought you said he was down?" Washington replies.

"He was but his body is gone. I only had my eyes away from him for a minute or so."

"We'll find him but you need to stay focused on the President right now."

"If he's alive then he's going to need help immediately. From what I saw...."

Before Michigan can even finish his sentence he hears two loud bangs coming from the door on his rooftop. The hair on his neck stands and he starts to sweat. He recalls what happened to Dakota and doesn't want to make the same mistake and end up like him.

"Michigan, are you there?" Washington asks.

"Yes, sir. I might have company though."

"What's happening?"

"It sounds like someone is trying to join me up here. I heard two kicks on the door. I'm checking it out."

"We need you up there, you're our last sniper. Quickly handle it and get back to your position."

All Michigan can think about is how Dakota handled his situation and how that ended. Not wanting the same outcome he decides to go with a different approach. He doesn't even think of sneaking up on the stairwell and taking his time. He pulls his gun, then attaches the silencer, and briskly walks to the front of the door.

He fires six shots, removes his magazine, and reloads right before he kicks the door in. With his gun drawn he quickly realizes two things. The stairwell is empty and when he looks down he realizes he's made a big mistake.

BEEP. BEEP. BEEP BEEP BEEP....

A red blinking light flashes on a round

piece of metal that is about the size of a cannonball. The top of it extends up by an arm in the center of the sensor. Instantaneously it shoots out shards of metal in the shape of tiny spears in every direction. Before he can even attempt to turn and run he is struck in the head, neck, arms, and legs killing him instantly.

"Michigan, check in." Washington says, hearing the gun shots and groans from his Agent. "Michigan, check in." He says more sternly.

The silence is deafening. Washington's greatest fear is happening right in front of him and it's happening quickly and precisely.

In the matter of minutes Di9 has lost four of its best Agents. Whoever this enemy is, they know the exact location of each Agent and has taken them down without breaking a sweat. He knows this isn't good, especially for an agency that is supposed to be unknown. As bad as this situation is, it will only get worse if they can't keep the President safe and he gets killed too.

Without wasting any more time he decides to make the call. It will be an unpopular decision and could cause chaos, but he has to do what he thinks is right.

"Agents Maine and Florida, get the President out of there right now. Use whatever force is necessary and shoot to kill if you have to. Meet at Rendezvous Alpha.

CHAPTER 4

Saturday, July 4th, 2026

4:05 P.M.

Agents Maine and Florida put their fingers to their ear trying to hear Washington's command over the noise of the crowd. Florida shrugs his shoulders and waits to see what Maine will do. Before either of them take a step, the sound of gunfire fills the air causing chaos and panic throughout the crowd of people. Screams fill the air while people scatter frantically searching for safety.

The commotion causes families to be separated as people try to flee the area. Men push women and children out of the way as they attempt to escape. Mothers hold their babies while hiding behind cars and in the doorways of buildings.

Maine sees the Secret Service has already surrounded the President and are on the move to Cadillac One. He watches them struggle to keep the President low to the ground and out of danger.

Both Di9 Agents scan the crowd to see if they can find the person responsible when another gunshot rings out. The sound echoes off the buildings making it impossible to decipher where the shots are coming from.

Out of the corner of his eye, Maine sees the head of one of the Secret Service snap back. He looks over and sees what remains of the cloud of blood that exploded from the back of his head above the now deceased body laying on the stage. Before anyone can react, the exact same thing happens to the other member of the Secret Service. This leaves the President alone and exposed.

"Sir, get down! Sniper!" Agent Maine yells to the President.

Without hesitation the Commander-in-Chief dives behind the stage and stays low to the ground as Agent Maine jumps down to protect him.

Florida has his gun drawn and is looking through the chaos but is unsuccessful in spotting the threat. All he can see is just a blur of people running scared and terrified.

"Florida, I've got the President behind the stage. The Secret Service Agents are dead, I need backup." Agent Maine yells.

"I'm a few yards in front of the stage, I'll be right there." Florida lowers his gun and begins to sprint towards the President. On his way, he notices a boy no older than eight years old sitting in the middle of the street all alone and crying.

"What are you doing? Get over here!" Maine barks.

Florida looks at Maine for a second and can only think of his own son. He runs to the boy to scoop him up and tries to calm him down while scanning the crowd. On the sidewalk to his left he sees a woman crying hysterically and overwhelmed screaming for her son.

"I think I found your mom, buddy." Florida says to the sobbing kid.

The child's enormous smile makes Florida happy, knowing he reunited the boy with his mother.

"Thank you so much!" She says, giving her son a huge embrace. "I thought I lost him for good."

With tears in her eyes she looks up at Florida and thanks him again. When he looks down at her he can see that her tears of terror have turned to tears of joy. He is proud of himself and feels a sense of pride as he watches the boy and his mother reunite.

Happy that he was able to reunite the child with his mom, he knows he has to get back to Agent Maine. He looks back down at the woman one last time but is perplexed by her face. Her tears have vanished and Florida can see the panic in her eyes. Before he can turn around to see what has caused the woman's look to change so quickly, he feels the pressure around his neck from a tight choke hold.

Florida grabs the man's arm to pull it off but is unsuccessful. He can tell the attacker is a skilled fighter from the technical grip. Instinctively he hits the man in the stomach three times with his elbow finally giving him enough slack on his neck to escape the hold.

Gasping for air he turns to face his assailant and sees a man dressed in all black just like the man from the alley described by Agent Montana. Florida catches his breath while his attacker stands and stares at him, almost as if the man doesn't care if he does or not. He knows the man is strong by the pressure put on his neck, but he can see the man is only average height and weight.

"What do you want from us?" He asks, rubbing his neck and trying to see any features on the man that can be used for identification. The only thing he can make out, other than the man in black being covered head to toe, is that there is a red stripe on each of his sleeves and a patch on his shirt with the letters DS.

He watches the man in black raise his thumb to his own throat and slowly move it from one side to the other.

"I hope you don't mind being disappointed." Florida says.

Charging at the man in black with his fists in front of his face, Florida throws a left jab, then another, followed by a right cross. He is astonished at his opponent's speed as the man has no trouble dodging every punch that comes his way.

Florida is further provoked when the man takes a step back, holding his hand out with his palm in the air to arrogantly wave Florida on for more. Reacting impulsively, Florida charges his opponent even faster this time, unleashing a flurry of punches, most of which are either blocked or dodged. His aggressive style of fighting causes him to become increasingly sloppy and out of control, playing right into the arrogant man in black's hands. As the fight progresses, Florida grows more frustrated and angry.

Fatigue begins to set in as the aggressive fighting style drains Florida's energy. His punches become slower and weaker, and his breathing grows heavier. A lazy jab is easily dodged by his opponent, allowing him to land a counter punch to Florida's nose, followed by a hard, straight kick to the stomach.

Struggling to concentrate and dazed from the relentless beating, Di9's longest active Agent gasps for air as he is struck in the throat, causing him to drop to the ground. The swift kick to the side of his knee leaves him writhing in pain from the torn ligaments caused by the perfectly placed strike.

Rolling back and forth in agony, Florida watched as the man in black, still silent, approaches him and stands above his head. They make eye contact before the man repeats the same motion he did before the fight, sliding his thumb from one side of his neck to the other.

"Please, I have a family." Florida pleads.

Now terrified, when he sees the man ignore his plea and pull a knife from its sheath, Florida watches his attacker drop to a knee and lift the knife over his head before thrusting down for the final strike. With every ounce of energy he has left, Agent Florida blocks the attack and holds his opponent's arm away just far enough for the blade to not penetrate his body.

Eventually, even the strongest man will run out of gas, and Florida is no different. His muscles just can't put forth any more effort. The strong knee strike to his ribs from his opponent causes him to expel his last bit of strength, ultimately costing him his life. The last thing he'll remember is the man in black standing up and waving goodbye while he gurgles and chokes on his own blood before finally passing away.

Agent Maine watches the whole fight unfold behind the stage, still trying to keep the President safe. He is shocked at what just happened and knows he is the last Di9 Agent left to get the President to safety. He sees Agent Florida's lifeless body in the middle of the street, oozing blood. His eyes look towards the man in black when he stands and purposefully turns his head towards the President.

"Sir, we need to move." Agent Maine says in a calm, authoritative way. "Cadillac One is just a half a block away."

Maine takes the President by the arm and puts his other hand on his head to keep him as low and as safe as he can. They begin their escape and stay behind objects the best they can to avoid being spotted or shot by either the man in black or the sniper who took out the Secret Service Agents.

Agent Maine begins to panic when he notices the man in black quickly gaining ground on himself and the President. Every time he looks back, he can see the enemy getting closer with each glance.

"Sir, we're going to have to move faster. Cadillac One is just up ahead on the left, then it's a quick five-minute ride to Rendezvous Alpha." he tells the President.

Just as they reach Cadillac One, the man in black grabs Agent Maine's arm from behind. Without hesitation, Maine turns around and reverses the hold before he drops an elbow on the man's humerus. A smirk shows on his face when he hears the bone break from the elbow strike. He then throws a hard right cross striking the man's jaw and dropping him to the ground, leaving him unconscious.

"Quickly, sir, get in." Maine tells the President, opening the door of Cadillac One. "I'm sorry I had to leave you for a second, I just had to settle a little disagreement."

"Yes, I saw. Remind me to stay on your good side."

"That would be wise, sir."

"Thank you, Agent Maine." The President says smiling.

As soon as the President finishes speaking, something catches his eye behind the Di9 hero. His smile turns to panic, causing Maine to frantically turn his head to see what is behind him.

Maine's victory in getting the President to safety is short lived. Another man dressed in the same black outfit walks towards them, his gun pointed at the Commander-in-Chief. Agent Maine turns as fast as he can and shoves the President in the car.

"Go! Go!" He shouts to the driver before closing the door.

POP!.....POP!

Maine drops to the ground from the first bullet that hits him in the shoulder outside his kevlar vest. The second shot hits his arm just above the elbow. Cadillac One speeds away with the President safe inside as the second man in black watches the car drive off before turning his attention back to Agent Maine. The President watches helplessly while the man in black fires two more shots towards Maine's head.

The President slumps in his seat,

devastated. Not only has there been an attack on U.S. soil, but many good Agents lost their lives because of it. He needs to find out who perpetrated the attacks and the motive behind them.

KABOOM!

The President's eyes widen and his heart drops. As he turns his head to look back, and all he can see is fire and a big cloud of smoke where Agent Maine was killed. A bomb has exploded in the middle of the city. As the Commander-in-Chief, he usually has nerves of steel, but this attack has him rattled. What the President is certain of is that he wouldn't be alive if it wasn't for Agent Maine.

CHAPTER 5

Sunday, July 5th, 2026

Washington D.C.

The loss of Travis eats away at Bryce. He is there physically, but mentally he is gone. All he can think of is his brother, and the countless stories about his missions. Unless his brother was embellishing, Bryce couldn't fathom how only two men could have taken him down. There wasn't a single viable threat or any chatter mentioning what happened yesterday. If it wasn't for Washington's gut feeling, Di9 wouldn't have been there and the President would be dead, not Travis.

And yet, his brother is gone. He gave his life and nobody will ever know except members of Di9. Another unknown hero that won't get the credit or accolades he deserves.

"Hey, we're almost there." His wife says, driving while he sits in the passenger seat. Bryce doesn't respond or move a muscle. He continues to stare out of the window with a blank look on his face. "Bryce." She calls again, putting her hand on his arm.

"Huh." Bryce reacts to her startling him.

"We're almost there. You were pretty zoned out there weren't you?"

"I'm sorry, were you talking for a while?"

"No, I just said we're almost there. You don't have to be sorry; I know this is tough for you."

"It is, but I'm sure it's tough for everyone, especially Emma."

"I can't even imagine what she is going through." Kayla pauses. "I know that if something ever happened to you, I wouldn't be able to function. I don't know how she is managing to get through losing her husband. She must miss Travis so much."

"That's why I think this will be good to go over there. I know it won't bring back Travis or make Emma feel better, but at least she knows we are here for her."

Tears begin to run down Kayla's face as she nods. Bryce knows she's been up all night trying to be strong and supportive for him, but she can't hold back her emotions anymore. He can see that she is beaten down and fragile emotionally, they both are. Putting his own feelings aside, he wipes away her tear before putting his hand on her shoulder. It is 11:59 as they arrive at Emma's house and she stops the car at the end of the long driveway.

"I can't do this." She says, sobbing.

"What do you mean you can't do this?" He asks.

"I don't know what to say to her."

"You don't have to say anything. You being here is all she needs."

"As soon as I see her I'm going to break down. I won't be able to keep it together."

"You won't have to. You'll give her someone to cry with while she grieves."

Bryce can only smile back when he sees Kayla look at him smiling through her tears. He hands her a tissue to wipe her eyes and knows she agrees that's she needs to be there for her sister-in-law. They start to drive towards the house slowly down the long driveway.

The car is filled with silence, driving towards the house. Bryce was always impressed with his brother's gorgeous house. He looks at the eight-foot-tall trees to the right as they pass, each one exactly the same height. They are bushy, not only to provide some shade but also privacy from the neighbors. On the left is a beautifully kept front yard. The grass is green, perfectly cut and trimmed, and there isn't a blade of grass out of place. Half way up the driveway, he looks up at the house and sees Emma through the front screen door as she stands inside waiting for them to arrive.

"There's Emma." Bryce says. "She doesn't look....."

KABOOM!

Without warning, a giant explosion annihilates the house. Wood and metal shrapnel fly in all directions. Massive flames engulf the house and burn what wasn't already destroyed by the explosion.

Bryce's face turns red, and his blood starts to boil. He clenches his fist and punches the dashboard startling his family. He is so zoned out and focused on the house that he forgot his wife and son were in the car with him. Quickly he composes himself and looks over to Kayla and then back at his six year old boy, Michael.

Kayla is shocked and doesn't want to believe what she just saw. Trying to process what just happened, she is left speechless. Her knuckles are white from gripping the steering wheel tightly, her entire body is shaking.

Michael is crying so hard, the noise is deafening. His face is red and tears stream down his cheeks as Bryce reaches back to unbuckle him and pull him onto his lap. Immediately he wraps his tiny arms around his Dad and lays his head on his father's chest.

Bryce comforts his son, holding him tight. He looks over at Kayla and places his hand on her arm, which snaps her out of her shocked state.

"Are you okay?" He asks, grabbing her hand to hold it tight while still holding Michael with his other hand. He breathes slow and steady and tries to keep his composure for the sake of his family.

"Why don't you sit with mom for a second." He says, putting Michael onto Kayla's lap.

"Where are you going?!" Kayla asks, frightened.

"I need to go check what's left of the house before it burns to ash."

"No, you need to stay here with us. What if something else happens?"

"If something else were to happen then it would've happened already."

"Don't go Dad!" Michael screams through his tears.

Bryce places his hand on the top of Michael's head and gently slides it down to his forehead. "Nothing is going to happen to me, I promise. I'll be right back." He tells Michael lovingly. He exits the car and notices the neighbors start to come out of their houses to see what's going on. "Kayla, pull the car to the end of the driveway and call 9-1-1. Tell them what happened and that I'm here at the house so they don't shoot me thinking I'm a bad guy. I don't have much time until they get here."

Quickly, Bryce shuts the door and rushes up to the house. There isn't much left to investigate and knowing how long it takes for the authorities to show up doesn't leave him much time. Most likely, there is nothing there for him to find, but he still has to look. The odds of this being just a coincidence after what happened in Philadelphia are very low. It seems like someone had it out for Travis, and they wanted him dead for some reason. This must have been the back up plan if they didn't kill him yesterday.

The area around the house is mostly rubble and dirt, the very thing he expected to see. He can hear the sirens blare and knows he doesn't have much time left alone at the house. As he makes his way around the back, he still doesn't see anything out of the ordinary. He wonders if maybe it was just a gas leak but his training tells him something different. He approaches the corner of the house, and the sun reflects off something catching the corner of his eye. He runs over and sees that it is something out of place. It's a small piece of metal in the shape of a trapezoid that is the size of the palm of his hand. There are also a couple singed wires coming out of it.

He takes off his shoe and sock, and slides the sock over his hand in an effort to maintain evidence. He puts his shoe back on and picks up the metal. It is still very hot even with the protection over his hand. After putting the metal in his pocket, still wrapped in his sock, he jogs back to the car. Just as he arrives, the police, ambulance, and fire trucks all pull up simultaneously.

"Here, put this under the seat. Make sure you touch it with the sock." Bryce tells Kayla, placing the metal on the seat inconspicuously.

"What is it?" She asks.

"I don't know but it seemed like it didn't belong where I found it." Bryce looks around and sees some police officers getting out of their car. "I'm going to go talk with the lead detective; I'll be right back."

Kayla and Michael watch Bryce walk over to the detective. They can see the firemen rush to the house to start to put out the flames. The two men talk for a couple minutes and then give each other a handshake before Bryce starts walking back towards the car.

"What did you guys talk about?" Kayla asks Bryce after he enters the car.

"I just told him the truth. I provided him with every detail from the moment we entered the driveway until their arrival."

"What about the piece of metal under your seat?"

"I left that part out."

"Why?"

"There's something I need to tell you." He says before pausing. "Nobody can know about this, not even Michael."

"You're starting to freak me out a little." Kayla says nervously.

"I got a new job at Di9. I'm not even supposed to be telling you about it, but I don't like to hide anything from you."

"What is Di9?"

"It's a government agency."

"Like the FBI or CIA?"

"Something like that, it's just kept off the books so nobody knows about it. We would be the equivalent of MI6 for James Bond or IMF for Ethan Hunt."

"Why didn't you tell me about this?"

"I just did. I just got the job a week ago. Nobody is supposed to know we exist. The only way to be part of Di9 is to be recruited by them."

"How did they find out about you?"

"Travis recommended me. He's been trying to recruit me for a couple years now."

Bryce watches Kayla look out the window and stay silent for a minute trying to comprehend what he just told her.

"What is Di9? What do you do there?" Kayla asks curiously.

"Think of all the *Mission: Impossible* movies. What do they do?"

"They usually stop some bad guy from blowing something up."

"Well that's what Di9 does too. We protect the world from any enemy that wants to destroy it. Whether that's in our country or abroad."

"What does Di9 stand for?"

"Dark Intelligence. The nine is for the nine sectors of the agency."

"Are you a spy?" Kayla asks nervously.

"No," Bryce says, chuckling. "I'm an analyst."

"What does an analyst do?"

"We take data from what our intelligence gathers and create metrics to prioritize threats and pass it along to the next sector."

"What did Travis do?"

"He was an Agent," Bryce pauses. "He was the top Agent in Di9. He would be the guy they would make movies about."

"You didn't want to be an Agent?"

"Yes and no. I think being an Agent would be amazing. I would get to travel the world and protect it from terrorists. But there are two reasons why I'm not an Agent."

"What are they?" Kayla asks.

"The first reason is that you don't just start out as an Agent. You need to work your way up the ladder and then pass the field test."

"And the second reason?"

"The second reason and most important is that I don't want to put you or Michael in any danger. I love you both too much."

"Do you think the explosion had anything to do with Travis being in Di9?"

"I'm not sure. It could've just been a coincidence but this piece of metal under my seat makes me wonder about that.

"Why didn't you tell the police about it?"

"Because sometimes you just have to know when something needs to be left out so someone else can handle it."

"Are you that someone?"

"Not me. Di9."

CHAPTER 6

Sunday, July 5th, 2026

Di9 Headquarters

12:25 P.M.

Normally, Di9 Headquarters is a noisy and busy building, but today, it's different. The building is silent and somber due to the loss of friends and colleagues. Everyone does their best to stay focused on their job because the slightest interaction with another person could cause an emotional breakdown.

There has never been an attack on U.S. soil since the birth of Di9. Yesterday was a huge failure, and their reputation has taken a hit. The Commander-in-Chief is still alive, but the attacks should have never happened.

The terrorists knew every move Di9 would make before they made it. They weren't there to make friends and have a cup of coffee. They came, attacked, and almost accomplished their goal of killing the President. If it weren't for

Agent Maine's heroic sacrifice the country would be mourning the loss of its leader right now. Instead they were able to take out every single Agent in the field that day and make it look easy in the process.

Agent Washington stands in the entrance of the main room of the building and feels more grief than anybody. Being in command during the attacks he knows he should've moved faster to get his men and the President to safety earlier. Now he's going to have to live with the fact that he failed his Agents and will remember that for the rest of his life. He looks around and sees the sorrow and pain on everyone's face and knows that he has to be the leader in this difficult time.

"Can I have everyone's attention?" He says, walking towards the center of the room.

Everyone stops what they are doing and looks at him. Silence fills the room as they wait for him to speak.

Now in the center of the room he stops and takes the time to look at each person present. He is not one to write down a speech and memorize it. Usually, he can read the room and know what to say. Today that skill is especially important to him because he wants everyone to know the words come from his heart.

"Yesterday we lost. We lost colleagues and we lost friends. We all lost people who are very important to us." He pauses, trying to maintain his composure. "But I promise you all that we will find who did this to us and we will not stop until we do."

Everyone in the room listens intently nodding theirs heads in agreement. They can see that Washington is choked up but his words start to get more intense with each passing second.

"These terrorists came into our country and attacked us. They went after our President, murdered Di9 members, killed our brothers and sisters from other agencies, and rubbed our face in it. I know you're scared, I know you're angry, and I know you're grieving, but don't give in to your emotions. Harness your feelings into something meaningful. Don't fear and do not quit." He pauses and lowers his voice before saying, "If you quit, if you give up, if you retreat, then our friends will have died for nothing." He looks at every worker at Di9 and sees their eyes glued to him, focusing on every word he says. "Things go wrong sometimes, life isn't always rainbows and sunflowers. People die and mistakes are made. But what makes each one of you a Di9 member is not how great you are when things are going well. What sets you apart from everyone else is that no matter how hard you get hit, no matter how hard you fall, no matter how much pain you are in that you will keep getting up and will continue on. And that, my friends, is why I know we will succeed." He pauses one more time and looks around the room before adding, "Now let's go find those bastards."

Washington can hear the room erupt behind him as he walks down the hall towards his office until he is around the corner and out of sight. Although the morale is still low from what happened yesterday, people are now ready to run through a brick wall for him. Men would follow him to their deaths just so they wouldn't let him down.

Once back in the office, he sits at his desk and wipes away his tears. He takes a sip of scotch and stares off wondering if his speech motivated anyone. Before he can think too much there is a knock at the door. Quickly he wipes his eyes and tries to regain his composure.

"Come in." He says. The door opens and his second in command stands at the entrance to the room. "Agent Texas, come in and have a seat."

"Thank you, sir." Texas says, walking to the desk and sitting across from Washington.

"You know you don't have to call me sir in private. We've been friends for many years. What can I do for you?"

"I just wanted to let you know that your speech was great. I think it's what we all needed."

"Thanks, Tex, but that wasn't just a speech, I meant every word of it. I have no idea who those men in black are or where to find them, but I won't stop until we do."

"Washington, I want to get these guys as bad as you do. I can't imagine how overwhelmed you must feel or how much pressure you must be under to get them."

"Do you know what the worst part is? After we catch these guys it still won't bring back our Agents that were murdered out there yesterday. It won't bring back the fathers or husbands or the sons or brothers of those families."

"That wasn't your fault. You didn't kill those men."

"I didn't save them either."

"What could you have done?"

"I could've got them out of there."

"But then the President would be dead, sir."

Both men stay silent for a second, avoiding eye contact with each other by looking down. Just as Agent Texas is about to speak again, there is another knock at the door.

"Come in." Washington says.

The door opens and Amy, Di9's Head of intelligence, is visibly shaken.

"What's wrong, Amy?" Washington asks.

"Sir, there's been an explosion at Travis's house. Emma was inside at the time." She pauses for a couple seconds before finishing the news. "She's dead, sir."

Washington drops his chin to his chest in disgust and rubs his head. People associated with Di9 are dying, and something needs to happen quickly to put an end to it.

"Thanks, Amy. Have you heard from Bryce yet?"

"No, sir. Nothing yet."

"Keep me informed. Let me know if anything else happens. That will be all."

"Yes, sir." Amy says as she leaves the room and shuts the door behind her.

"I need you to do something for me." Washington says looking up at Texas.

"What do you need?"

"Get me Bryce Stone."

CHAPTER 7

Monday, July 6th, 2026

Di9 Headquarters

9:10 A.M.

Bryce has had a couple of tough days in a row, the loss of his brother and sister-in-law eats at him. Staring at his computer, he can barely muster up enough energy to say 'thank you' as people offer their condolences. He hasn't said good morning to anyone, and doesn't want to be bothered. It seems like he's been there for hours and yet the clock tells him it's only been ten minutes. Despite his efforts to stay motivated, he just wants to go home and be with his family.

He glances at a picture he has on his desk of Travis and Emma sitting across from himself, Kayla, and Michael at Thanksgiving last year. At first it soothes his pain, but the more he looks at it, the angrier he gets. He pushes some papers off his desk and they fly into the air and float to the ground. Colleagues in the area awkwardly ignore his outburst as he wonders why his brother and sister-in-law had to die. The more he looks at that picture the more he wants to flip his desk and start smashing things. He decides the best thing to do right now is to walk away and take a break.

Everything is a blur, and his mind is foggy as he makes his way to the kitchen. He is so absent minded that he hasn't even noticed Amy quietly trying to get his attention by waving. Just as he is about to enter the kitchen Amy puts her hand on his shoulder which snaps him out of his daze.

"Bryce, I'm so sorry. I know that you and Travis were close. If there is anything that you or Kayla need then please let me know." Amy says with sympathy in her voice.

"Thanks, Amy, I appreciate that." He responds while turning towards the kitchen again.

"You never answered your phone, we've been trying to get a hold of you since yesterday."

"I wasn't really in the mood to talk to anyone yesterday, It's been a little hectic the last couple of days." He says, turning around to face Amy.

"I know and I hate to nag you about it, but Washington wants to see you. That's why we were calling."

Bryce nods to acknowledge what he just heard and continues on his way into the kitchen.

Even though there are a few people in the room it seems empty. The colleagues that are there give their condolences and he does his best to fake a smile and tell them thanks. At this point he is just going through the motions, he has no idea what is being said or who is there.

"Bryce, Washington needs you in his office now." Amy says, a little more stern this time.

"Yeah, alright. The donuts are gone anyway." He responds, looking down at the empty box sitting on the counter.

Brusquely, he walks right past Amy and through the kitchen door, making his way to Washington's office. Normally he'd wonder if he's going to get chewed out for not showing up yesterday but deep down he really doesn't care. Now at Washington's door he wipes his face and brushes off his shirt, knocking twice.

"Come in." Washington says.

"You wanted to see me, sir?" Bryce asks, entering the room.

"I did. Have a seat."

Bryce closes the door behind him and walks past the many plaques and awards on the wall towards the massive desk where Washington sits in his executive leather chair. The Master's degree in Politics and International Studies from the University of Oxford and the shine of the Silver Star stand out. What really catches his eye is the Purple Heart that

Washington received when he was in the Army. And here he thought that he was important because he got a 'World's Greatest Dad' coffee mug for Father's Day from his son last year.

He gets to his chair and sits vulnerably across from his boss. His eyes stare down at the desk, not once looking up. All he feels right now in this moment is emptiness. Not until Washington begins to speak does he snap out of his funk.

"Bryce, I know what you are going through right now. I've lost many people that are close to me. Friends, colleagues, and even family members." He says, before pausing. "We all loved Travis. He was an excellent Agent and even better friend, I can only imagine how great of a brother he was. I'm truly sorry for your loss, we all are. If there is anything you need then don't hesitate to ask, even if it's time off."

"Thank you, sir. But I'd like to continue working to do my part to find these guys. Sitting at home won't help me at all. If I'm here then my mind will be occupied. Yesterday I was going crazy at home, I'm not going to sit back and do nothing."

"That's good to hear, and believe me, we all want to find the people behind this attack. We are a unit here, we all work for the same goal. When one of us hurt we all hurt. When one of us grieves we all grieve. We don't give out medals here and we don't do anything for glory.

Our job is to protect not only our country but every single person that works for Di9. I give you my word that we will get the people responsible for the attack and we won't stop until we do." Washington pauses to gather his thoughts before saying, "Bryce, we all love you here. Your work ethic is hands down the best I've ever seen. I know you're new here but you've succeeded at everything you've done in the past according to your profile. I need to ask you a favor."

"What is it, sir?"

"I know your stance on becoming an Agent. Believe me, I understand it." Washington says almost nervously.

"But?"

"But I'd like you to reconsider. I have no doubt that you'll……."

"I'll do it." Bryce interjects.

"Really? You don't want to think it over?"

"No, sir. I've always wanted to become an Agent and what better time than now? I mean, what kind of brother would I be if I didn't find whoever did this and make it right?"

"I'm glad to hear that, son. Before we can make it official I need you to go see our psychologist to make sure you are ready. If you pass the test then you will be an Agent. Go down and see Mike and he will give me your results when the evaluation is over."

"Yes, sir. Thank you, sir." Bryce says, standing. For the first time in two days the smile on his face is real. It's not fake and forced like it has been all morning.

As he heads towards the door to leave Washington's office he can still feel the pain inside. His brother will never come back and his absence will always be a reminder of what happened to him. Now he has a chance to become an Agent just like Travis and what better way to honor him. Walking into the hallway, he remembers the last movie quote from *Braveheart* that Travis tried to stump him on right before the attacks in Philadelphia. "Every man dies, not every man really lives".

CHAPTER 8

Monday, July 6th, 2026

Di9 Headquarters

9:30 A.M.

Bryce walks to his meeting with the psychiatrist with a little more pep in his step, slightly smiling at people as they pass. The destination is the second to last door at the end of a long hallway adjacent to Washington's office. His mind is racing with so many questions that he doesn't even realize he walked past the psychiatrist's door. *"What it's going to be like to be an Agent, what is Mike going to ask about, and when he will start."*

He backtracks and finds himself in front of the correct door, which is cracked open. Not thinking anything of it, Bryce knocks three times and waits for someone to answer. Twenty seconds go by, and he is still standing at the door waiting for an answer. Again, he knocks three times, but a little louder. After a few seconds, there is still no answer. He looks through the crack of the door to see if anybody is inside, but it is empty.

"Hello?" He says, slowly opening the door open.

The room is empty. An unoccupied desk is towards the back of the room in front of another door. Two chairs sit in front of the desk and there is a couch to the left. Just as he starts to wonder if Mike didn't know about the meeting, the lights in the room and the hallway go out. He flips the light switch up and down, but it is useless.

It doesn't take long for his eyes to adjust before he starts to move around but it doesn't matter, it is pitch black inside the room. Suddenly, he hears footsteps coming from the area where the desk is. He can tell it is just one set of footsteps and the person is moving slowly. Quickly Bryce crouches next to the couch and stays silent and very still.

He can remember the layout of the room and where each piece of furniture is after seeing it for only a few seconds. All the different scenarios play out in his head and he comes up with a plan for how to react to each. Prepared for what might happen, he is surprised when he notices the footsteps have stopped. He extends his hand until it is even with the front of the couch and remains still. He won't be able to see the person in the room with him, but he will feel the air move if they walk by.

After a few seconds his plan works to perfection. He feels a light movement of air on his hand and waits for the perfect moment to stand and make his move. In one swift motion he grabs the person's right arm and pins it behind their back while grabbing a handful of shirt with his other hand. Forcefully he slams the person into the wall face first and pins him tight so he can't move. He pulls a pen from his pocket and holds it to the person's neck.

"Bryce, it's Mike!" He yells.

The lights turn back on causing Bryce to squint while his eyes readjust. He turns Mike around to see his face but keeps him pinned against the wall with the pen to his throat.

"What's going on?" Bryce asks.

"That was just a test to see how'd you react. Please put the pen down." Mike answers.

Bryce loosens his grip and puts the pen back in his pocket. He can see that Mike is shaken from what he did. "I'm sorry about that, I feel bad now. You're very lucky though, I almost killed you."

"I'm glad you didn't." Mike responds, rubbing his arm that was pinned behind him.

"Do you think that was a good idea to give me a test like that after the stuff that happened the last couple of days?"

"Not so much now. At the time we decided to do it we thought it was."

"Why?"

"Look, we're all very sorry about what happened, but we thought if you couldn't focus and react because you had some stuff on your mind then you wouldn't be ready."

"Are you saying I'm ready then?"

"Not yet, but you passed the first test for sure."

"So what now? Do I have to fight a bear while I'm juggling chainsaws?" Bryce asks sarcastically.

"No, but that's a good idea for the future." Mike responds with some sarcasm of his own. "Come have a seat."

Bryce follows Mike over to the desk in the back of the room and they each take a seat across from each other.

"So what's next? Are you going to make me lay on the couch? Am I going to have to take a written test?" Bryce asks.

"Not yet. First I need to fill out some paperwork about how you handled the situation with me when you came in. You know, just how you handled your fears and how you reacted."

"Wait, do you think I'm afraid?" Bryce asks, annoyed.

"You tell me." Mike responds, looking at Bryce's eyes.

"I'm not afraid. I want to go after every single one of the people that killed my brother and I want their blood."

"It doesn't sound like you are afraid at all."

He says, listening intently while sitting back in his chair.

"I'm not."

"That's not always a good thing."

"How not? If I'm fighting someone and they see that I'm scared then they have the mental edge. They could use that against me."

"Well that is true. In hand to hand combat showing fear is never a good thing, but being afraid beforehand is never a bad thing either."

"How is that?" Bryce asks, confused.

"A man that is afraid has respect for his opponent or the mission. He is more careful and more precise, he has something to lose. You are a man full of rage and that is dangerous, not to your opponent, but to yourself."

"Did I seem dangerous to myself a couple minutes ago when I had you pinned against the wall?"

"No you didn't, you seemed dangerous to me. How did you do that anyway? You had me tied up and pinned against the wall in a matter of seconds."

"Years and years of Jiu-Jitsu."

"You took Jiu-Jitsu? When did you start?" Mike asks.

"I was ten when I started."

"What made you get into that?"

"After my mom died I was pretty messed up mentally, we all were but I think it hit me the hardest. My grades dropped and my attitude changed for the worse. My dad used to call me a loose cannon because he never knew what I was going to do or say. Well one day I said the wrong thing to the wrong kid and I came home with a black eye and bloody lip."

"So you started taking Jiu-Jitsu to defend yourself?"

"That was one of the reasons. My dad didn't like the fact that I came home that day beaten up that badly. He didn't want that to happen again so he signed me up for lessons the next week. He said if I was going to shoot off my mouth that I better be able to defend myself."

"It looks like it worked."

"It did. It also taught me discipline and respect. I think my dad didn't know how to raise me and my brother alone without my mom. It was just as much for his benefit as it was for mine. He had his own demons to deal with and didn't want to have to worry too much about mine."

"So he signed you up so they can train you and keep you disciplined. Maybe conquer your fears as well?"

"I told you I'm not afraid."

"No, you are not. You are so keen on exacting revenge that you will do anything in your power to get it. Having rage will make you reckless which could cause you to miss something. Perhaps a small detail that could be the difference between completing the mission and failing. The difference between life and death."

Bryce leans forward and places both arms onto the desk. Trying to control his emotions he stares at Mike and taps his foot repeatedly on the ground.

"You're right, I do have rage for what they did to my brother. I am afraid of what will happen to my family if something happens to me." He pauses to gather his thoughts as Mike looks on. "I will not allow my son to grow up without a father. I know what that's like and that will not happen to him."

"I thought you just said your dad took you to jiu jitsu after your mom died." Mike says, confused.

"He did, but as time when on so did his drinking. I had a great Dad when I was younger, but when my mom died we didn't just lose one parent, we eventually lost both. My Dad would go to work every day and work his shift and then he would go to the bar after work every single night. He would drink his money away instead of coming home to his sons and we had to fend for ourselves. When he did come home he would take out his frustrations on Travis. I can still hear the beatings and screams that he had to go through."

"He would beat your brother? Did he ever hit you?"

"Only Travis. I don't know if it was

because he was older than me or maybe Travis would make sure he got our Dad's attention first to protect me, but he took it all. I can still hear him say after every beating when he'd come back to our room that 'I'm your older brother. I'll always be there to protect you. I'll always have your back'."

"He sounds like a great brother."

"He was." Bryce drops his head and pauses. "He is."

"So why the different last names then?"

"Once Travis was old enough to do so he moved out and changed his last name and never spoke to our Father again. He didn't want anything to do with him so he changed his last name to Wolf."

"You don't feel the same way?"

"I'm devastated by it. I get why Travis feels the way he does, I don't blame him and I have the same feelings. But I have to give my Dad a little bit of a pass. He just lost his wife and didn't know how to cope. It's no excuse but I can see why he reacted that way."

"You try to see the good in people don't you."

"I try. Everyone has a story and you can never know what is going on in someone's life until you talk to them. I still remember the good times with my Dad. I remember not being able to wait for him to come home and hear some of the stories he had for us. He was such a good detective. A couple times a month he would set up a game or a scavenger hunt and have me and Travis look for clues to try to figure out and solve the riddle. They were so much fun and I think it's one of the reasons why I advanced as far as I did with the Metropolitan Police Department (MPD) in Washington D.C. Travis and I both benefited from them. But then it always comes back to how he basically abandoned us after my Mom died. Me and Travis had to raise ourselves."

"So tell me, are you afraid that you might turn out like your father too or are you full of rage because of him?" Mike asks.

"I'm afraid of what my rage will do to my enemies." Bryce says with a death stare. "Now you tell me, what do you think I am?"

Mike nods and puts his pen down. He stands up and walks around to the side of the desk and holds his hand out.

"I think you're ready." Mike says as he shakes Bryce's hand. "Welcome to Agent status."

"That's it?" Bryce asks, shocked. "You aren't going to evaluate me or test me at all?"

"Those were the tests. We do things a little differently here. There are no right or wrong answers. We base our results on responses and reactions, with a little bit of a background check."

"So I'm good to go then?"

"You just have to wait for Washington to sign off on it and put some paperwork in. That shouldn't take long, it was his idea to make you an Agent. He's been pushing for you for a while."

"What do I do now?"

"Head back to your desk. Washington will come get you when everything is approved and then he'll tell you what to do next."

"Mike, thanks a lot. I apologize again for how I reacted earlier and for what I did to your arm."

"No worries, I expected something like that. Just hopefully it doesn't affect my bowling."

"You're a bowler?" Bryce asks, stopping in his tracks by the door.

"Nope." Mike replies with a straight face. "You better get going. We'll talk soon."

Bryce stands in the doorway confused. Before he can even ask why Mike contradicted himself about bowling the door shuts behind him. He shakes his head and chuckles as he heads back to his desk. The smile on his face would light up a dark room. All he can think of is how he is almost officially an Agent in Di9.

CHAPTER 9

Monday, July 6th, 2026

Di9 Headquarters

10:03 A.M.

As soon as Bryce turns the corner he can see Washington pacing back and forth holding a folder waiting for him to return to his desk. He picks up the pace when he sees his boss check his watch.

"There you are." Washington says with a smile, seeing Bryce approach the desk.

"I'm sorry, sir, I came right back from my meeting with Mike."

"I know you did. This is just one of my favorite things to do."

"What is?" Bryce asks.

"Telling a Di9 member they're becoming an Agent."

"I'm an Agent now? There are no tests or a field exam? No big background check?"

"All of that was done before you were

hired. I've wanted you to become an Agent for a long time. Why do you think Travis was bugging you for so long?"

"You always knew I would become an Agent?"

"I knew you could be an Agent. Becoming one was always up to you. I usually have a hunch about those kinds of things."

"Travis told me about your hunches. He even told me that you had a hunch about something bad happening in Philadelphia."

"That's true. I had a hunch and I still couldn't stop the attack." Washington says as his eyes start to tear up.

"Sir, there was nothing you could've done about that. You had no idea what they were going to do or that anything would happen."

"I had a hunch and I could've stopped it sooner instead of letting everyone die."

"You can look at it that way I guess, but I see it another way."

"What way do you see it?"

"I see that your hunch brought Di9 to Philadelphia. Yes, our Agents died out there, but that's what we signed up for. We know the risks. You see the attack in Philadelphia as a failure, I see it as a success."

"You think July 4th was a success?" Washington asks, befuddled.

"If our Agents weren't there because of your hunch then not only would the President be dead but most likely hundreds of civilians as well. Our mission was to protect the President and we succeeded."

"That's where we differ. Yes, it was our mission to protect the President, but it was my mission to protect my Agents." Washington pauses, looking away from Bryce. "I failed them."

"Then let's make it right." Bryce says, sticking his hand out.

Washington looks back at him and shakes his hand. Like a father looking at his son, Washington looks at Bryce, smiles, and straightens his posture. He nods as his chest fills with pride. The failure of the mission remains with him but Bryce's words make it seem like less of a burden.

"I want you to head down to Weapons and Gadgets and get your weapons and tech. Chase knows you're coming, he runs the W and G sector. I was going to have you fill out this paperwork now but you can do that when you come to my office after you see Chase."

"Yes, sir. Thank you, sir." Bryce says, smiling so big it almost looks fake. "Which way is W and G?"

"There is only one way in and one way out of that room, and it's the elevator at the end of the hall." Washington says, pointing to a long hallway across the room.

Bryce looks over and sees the elevator doors in the distance. All he notices besides the elevator is that the hallway is very long and wide enough for only two people to walk side by side.

"Oh, and one more thing, your field name will be Agent Nevada."

Bryce looks back at Washington in silence with a fake smile on his face.

"What's wrong?" Washington asks.

"If it's alright with you, sir, I was hoping I could be called Agent Maine so I can honor my brother."

"I think that's a great idea. What better way to honor him?" Washington responds, shaking Bryce's hand. "Now get going, we have work to do."

As Bryce walks down the hallway he notices the empty walls on either side of him. There are no doors, no paintings or pictures, and no signs. Only lights hang from the ceiling and they are very bright. He finally reaches the far end until he is standing in front of the elevator. His hands are shaking from the excitement of being able to see the Weapons and Gadgets sector. The energy quickly changes when he notices no button on the wall, just a small glass panel about the size of a business card.

Bryce pushes the panel, expecting it to act just like a button, but nothing happens. He waves his hand in front of it thinking that maybe it's a motion sensor and still the door doesn't open. Sweat runs down his face from embarrassment hoping nobody is watching him. Finally he pulls out his Di9 ID and taps the panel with it, waves it around a bit, and then holds it up thinking that the glass is a camera but the doors remain closed.

Now perplexed he looks around for anything that could help him figure out how to get into the elevator. All of a sudden his phone rings and he sees that Washington is calling after pulling it from his pocket.

"Sir?" He answers.

"Bryce, the glass is a thumb scanner." Washington informs him.

Bryce drops his head to his chest like a beaten man. He doesn't know what is more embarrassing, the fact that he couldn't figure out how to open the elevator or that Washington was watching the whole time. He places his thumb on the glass and a red light appears, scanning his fingerprint. The screen turns green indicating the biometric scan was accepted and the doors begin to open.

"Thank you, sir, that worked." He says before hanging up the phone.

The ride down is a fast one and he has no idea how many floors he has traveled when he feels the elevator stop. He steps out into a big, open room that is about twenty feet wide and twice as long as it's width. There is a single desk surrounded by glass at the far end of the room. A lone, middle aged woman sits there with one hand underneath. He also can't help but notice the massive trench in the ground only ten feet from the elevator going from one side of the room to the other. There would be no way for anyone to get across it without falling in.

"Retinal scan." The woman says before Bryce can even take a step.

"I'm sorry?" Bryce asks, befuddled.

"Retinal scan please." The woman says again, moving her eyes from him to the scanner.

Bryce turns and sees the retinal scanner in the corner to his right. He looks back at the woman and nods before making his way to the scanner. The machine doesn't take long to read the eyes. Within seconds the scanner beeps twice and the light on top turns green. He steps away from the scanner and turns towards the woman seeing that the trench's floor is rising. It stops even with the regular floor.

"Bryce Stone, it's good to meet you." The woman says.

"How did you know who I am? Was it from the retinal scan?" He asks.

"No, from the thumb print at the top of the elevator. The retinal scan just confirmed it."

"That's a nice little security measure you have there. I assume if someone got down here somehow and didn't belong there wouldn't be a way across the gap in the floor?"

"That's right. The only way to get across is by the retinal scan. Once you are confirmed, the floor starts to rise."

"What if I didn't belong and brought

down a gun? I wouldn't be able to get to you but I could very easily shoot you from here."

"That's what the bullet proof glass is for around my desk."

"So you'd be safe but you'd be stuck in here with me. There is no way you could get to the door behind you without getting shot. Do you have a panic button or something?"

"There is a panic button to let others know of the danger. I wouldn't have to wait for help though."

"Why is that?"

"If I hit the panic button under my desk, not only does it send out an alert but it will also fire a heat seeking defense at whoever doesn't belong down here."

"A heat seeking defense?"

"That's right. No bullets are fired and the assailant will not be harmed. What is fired are multiple, well, I call them gum balls."

"Gum balls?"

"They are about the size of softballs and very sticky. Once they hit the target they quickly expand trapping them and rendering them unable to move. After they are down, an electrical net is fired from the ceiling which sends out a current with the strength of five taser guns."

"That doesn't sound pleasant."

"We've never had to use it yet, but I wouldn't want to be the one that it is tested on."

"I don't blame you. So what now?"

"What do you mean?"

"I was told to come down to W and G."

"Oh, that's right. I'm so sorry, I don't get a lot of visitors here and most people don't really stop to talk to me. They are all too busy."

"I'm sorry to hear that. By the way, I didn't get your name."

"My name is Deb, but everyone here calls me The Protector. I'm not very fond of that."

"Well, Deb, it was very nice to meet you and I'd love to talk some more but Washington wants me in W and G as soon as possible. I already wasted time at the top of the elevator trying to figure out how to open it."

"Yes, of course. It's just right through the door." She says, pointing to the door behind the desk.

"Thanks, Deb. I'm sure we'll be seeing each other more often from this point out." He says opening the door and walking through.

CHAPTER 10

Monday, July 6th, 2026

Weapons and Gadgets

10:27 A.M.

Bryce shuts the door behind him and stands in awe at the size of the room in front of him. It is as long as a football field and three times as wide. He notices the many different areas, each with it's own specialization.

Multiple cars are being fitted with weapons and gadgetry to the left. On the right is a firing range for shooting and testing weapons. Sitting in front of him in the middle of the floor are dozens of work stations and computers for the IT department. As he continues to scan the room he sees an area past the IT department on the far end of the room. It is a solid wall with a single door with no windows or additional entry points into that area. He watches two men walk through the door and quickly close it behind themselves.

Just as his intrigue heightens, he spots a man walking towards him from the center of the IT department. The guy looks like he hasn't slept for days. His hair is disheveled and the bags under his eyes are big enough to hold groceries.

"Are you Bryce?" The man asks, holding a gigantic travel mug filled with coffee.

"Yeah, I'm Bryce."

"It's nice to meet you, I'm Chase."

Bryce smiles and sticks out his hand waiting for Chase to do the same. The two men stand and stare at each other for a few seconds before Bryce drops his hand.

"I'm sorry, I just don't like to share my coffee." Chase says.

"What? I don't want your coffee." Bryce says, confused. "I was trying to shake your hand."

Chase shakes his head embarrassed at himself for not realizing what was going on. "I'm sorry, I've been here for a long time." He says, rubbing his eyes.

"To be honest, it looks like you haven't slept for a while."

"That would be an understatement. I'm already on my sixth coffee this morning."

"What time did you get here?" Bryce asks.

"What time is it now?"

"10:30."

"Oh, I've been here since Saturday afternoon."

"You don't get to go home?"

"Not when I'm busy."

"When do you sleep?"

"I get some time here and there. I have a cot in my office. When you are down here long enough you tend to lose track of the time and day. As you can see there are no windows to the outside world."

"I don't think I could do that."

"Yeah it's not for everyone. Now what do you say I show you around and get you all set up with your gear. Where do you want to start?"

"Wherever you want to take me first is fine by me. You're in charge."

"Follow me."

Bryce follows Chase through the IT department and past the firing range before heading down a hallway. The men walk in silence as the hallway leads them past the firing range.

"Where are we going?" Bryce asks.

"The place where all Agents want to go first." Chase stops at the double door at the end of the hallway and looks back at Bryce with a smile on his face. "You're going to like this." He says, swiping his ID card which opens the doors.

With one hand on each door, Chase pushes both open with a swagger. He continues into the room with both arms held away from his body showing off just a bit. Bryce follows closely behind him and is confused by what he sees. Of all the things he thought might be there he definitely wasn't expecting to see an empty room. There is no furniture and no windows. The only thing he notices in the room other than the lights is a dial on the wall just inside the door.

"What do you think?" Chase asks.

"Think of what? There's nothing here." Bryce responds.

"Everyone always says that their first time." Chase says, walking over to turn the dial one click to the left.

Immediately the empty walls slide open to reveal a hidden panel that begins to emerge. Bryce's jaw drops when he sees the once empty room now filled with hand guns of every shape and size he could imagine.

"You have to have every kind of gun ever made in here." Bryce says, astonished.

"And we've customized some of them." Chase says, proudly.

"What if I needed an assault rifle?" Bryce asks, quizzically.

Without answering, Chase turns the dial one more click to the left. Again the walls slide open revealing an assortment of assault rifles.

"Before you ask....." Chase turns the dial one more time to the left revealing sniper rifles.

"That is amazing." Bryce says.

"Thanks, it took a lot of work but it makes everything easier to find this way. Now which gun do you like?"

"I am a big fan of the Glock."

"That's a good gun," Chase says, turning the dial back to the first position bringing all the hand guns back into view. "Back left corner of the room."

Bryce walks over to the corner and sees all the Glocks. He scans them thoroughly and picks a couple up before putting them back down.

"Find anything you like?" Chase asks impatiently.

"A few caught my eye but the balance was off. If it doesn't feel right in my hand then it won't feel right if I have to fire it. Your gun is your best friend out there. If you aren't getting along with your best friend in the field then things could get awkward."

"So all the Glocks in here, and you can't find one you like?"

"Is this all the Glocks you have?"

"This is all of them except for one. An Agent is testing it at the firing range now. It's actually the one your brother used."

Bryce whips his head around and looks Chase right in his eyes. "Show me."

CHAPTER 11

Monday, July 6th, 2026

Shooting Range

10:42 A.M.

...........POP! POP! POP!

Bryce and Chase watch the Agent in the room finish testing the Glock. His target is about 75 feet away from where he was shooting and most of the bullets hit center mass. Both men watch the Agent bring the target in before they approach him. The man looked big from afar, but the closer he gets the bigger the man seems. Not only his height, which has to be about six and a half feet tall, but his muscles too. They bulge and tighten with every move as he unhooks his target from the range. The guy looks like he spent the last year training for a UFC fight.

"John Palmer, I'd like you to meet Bryce Stone. He just became an Agent today." Chase says, introducing the men.

"Bryce Stone." John says, extending his

hand. "I'm sorry to hear about your brother."

"Thank you. I heard stories about you from Travis. He always spoke highly of you." Bryce responds while shaking John's hand.

"We were very close, he was my best friend here. I just wish I was with him in Philly fighting along side him."

"Why weren't you there?"

"I was on assignment for two weeks in Beijing. I just got back last night."

"What were you doing there?" Bryce asks curiously.

"I don't remember."

"You don't remember what you did on your assignment?"

"Look, man, I don't know you. I'm not telling you anything unless I'm ordered to."

"Okay, take it easy. I was just making small talk."

"I brought Bryce down here to test out the Glock you're using." Chase says after an awkward silence, trying to defuse the tension.

"Well, that's too bad, I like this gun a lot. I think I'm going to make it my own." John replies.

"I just want to try it out. You can have it back when I'm done." Bryce pleads.

"I think you guys should get moving before I get angry." John says with a snarl.

Both men stare each other down and refuse to give an inch. It gets tenser by the second with each man trying to stake his claim on the gun. Before things escalate further, Chase steps in between them and puts his arm around Bryce's shoulder.

"Come on, we can find a gun that's just as good." He says, trying to walk Bryce towards the door.

"Smart thinking," John says. "By the way, what name did they give you? Agent Pipsqueak?"

Bryce stops in his tracks and slowly turns around. Chase tries his hardest to get him to continue to the door but he has no luck.

"Agent Maine." Bryce says, taking a step towards John.

"No, that can't be true. They wouldn't give away Travis's name to some noob." John says, shaking his head in disgust.

"Maybe they gave it to some noob because the Agents that were here already weren't worthy enough to have it." Bryce says with his fists clenched, ready to fight.

He can see that John is taken aback by what he just said. His blood boils more with each second that passes thinking that John doesn't think he's worthy to carry on his brother's code name.

"I'll tell you what, if you beat me right now at the range then you can have the gun. There are fifteen rounds in the clip and one in the chamber. We'll empty the clip and the best score will win. The round in the chamber will be your practice shot. The last fifteen rounds will count."

"Sounds good to me." Bryce says, walking over to John.

"I'll let you decide if you want to go first or second." John says.

"You can go first. At least then you'll feel like you still have an opportunity to win."

John nods and hangs his target before moving it back 75 feet, about half the distance of the range. He takes off his shirt revealing both arms covered in tattoos, with some peeking out of his tank top on his chest and back. Bryce just gets angrier when John smiles at him while pointing his gun towards the target.

"Make sure you take notes. Watch how a real man shoots." He says to a silent Bryce.

Bryce watches John fire his practice shot at the red dot in the upper left corner of the target. He then unloads his clip into the target hitting thirteen of fifteen shots in center mass. John arrogantly brings his target in and holds it up for Bryce to see smiling from ear to ear causing the skin on his bald head to wrinkle.

"If you want to walk away now I won't blame you." John says.

"You know, you're awfully cocky for a guy who hasn't seen me shoot yet."

"This ain't Call of Duty, Agent Pipsqueak. This is where real men come to shoot."

Bryce grabs his target, hangs it, and moves it back 75 feet before locking eyes with John to load his gun. While maintaining his eye contact he pushes the button to move the target back the length of the range. He aims his gun as John and Chase look on and fires the first shot, hitting just left of the red practice dot. Making his adjustment he fires two rounds at a time until the eighth bullet. From then on he continuously fires until the clip is empty.

He places the gun on the counter and brings the target back in. "I believe the gun belongs to me." Bryce says, holding the target up for both men to see.

Chase and John stand in silence with their mouths open in disbelief, 14 out of 15 are head shots.

"I'm a man of my word. It's yours." John replies, frustrated before angrily turning and walking towards the door with his shirt draped over his shoulder. He stops in his tracks right before the door when he hears Bryce speak.

"Hey, John, you never told me your Agent name. Is it Agent Gigantor?"

"Agent Utah." He replies, turning back towards Bryce with a smirk.

"Nice shooting, Agent Utah."

John nods and then turns to leave the room while Chase stands in shock, holding Bryce's gun.

"I've never seen anyone shoot like that." Chase says.

"This isn't the first time I've shot a gun."

"Come with me, I think it's time to do the

training program."

CHAPTER 12

Monday, July 6th, 2026

Training Program

11:01 A.M.

"Okay, Bryce, you are good to go." Chase says, putting a vest on Bryce.

"What is this for? What kind of training program is this?" Bryce asks.

"Think of it as a game of laser tag with objectives."

"Is that what the vest and hat are for?"

"Yup, just like in laser tag, if one of the sensors on your body pick up a laser being shot at you then you are dead."

"The five bad guys have the same thing on them that I have to shoot?"

"They do, just theirs are a lot smaller and they only have one on the chest, one on the head, and one on the back."

"I have a lot more targets on me than just those three."

"That's true. We try to make it a little harder for the Agents to help them train."

"Train to do what?"

"To not get shot."

"How will I know if I'm shot or if I take down one of the assailants?"

"You'll know."

"How?"

"See those five lights on the wall above you? Once the program starts all five will light up. Every time you hit one of your targets a light will go out. When all five are out then there are no bad guys left."

"And if I'm hit?"

"You'll feel a little zap of electricity."

"Wait, what? Are you serious?"

"It's not that bad, I mean it will knock you down, but it won't do any damage."

"I'm starting to have second thoughts about this."

"You'll be fine, just don't get shot."

Bryce looks at Chase out of the corner of his eye and adjusts his vest to feel more comfortable. He grabs the gun he's going to use for the program and gets a feel for it before putting it in his holster.

"So what's the objective?" He asks.

"In this program you need to rescue a hostage from five assailants in an abandoned building. You don't know where the bad guys are or where the hostage is being held. You only have ten minutes to complete the task."

"A whole ten minutes without knowing the layout of the building or where anyone is? Gee, thanks." Bryce says sarcastically.

"You'll do fine." Chase says, patting Bryce on the back. "Ready to begin?"

"Yeah, let's do it."

"Okay, I'll head into the other room. You'll know when to start when the assailant lights go on above you. After they are on you will have ten minutes to rescue the hostage. The clock will stop if you are shot or if you hit the button behind the hostage."

"What button?"

"It's right behind her, you won't miss it. Hitting the button means you completed the mission." Chase says, leaving to watch on monitors. "Oh, by the way, the hostage is in the building in front of you."

The building is three stories high with a lone door on the first floor three steps up from the ground and perfectly centered on the building. Each floor has four windows with two on each side of the door.

"Ready to begin?" Chase asks through the ear piece.

Bryce turns and gives a thumbs up signaling he is ready. He turns towards the building and pulls his gun from his holster.

"Good luck, Bryce. Let's start in five...four...three...two..."

The overhead lights go out and a dim light turns on simulating the moon on a dark night. Just as Bryce adjusts to the nighttime lighting, the five red lights on the wall turn on signaling the start of the program. Immediately he clicks a button on his watch starting a ten minute timer before sprinting to the back of the building. He doesn't have time to assume the hostage is on the third floor and be wrong. Without knowing where anyone is, he decides that he has to check each floor thoroughly and do it quickly.

The back of the building is set up just like the front, with a door in the middle and two windows on each side. As Bryce approaches the door he sees it is slightly open causing him to stop in his tracks. He pulls a small mirror from his pocket and backtracks until he is directly under the window just left of the door.

He looks through the window with the mirror realizing his instincts were correct. One of the five bad guys is waiting in the hallway wearing a ski mask with his gun drawn, ready to shoot. Quickly Bryce makes his way back to the door slowly nudging it open and then heads back to the window. The door opens about half way before coming to a stop. He watches in the mirror as the bad guy raises his weapon and aims it at the door.

"I hope these things shoot through glass." He thinks to himself.

In one motion he stands, aims, and shoots

twice hitting the bad guy in the sensor located on his chest. Bryce watches him drop to the ground from the electrical shock. His body convulses waiting for the shock circuit to finish.

"Good job on the first kill. Nine minutes left." Chase says through the ear piece as one red light turns off.

Bryce enters the building with his gun drawn scanning the area. The first floor is an open concept office with a couple of glass conference rooms. He searches the room on the left side of the building followed by the one on the right. Once clear he heads down the hallway in the center of the building towards the front.

Now past the conference rooms he sees a floating stair case on his right with an elevator at the base of the stairs. The rest of the first floor is wide open with limited places for someone to hide. There is a receptionist desk by the front door with a few chairs in front of the desk and some tables and filing cabinets against the wall.

"Eight minutes left." Chase says again through the ear piece.

Confident the first floor is clear, Bryce focuses on the stairs. They go half way up before reaching, then turn 180 degrees to continue to the top. He knows either way he goes up to the second floor is trouble. If he takes the stairs then he is out in the open with no cover while the enemy could be waiting for him from an elevated position. If he chooses the elevator then he will be trapped in a box while the enemy waits for the doors to open.

With the clock ticking and losing valuable time he decides to take the elevator. The enemy will know he's coming but at least he'll have a little cover to try to defend himself. He reaches for the button to open the elevator doors but stops just before pressing it.

He sprints towards the first bad guy that he already shot and drags him back to the elevator, pushing the button to open the doors. Laying the bad guy on his stomach, Bryce stages it to look like he is about to shoot. He pulls off the mask of the bad guy and reaches up to push open a panel on the roof of the elevator. Pressing the button for the second floor he jumps up to grab the roof and pulls himself up through the open panel.

The elevator slows as it approaches the second floor and he pulls the panel back into place just before the doors begin to open but leaves it pried open a crack to see what is going on. Not even a second goes by before a red laser is pointed at the bad guy on the floor. He watches the decoy shake from being shocked again from a gunshot.

"Hey, Jimmy, I got him!" A voice says in the distance.

Bryce watches the bad guy slowly come into view as he approaches. Through the panel he can see the masked bad guy enter the elevator and look straight down at the man he just shot.

"What the….."

Before the man can finish his sentence Bryce shoots him in the target on his hat and jumps down. He grabs the second bad guy before he can even fall to the floor and holds him up as a shield waiting for 'Jimmy'. A couple seconds go by and Bryce hears footsteps getting closer and closer. He inches into the back corner of the elevator still holding the second bad guy.

"Randy, are you okay?" Jimmy asks.

"I'm in the elevator. Come check this out!" Bryce says, disguising his voice to sound like Randy.

He waits with his gun in his right hand as the footsteps get closer. With every footstep he hears he slowly lifts his gun higher to be ready to fire immediately. The third bad guy finally reaches the elevator and walks right into the opening.

"Hey, Jimmy." Bryce says with a smile.

Jimmy fires two quick shots that hit Randy in the target on his back causing him to feel the electric shock again. Bryce fires one shot hitting Jimmy in his chest which drops him to the ground shaking and convulsing. He lets go of Randy and sprints into the hallway to take cover and waits for a couple seconds to make sure nobody else is coming. The second floor is laid out exactly like the first.

"Only four minutes remain." Chase

informs Bryce.

With not much time left, he has to make a decision. Should he check the rest of the floor to ensure it's all clear before heading to the third floor, or should he just assume the floor is clear. If his kindergarten math is correct, there are a total of five guys and he already shot three meaning two remain. From his experience bad guys never leave just one man guarding the hostage, there are always two or more.

He runs to the stairs and takes them two at a time to get to the third floor as quickly as he can. Once he gets to the third floor he realizes it is laid out differently than the first two floors. There are no glass walls and there appear to be apartments on this floor. He's going to have to check each room carefully but very quickly.

He goes to the closest door and quietly puts his hand on the handle. He tries to turn it but realizes it's locked. Before trying anything else he stops and thinks for a second and then heads to the next door. Again he quietly tries to open the door but again it is locked. He swiftly walks down the hall looking at each door as he passes but not even stopping to check them.

"Three minutes left." Chase says.

Now almost at the end of the building, there are only two more doors on each side of the hallway. Passing the second to last set he stops in his tracks and takes two steps backwards. He looks at the door on his left and then stands next to it with his back against the wall. Taking a deep breath he grabs the door handle and quickly swings it open to take a peek inside the room.

"Two minutes left, Bryce." Chase whispers in his ear.

With only the moon light from outside the building shining in, Bryce sees the hostage sitting in a chair in the middle of the room with a bad guy standing directly behind her using her as a shield. A second guy stands in the back corner of the room behind a book shelf with his gun pointed at the door. Just like the other bad guys, these two are also wearing ski masks.

He goes over the options in his head and realizes the odds aren't in his favor. He pulls the mirror from his pocket and has another look in the room. Both men are covered and pointing their guns right at the doorway.

"You know you have less than two minutes left. Why don't you just come in here and get it over with?" One of the men yells out.

Knowing that he can't just stick his gun in the room and take a shot or two hoping to get lucky, Bryce decides to try a different tactic. He goes to the end of the hall and unplugs the emergency flood light fixture and takes it off the wall.

"One minute left, Bryce. You need to hurry!" Chase says one last time into the ear piece.

Bryce runs back to the door and plugs the

emergency flood lights into a hallway outlet. He looks at the back of the light and switches it to off and holds it in the doorway. Quickly he turns it on high, then off, and back on high. All three people in the room squint as their eyes try to recover from the blast of light. Bryce sprints into the room and fires two shots into a target of the man in the corner knocking him down. Before the last bad guy can figure out what is going on Bryce is already standing next to him holding his gun to the target on his head.

Turning his head towards Bryce he drops his gun in defeat. Bryce shoots the target on the ski mask dropping the last bad guy to the floor from the electricity coursing through his body. He looks at his watch and sees he only has fifteen seconds left. Quickly he cuts the zip ties that were holding the hostage to the chair and makes his way over to the button on the wall.

"Hey, Bryce." The hostage says. "I'm sorry."

Bryce stops in his tracks and turns around. The hostage fires a shot, hitting him in the chest seconds before he presses the button. As he lays on the floor twitching and shaking he hears the alarm on his watch going off indicating that he ran out of time. The lights turn on announcing the simulation is over. Medics come into the room to check on the electrocuted Agents while Chase walks over to Bryce and stands above him making sure he is okay.

"You said there were only five bad guys."

Bryce struggles to say, still shaking from the zaps of electricity.

"That's true. But you see Bryce, you weren't supposed to be successful. You were meant to fail this one." Chase replies.

"Why? What's the point of that."

"As good as our intel is you can never assume that there are no more bad guys. You can't always trust who someone says they are. You need to always be aware and have your radar up. Do that and you can survive."

Bryce nods in agreement with Chase. He knows he should've checked the hostage for weapons or at least hit the button on the wall first before he untied her.

"Come on, Washington is waiting for us." Chase says, holding out his hand to help Bryce stand up.

Bryce doesn't reach up for help. He lays still and stares up at Chase embarrassed.

"What's wrong?" Chase asks.

"I think someone peed my pants."

"No worries there." Chase says, chuckling to himself. "It happens to a lot of people the first time they get zapped. You can take a shower in my office. I'll grab you some new gear and then we'll go see Washington."

Bryce nods and grabs Chase's hand to stand up.

"Thanks, Chase." Bryce says, jogging out of the room and down the hall to get to Chase's office.

Chase pulls out a phone and calls Washington who is waiting for them in his office.

"Washington." He says, answering the phone.

"It's Chase, there's going to be a slight delay. We'll be there in a few minutes though."

"Did Bryce pee himself?"

"Yes, sir."

"How do you think he did?"

"I would say from the zap of electricity. It happens quite often."

"No, I mean in the training program."

"Sir, he was feet away from hitting the button. It's the farthest I've ever seen anyone make it in that program."

"You gave him the hardest one with the hostage?"

"Yes, sir. It was the best run I've ever seen."

"Good, my hunch was right about him. I can't wait to see what he can do in the field."

"Me neither, sir."

"Is he getting cleaned up now?"

"Yes, sir. We'll be up shortly."

"Make it quick. We have some stuff to discuss."

CHAPTER 13

Monday, July 6th, 2026

11:28 A.M.

Bryce stands in front of Washington's door and has yet to knock, something doesn't feel right. He knows he was a good detective, some would say great. For some reason he feels he might not be good enough to be an Agent in Di9. Finally, he knocks, realizing it's better to talk to Washington than to stand out in the hall like an idiot staring at a closed door.

"Come in." Washington says from inside his office.

Bryce enters and closes the door behind him. He sees Washington standing at his drink cart pouring himself a glass of Johnie Walker Blue scotch.

"Have a seat, Bryce. Can I fix you a drink?" Washington asks.

"No, thank you. I'm not a big drinker." Bryce says, heading over to Washington's desk to take a seat.

"Well you just became an Agent, give it

time," He walks over to his desk and puts down his drink as Bryce settles in. He pulls a couple files out and places them in front of his newest Agent. "Have a look at them." He says, picking his glass back up. "Are you sure I can't get you a drink? I'd rather not drink alone."

"Sure, I'll drink one with you." Bryce says after thinking for a second.

"Excellent." Washington says, walking over to the cart to pour another glass of scotch.

"Sir, before I look at these files I think we need to have a conversation."

"What's on your mind, son?" Washington says, pouring the scotch.

"I'm going to be honest with you and I'm not sure if I should say this to you or not, but I feel it's better to tell you now then wait until it's too late."

"Well what is it?" Washington asks, setting the drink down in front of Bryce.

"When I was standing outside your door I was wondering if I was ready to be an Agent."

"What makes you think that?" Washington says, standing next to his desk.

"When I became a detective I was excited. There was nothing else I wanted more at that time and I knew I was ready. I'm excited to be an Agent too, but I'm just not sure I'm ready to be one yet."

"Why do you think you aren't ready?"

"I don't really have an answer for you on

that. It just feels different, almost like I'm not supposed to be here, like I don't belong."

"Bryce, let me tell you something. You wouldn't be here if you weren't supposed to be here. We don't just pull random people off the street to be in Di9. You definitely wouldn't be an Agent if I didn't know that you are ready. My hunches are usually spot on and I have a hunch that you are going to be an outstanding Agent."

"Thank you, sir. Maybe it just feels different because I failed the one test you gave me."

"You were supposed to fail that. Those are more for learning purposes than practice. Now you know in the field to never let your guard down and rely on more than just the intel." Washington pauses to think if he should tell Bryce the next sentence before deciding to do it. "Don't tell anyone I told you this, but you scored the best out of any Agent that has ever taken that test."

Bryce smiles and sits up in his chair after hearing that. In a matter of minutes he went from doubting himself to feeling like he is ready to conquer the world.

"Trust me, we do our homework on every single person that walks through those doors. You are the person I was most excited about becoming an Agent by far." Washington says to reaffirm his faith in Bryce.

"I think I'm ready to look at that file with

you now." Bryce says with confidence, finally taking his first sip of the scotch.

Washington opens a drawer on his desk and pulls out a remote and points it behind him to press a button causing a big screen to come down out of the ceiling behind his desk. Bryce watches the screen descend into place while both men take a sip of scotch. He opens the file and sees a report and picture of Tiffany Peterson. The first thing he notices about her is the big scar on her right cheek followed by the fact that she looks like Legolas from *Lord of the Rings*. He studies the file and is impressed by the things he is reading about her.

"Why am I looking at her? According to her file she doesn't seem like a threat at all. Her father is German with a 140 I.Q. The mother is Scandinavian and an ex-Olympic athlete turned model. There are no signs of any terrorist affiliations or known associates." Bryce states.

"We have algorithms that our intel uses to pick up many words or phrases that might be said over the phone or written in a text or email. Things like Al-Qaeda, Allah, and anything that deals with harming the President or an act of terrorism. Every time our computer picks up one of those words it gets flagged and analyzed. If a person gets flagged more than once then they get investigated."

"Is that why you want me to look at this file? She's been flagged?"

"Not only has she been flagged but she has been in the same area of some pretty bad people more than once. Maybe it's just a coincidence, but maybe not. That's what we need to find out."

"The file says she's in Germany. Do you want me to go there to tail her and find out what she's up to?"

"Not yet. We know she's traveled to Russia twice in the past week and we believe she has met with an ex-FSB Agent, formerly the KGB. We don't know who she met or why."

"Why would they want to meet with her, she's not Russian and she's not a terrorist that we know of."

"I have a hunch that she might've been involved in the attacks in Philly the other day. I believe she met with a Russian Agent to provide funding for an attack."

"What makes you say that?" Bryce asks.

"When she was younger her father worked for the President of the United States. He was the right hand man and very trusted. The President would never make a big decision without speaking to her father. The two men were best friends."

"It doesn't say that in the file anywhere." Bryce says, shuffling through the papers looking for that info.

"That's true. There is no evidence of him ever working for the President and not many people even know he did. It's almost like his identity was erased and he never existed."

"Why?"

"Story has it that one day Tiffany's father made a very poor decision or had a lapse in judgment. The President was so furious that he deported Tiffany and her family back to Germany and cut ties with them completely because of what her father did. She was only eight years old. Imagine losing everything you have and deported from the country with nothing but the clothes on your back and the money in your account."

"Nobody ever got the truth about what happened?"

"Not that I'm aware of and I know a lot of things about a lot of people. This happened back in 1992 so it's been thirty-four years and still nobody knows."

"You said they were left with nothing when they were deported. How did they get their money?"

"They did enough to survive the first few years there. Word has it that her father worked his tail off to provide for his family and for them to live comfortably. Once he had a little money saved he did some research and started investing in some stocks. He was doing okay until one day he hit the jackpot."

"Did he invest in Apple or Amazon?"

"He did better than that. He bought stock in Bitcoin when it first became public and everyone knows how well that did. The family is now worth billions."

"Did you say billions with a 'B'?" Bryce asks, stunned.

"That I did, and because of her father's smarts and business savvy he kept investing in other things with the money he made from Bitcoin. The next twenty generations of Peterson's will never have to work a day in their life if they don't want to because of that man."

"So because they got deported and because of their money you believe Tiffany is involved with the attacks? You think she has some sort of vendetta on the U.S.?"

"I believe so." Washington says, leaning back in his chair.

"Why would she go through all that trouble? Wouldn't there be easier ways to get back at us?"

"For most people, yes. Take a look at this though." Washington says, hitting a button on the remote that brings up some pictures of Tiffany Peterson.

Bryce is shocked by what he sees on the screen as Washington shows him one picture after another. The picture of Tiffany in the file looks nothing like the ones he is looking at now.

"Is that Tiffany?" Bryce asks in disbelief.

"It is. The picture in the file is from five years ago. These are more recent ones."

"What happened to her?"

"Her father was so smart and so busy making a living that he never had time for her. Her mother was so beautiful, loved, and well known that it caused Tiffany to have doubt about herself. She felt like she could never live up to her parents. She wanted more attention from her parents and was jealous of the attention they were getting from the public. So she started having plastic surgery to make herself more beautiful."

"Is that what the scar is from?"

"Yes, it was a botched surgery which caused her to have another surgery to repair the scar and then another and then another. Before she knew it she had so many surgeries that her face and body turned into a big pile of scar tissue that wouldn't heal. She is in constant pain and needs help getting around. That girl takes so many pills I don't know how her body doesn't shut down. She needs an oxygen tank just to walk and most of the time her two body guards have to help her get around by carrying her."

"Where are her parents now?"

"They died in a mysterious plane crash eighteen months ago. They were flying their private jet from Germany to Switzerland and their plane went down in the Alps. By the time responders got to the plane most of the wreckage was burnt and gone."

"What makes it mysterious then? Don't planes go down sometimes?" Bryce asks quizzically.

"What makes this so mysterious is that there was no distress signal, no call for help, and not a word was said about anything going wrong during the flight. When the responders finally got there they realized that the electronic flight data recorders, or black box, was gone. They spent six months looking for it but they never found it."

"Don't they usually get found?"

"They do. Almost all of them get found. Where the plane went down in the Alps would make it difficult to find but they should have found it."

"What do you think happened?"

"I think it was removed before the flight by someone who knew how to work on them and they disabled it so it wouldn't ping."

"You think Tiffany was involved in that? You think she killed her own parents?"

"I'm not certain but it is very coincidental. Especially when you factor in that Tiffany inherited everything after her parents deaths. Now she is a billionaire and owns the rights to everything her parents owned."

Bryce looks down and thinks about all the details Washington just told him. There is no hard evidence to support the theory but he knows this is more than just a coincidence and agrees with his boss.

"What do you want me to do?" Bryce asks,

looking back up at Washington.

"For now I need you to go back to Philadelphia to see if there is anything you can find. We need to find out who those men in black were and maybe we can figure out if Tiffany is involved and who exactly she might be funding."

"When do you want me to leave?"

"Now. Bring back anything you think might be of help."

Just then Bryce remembers the metal piece he found at his brother's house after it exploded. He's not sure if it will help at all but he knew it didn't belong where he found it.

"Sir, I found something at Travis's house that seemed out of place. I don't think it was a coincidence that his house blew up the day after the attacks on Philly but I also didn't think what I found would give us any helpful intel."

"Where is it?"

"It's in the bottom right hand drawer of my desk. Want me to go get it?"

"No, I need you to get to Philly. I'll retrieve it from your desk if you are okay with that. What does it look like?"

"It's the only thing in that drawer. You'll know it when you see it."

"I'll bring it down to get analyzed while you are gone. I want Agent Utah to go with you so you have another set of eyes."

"Yes, sir." Bryce says with his best fake smile, finishing his last sip of scotch.

He knows his first encounter with Utah was not the best and he is a little intimidated by him, but two sets of eyes are better than one. If Travis's stories are true about Utah then he knows he's working with a great Agent.

"Dismissed." Washington says.

Bryce stands, leaves the room, and walks down the hall with a swagger. The weight on his shoulders seems much lighter now and he doesn't feel the helplessness of not being able to do anything about his brother's death anymore. Now everything feels real again.

Walking by his desk on the way to his car he sees a picture of Michael that makes him smile. He glances at a picture of Kayla and knows he messed up causing his heart to drop. Her voice runs through his head as he remembers her saying, 'I don't want you to jump into anything without talking to me about it first.' Bryce knows there are many dangerous things that an Agent encounters. He never thought he would have to worry about his wife killing him before he even goes in the field.

CHAPTER 14

Monday, July 6th, 2026

Bryce and Kayla's Home

12:20 P.M.

"Kay?" Bryce says, entering his house and closing the door behind him. "It's me."

He can hear his wife singing over the blaring music in the kitchen which causes him to smile. She isn't a very good singer but that doesn't stop her.

"Kayla!" Bryce yells to try to get her to hear him over the music, but there is still no answer.

He looks in the living room to his left and then proceeds past the stairs and down the hallway towards the kitchen. He glances into the dining room on his right, causing him to shake his head in disappointment. "Such a waste of a room." He says to himself, trying to remember the last time it was used.

Entering the kitchen he sees one of the greatest things he's ever seen. Kayla is holding a wooden spoon, using it as a microphone as she dances. She is an even worse dancer than she is a singer but she does it with such conviction. He takes a couple steps towards Kayla, who is still unaware that her husband is home, and stops in the middle of the kitchen to do what any husband would do. He claps his hands once, scaring Kayla, and breaks into his best dance moves.

His plan works to perfection. A startled Kayla turns to see him doing the running man which quickly turns into the cabbage patch followed by the roger rabbit.

"You're so corny," Kayla says, smirking and shaking her head. "You almost scared me to death. What are you doing home, is everything okay?"

"I'm sorry to scare you. I was calling for you from the time I walked in the door." Bryce says, continuing to dance.

"Alexa, stop." Kayla says, making the music come to an end along with Bryce's dancing. "Why are you home?"

"They're sending me back to Philadelphia to investigate. I needed to come home to get a few things and pack a bag."

"When are you leaving?"

"As soon as I'm packed."

"Why are they sending you to Philly? I know you used to be a detective but you are just an analyst now."

"I'm not an analyst anymore. They promoted me to Agent." Bryce says excitedly with a huge smile on his face.

"What?" Kayla asks, annoyed with a new tone in her voice.

As much as Bryce hoped Kayla would let it slide and be happy for him he knows he messed up. He drops his head in embarrassment and knows he let down his wife.

"I'm an Agent now." Bryce says softly. "The gave me Agent Maine as a call sign so I can honor Travis."

Kayla turns her back to Bryce, puts down the wooden spoon, and places both hands on the kitchen counter. She grits her teeth and slams her hand against the granite countertop.

"What was the one thing I asked you?" Kayla says angrily, turning to face Bryce.

"You told me to talk to you first." Bryce responds sheepishly.

"So did you not listen to me or was it that you just don't care enough to talk to me first?"

"I'm talking to you now." Bryce says, hoping to defuse the situation.

"It doesn't matter now, you're already an Agent!" Kayla screams.

"Look, I know you're angry and I get it. It's not like they asked me to think it over and get back to them and I just disregarded how you felt. It happened this morning and it happened really quickly."

"So is there a rule that you can't call or text your wife while you're at work?"

"I didn't have time. I honestly was running around all morning getting trained and tested so they could make me an Agent."

"It's nice to know that you can't take two minutes out of your day for me." Kayla says sarcastically.

"You said you would be okay with me being an Agent. Why the sudden change of heart?"

"It's not that you became an Agent. It's that you didn't care enough to do the one thing I asked you to do before you became one. I'm your wife, but sometimes it seems like you only think about yourself."

Bryce walks up to Kayla and stands right in front of her. He places both hands on each of her shoulders and bends down slightly to be eye to eye with her.

"You know I love you and Michael more than anything in the world and I would never willingly do anything to hurt or disappoint you or him in any way." He says calmly and lovingly, hoping to calm down his wife.

"Is that alcohol I smell on your breath?" Kayla says, pulling her head away from his with a worried look on her face.

"Yes. I had one drink with my boss." He responds after standing up straight, knowing there is no point trying to hide it.

"So you're drinking now?"

"No, I'm not drinking. I was in his office with him and he asked if I wanted a scotch. I politely declined and then he said he didn't want to drink alone. So I had one glass with him."

"Oh I see. So that will never happen again, right? He'll only ask you just this one time?"

"I don't know." Bryce says.

"You don't know? You don't know?!" Kayla screams again. "How about you just say no, thank you! I'd rather not have a drink because I don't want to become my father!"

Bryce is taken aback by that comment. Kayla has never said that to him before. The more he thinks about her words the angrier he gets.

"Don't you ever say that to me again!" Bryce yells. "My father was a good man and a great cop. He taught me everything I know."

"Did he teach you how to drink until you forget about your family too?"

"He was going through a tough time then!" Bryce screams.

"So what's your excuse?"

Bryce's face turns red and he clenches his jaw. He's not mad at Kayla, he's mad at himself because he knows she is right. He takes a deep breath and exhales. Then without saying another word he turns and walks down the hall towards the stairs.

"That's it? You aren't going to answer

me?!" Kayla yells in disbelief.

Bryce keeps walking and shakes his head. He is embarrassed and disgusted with himself. Although unintentional, he just let down and hurt the person he loves the most.

"You are unbelievable! You really are becoming your father!" Kayla screams angrily. "I'm not going to be here when you get back and neither is Michael! I will not put him or myself in danger when you come home drunk!"

"I would never lay a hand on you or Michael. I love you both." Bryce says, standing at the bottom of the stairs.

"I bet your dad used to say the same thing to Travis before he would go to work too."

Bryce has never been this mad before. He stares at Kayla, shakes his head, and heads up the stairs to their bedroom. After he packs his bag with the things he needs he walks towards the door. Before he leaves the room he notices a pad of paper on the bureau. He stops in his tracks and drops his bag to grab a pen from his nightstand to write a note. Bryce folds the note in half, writes Kayla's name on it, and places it in on her nightstand.

Just then his phone buzzes. He looks down to see Agent Utah just texted him. It says:

You coming or what?

Bryce grabs his bag, heads out of the

bedroom, and down the stairs. He stops at the bottom and turns towards the kitchen to see Kayla sitting at the table sobbing.

"Kayla." Bryce calls.

She doesn't move a muscle or respond to her husband.

"Kay?"

A couple seconds pass before Kayla finally says, "Alexa, play *Had Enough* by Breaking Benjamin.

Bryce knows the song very well, as it is one of his favorite songs by one of his favorite bands. He doesn't need to hear the lyrics to understand what Kayla is trying to get across to him.

"Can we talk about this please?" He says, taking a couple steps towards the kitchen.

Kayla looks up at her husband before responding with, "Alexa, volume up."

The music plays even louder than it already was and Bryce gets the hint. He drops his head and turns to walk towards the front door. Today will be the first time that he won't get to give his wife a kiss and tell her he loves her before he leaves the house.

There is still a job to do in Philadelphia whether he is on good terms with his wife or not. He closes the door and leaves the house to get in the car. He knows he'll have to deal with this problem when he gets back, but for now it's on to Philadelphia.

CHAPTER 15

Tuesday, July 7th, 2026

Philadelphia

9:03 A.M.

Bryce and John stand quietly in front of the Masonic Library and Museum looking towards City Hall. Neither of them has seen a major city this quiet. A police officer walks by and they can only wonder why the cop is staring at them the entire time as he passes.

Three days after the attacks there are no trains running, hardly any cars on the street, and it is eerily silent. They choke up thinking of what their fellow Agents did to protect not only the President but also the people of this city. The loss of their close friends will stay with them for a long time. John knows this, but can only imagine how hard it would be if one of those friends were also his brother.

"You okay?" He asks, placing his hand on Bryce's shoulder.

"Yeah, I'm good." Bryce says, wiping away the moisture from his eyes.

"What do you say we get to work?" John asks, trying to draw Bryce's attention away from his brother for just a moment.

"Sounds good, where do you want to start?"

"Why are you asking me? You're the detective."

"Well then let's start on the roof where Dakota was killed."

The two Agents walk down the street towards the building where Dakota was stationed. Along the way they pass the alley where Agents Oregon and Montana were killed and Bryce recalls the conversation between Montana and Washington over the coms on the day of the attack. Based on the memory of the conversation and field reports he pictures a silhouette of the man dressed in black who lured Montana to his death.

"What's wrong?" John asks, seeing Bryce stop in his tracks and staring down the alley.

"Nothing." Bryce responds, trying to shake the vision out of his head. "I was just trying to visualize what Agent Montana saw when he followed that man down this alley."

"How can you see that?"

"I just put together what we know happened that day and play it out in my head. Sometimes it helps me with an investigation.

Come on, let's get to the roof." Bryce says, trying to change the subject.

Both men keep to themselves as they climb the stairs to the top of the building.

"How do you want to go about this?" John asks Bryce before they exit the stairwell and open the door to the roof.

"Why are you asking me? You're the senior Agent here."

"You're the detective, tell me what you would do."

"I think the best thing to do would be a grid search. Do you know how to do one of those?" Bryce asks.

"No, please tell me how to do that, it's my first day." John says sarcastically, rolling his eyes.

"Alright, take it easy." Bryce responds. "You take the far corner and walk east to west. I'll start in this corner opposite you and walk north to south."

John nods and walks to his corner while Bryce does the same. The men begin searching, making sure to take their time so they don't miss anything. As boring and mundane as the search is, the Agents stay silent and focused on the task at hand but after fifteen minutes they have yet to find anything of importance. They walk to the edge of the roof overlooking the street below and look towards City Hall.

"The only thing I saw that might have been something were a few small, concave holes in the wall near the door to the stairwell. That could be from many things though. I took a couple pictures of them just to be sure." John says.

"Yeah, I saw them too. There were no reported gun shots up here so it can't be from that. It's probably nothing." Bryce responds, staring off towards the other buildings.

"What's wrong?" John asks.

"I was just thinking." Bryce says, avoiding eye contact.

"Yeah, I can see that. What about?"

"I was wondering why every Agent was recovered after the attacks except for Dakota."

"What do you mean?"

"I mean they left every dead body right where they were killed. Every single one." Bryce pauses before looking at John. "Why wasn't Dakota's body ever found?"

"Dakota was my friend. You better be very careful with what you say next."

"Look, I'm just saying we need to consider all options. Why would these guys leave every body but one? It doesn't make any sense. In my experience, bad guys are either really good at covering their tracks or really bad. There's no half way."

"So you're saying we need to consider that Dakota was a double Agent?" John asks, annoyed.

"That's one option." Bryce responds, trying to calm his partner down.

"What's another option?"

"Maybe they did take his body. For what, I'm not sure. Perhaps they have something else planned and needed his finger prints, his ID card, or maybe they just took him to question him so they can find out everything that Di9 knows."

"I like that option better." John says.

"Believe me, I do too. I'm just keeping all things open until we find out what happened. I'm sorry, but it's how I was trained."

"So what now?" John asks.

"We need to head to the other roof where Michigan was stationed."

"Another grid search?"

"Another grid search." Bryce says with a smirk.

John does his best to fake a smile, nodding begrudgingly. "Lead the way."

CHAPTER 16

Tuesday, July 7th, 2026

Philadelphia

9:41 A.M.

Bryce and John walk up the stairs of the building where Michigan was killed. They reach the last landing before they get to the top and already there is a huge difference in what this area looks like compared to the other building. Bryce's eyes widen when he sees what looks like a war zone at the top of the stairs.

"Did the report say anything about a gun fight up here?" He asks, continuing to climb the stairs.

"I know Michigan emptied his clip before he kicked the door open, but there was no report of a shootout." John responds, looking around at the walls.

"Well then what do you think happened in here?"

The Agents stop at the top of the stairs

and can't believe what they see. They count forty-eight concave holes in the wall that are all the same size and shape.

"Can you pull up the pictures you took from the other building?" Bryce asks.

John pulls out his phone, quickly pulls up the pictures, and starts swiping through them.

"Wait, go back." Bryce says.

"What are you looking for?" John asks, scrolling back to the picture Bryce wanted to see.

"That right there. That was on the wall on the other roof. It's the same type of hole that is in here. What is that from?"

"I'm not sure. It wouldn't be from a gun though, that wouldn't leave damage like that. It would either ricochet or shatter the area on the wall that it hits. It wouldn't look like that."

"I agree, but all the holes in here from the ceiling to the floor are exactly the same. It wouldn't be from wear and tear."

"Why don't we go outside and do the grid search and see what we can find. Maybe we'll see something that will help us figure out what these holes are from." John says.

Just as the men are about to exit the building Bryce notices a hole about the same dimension of an average sized cantaloupe in the drywall ceiling. He stops to examine and wonders what it could be.

"What are you looking at?" John asks.

"Something about that hole doesn't seem

right."

"You want me to hoist you up to take a look?"

"If you don't mind."

John interlocks his fingers and Bryce steps into his partners hands so he can lift him up to take a closer look at the hole. Bryce pulls his flashlight out and shines it into the hole to looks to his left, behind him, and to the right. Just as he thinks there is nothing there he spots something leaning against the wall.

"You can put me down." Bryce says.

"Didn't find anything?" John asks, dropping Bryce to the ground.

"Not sure. Stand back a little."

Bryce reaches up, grabs the ceiling where the hole is, and rips a big piece of drywall down. Some dust and dirt falls and so does the thing that caught his eye. It looks to be a half of a metal ball that was hollowed out. There are some wires on the inside still attached.

"Is that what you wanted?" John asks.

"Yup, I have no clue what it is, but it didn't look like it belonged." Bryce says, picking it up.

"What are you thinking?"

"I'm thinking this is what put that hole in the ceiling." He says, looking at the metal and then the hole.

"How can you tell?"

"Just a hunch." Bryce says, holding the metal up to the remaining drywall where the hole was.

"It's the same size as the hole."

"I think we're getting somewhere. Let's go do the grid search outside."

Bryce puts the piece of metal in his bag heading out to do another grid search. He heads to the northeast corner of the roof and John heads to the southwest corner.

It's getting hotter and hotter by the second, and neither man wants to be up on the roof in the middle of summer. They know they are going to be hot no matter what so they might as well do their jobs the best they can. Without saying a word, the men begin another grid search walking the same direction they were on the other building. A few minutes go by before John spots something at the building's cooling tower.

"I think I got something over here."

"What is it?" Bryce asks, walking over.

"It looks like a tiny spear to be honest. Maybe two, two and a half inches long. I'd say about a quarter inch in diameter and very, very sharp on the end."

"Where did you find it?"

"I saw a small dent on the cooling tower and just thought I'd look around the area. I found it laying behind the pipe right there."

Bryce picks up the tiny spear and examines it. He notices that it's heavier than he thought it would be for something of that size. It also has a small taper that makes the back of it slightly smaller in diameter than the end with the point.

"No." Bryce says.

"What is it?" John asks, confused.

Bryce takes the tiny spear over to the top of the stairs and holds it up to one of the forty-eight holes in the walls. John follows him and doesn't believe what he is seeing. The spear fits in the hole exactly. Bryce holds it up to another hole, and then another, and another. Every single one matches the spear exactly. John wipes the sweat from his lip and chin and shudders at what the spears did to his friends and fellow Agents if they caused this kind of damage to a concrete block.

"I don't know who or what we are dealing with here, but we need to find out quickly. This isn't just a terrorist group with a bomb. Whoever planted this wanted to send a message."

"What message?" John asks.

"I think they wanted to let us know that they know about Di9. They wanted us to know how easily they can take us out and I don't think they are done yet."

"How could anyone know who we are?"

"You still think that nobody on the inside could be a double Agent?"

John takes a deep breath and looks down contemplating what Bryce is saying. He looks back up at his partner and turns to face the first building they investigated.

"I still don't think Dakota was a double Agent. I am curious how these guys knew about us though. I mean they knew every single Agent's location that day. That couldn't have been a coincidence."

"I hope I'm wrong, but we have to take that into consideration." Bryce says, putting his hand on John's shoulder. "Come on, lets go check out the alleyway and see if there is anything we can find there that proves me wrong."

John nods as he and Bryce grab the evidence, put it in their bags, and head down the stairs to the alley.

CHAPTER 17

Tuesday, July 7th, 2026

Philadelphia

12:10 P.M.

Bryce and John sit outside of City Hall on the stairs leading to the front door. They are only a few feet from where Travis gave his life to save the President and Bryce is struggling to hold it together. He looks to where the attack happened and watches it play out in his mind.

"How do you do it?" John asks.

"Do what?"

"How do you stay so calm? I would be a wreck right now if I was in your shoes. We spent almost two hours investigating an alleyway that gave us absolutely nothing. We searched two rooftops that gave us a piece of metal that may or may not be useful. You're staring at the exact location where your brother was murdered and I can't tell if you are holding a full house or you're bluffing."

"I'm going to be honest with you, it sucks being here. I'm doing all I can mentally to not check out and break down. But you know what, it doesn't matter if I'm here or at home, holding it together or being emotional. It doesn't change anything that has already happened. I can grieve and be sad when I get home, right now I have a job to do."

"So what's the next move?" John asks, nodding in approval.

"I want to take a break and eat lunch. Then I think we should investigate where the President was when the attacks happened."

"Sounds good to me." John says, looking around for a vendor on the street. "I'm going to go get a hotdog, you need anything?"

"No, thanks. I have some stuff in my bag."

Bryce takes a couple peanut butter to-go cups out of his bag along with some celery sticks and a six pack of powdered sugar, mini donuts while he watches John walk off to grab his food.

By the time John gets back he has already eaten half of his hotdog and he sits down next to Bryce to stare off in the distance.

"I know what you just said about being calm, but I still don't understand." John says. "I could never be as calm as you are in your situation."

"Thanks?" Bryce says, not knowing if that is a complement, a question, or something else entirely.

"I guess what I'm trying to ask is how?"

"Are you a religious man?" Bryce asks, looking over at his partner.

"No." John replies bluntly. "I grew up in church but I haven't been for a long time."

"Maybe that's why you don't understand then. I am a religious man, I believe in God and I know that He is in control. I believe that He was dead, buried, and rose again. So I guess what I'm trying to say is that if God is on my side then who can be against me? What do I have to fear?"

"That's what keeps you calm? Your belief in God?"

"I know that He will take care of me and protect me."

"So you're saying that you'll never get hurt or shot in the field? Are you saying you'll never die?"

"No, not at all. What I'm saying is that I'm not going to worry about any of that. When it's my time then it's my time whether I'm in the field or sleeping at home. Everything happens according to His will."

John shakes his head and turns away from Bryce. He's heard all this before when he was young but has seen too many things to believe it anymore. They are just fairy tales to him.

-TCKK-

John puts the last bit of hotdog in his mouth and opens his bottle of water.

-TCKK-

"What is that noise?" John asks, turning towards Bryce.

"What noise?"

John watches Bryce dip a celery stick into his peanut butter, lick the peanut butter off, and drop the celery stick onto a plastic bag sitting in front of him.

"What are you doing?" John asks, confused.

"I'm eating my peanut butter."

"Yes, I can see that. Why are you not eating the celery too?"

"I don't like celery."

-TCKK-

"Then why did you bring it?"

"The hotel ran out of spoons."

John stares at Bryce for a couple seconds wondering if he's just messing with him. "Why so many celery sticks then?"

"If you use the same one over and over it starts to get soggy and gross. I don't want the celery to ruin the flavor of the peanut butter."

"You're a weird guy."

-TCKK-

Bryce drops his last celery stick onto the bag, looks at John, and gives him the cheesiest smile he could think up. John shakes his head and smirks looking at what else Bryce has to eat.

"I assume the donuts are dessert?"

"Yup, lunch of champions right here." Bryce says, opening the package. "You don't get a body like this by not working hard." He says sarcastically.

Just then a pigeon swoops in and grabs the package of donuts right as Bryce is about to take one out to eat.

"No! Get back here!" Bryce yells, quickly standing and trying to get his donuts back.

John laughs hysterically watching his partner chase down a bird that just stole from him. After a second or two the pigeon is out of reach and flying away as quickly as it swooped in.

"Stupid pigeons!" Bryce screams as John falls back onto the stairs, holding his stomach in pain from all the laughter.

"You remind me of my neighbor who yells at squirrels for eating the food she puts out for the birds. The only difference is that you weren't chasing it around with a broom." John says, wiping the tears from his eyes. "She's also eighty-two years old."

Bryce looks at John and can't help but laugh at himself. Both men needed a good laugh and John's laughter is contagious. After a couple minutes of shared laughter the Agents finally compose themselves.

"That was good, thanks for that." John says happily.

"It wasn't that good, I lost my donuts. I love my pastries."

"Yeah, I can see that."

Bryce shakes his head and looks to where

the pigeon flew off. He knows the donuts are gone and just wants to continue with the investigation. Just as he is about to grab his bag John interrupts him.

"So you were a cop, right? What made you want to become on officer?"

"Long story short, I became a cop because my Dad was a cop."

"Following in his footsteps huh?"

"Yeah I guess. It was more for approval than to be like him though."

"What do you mean?"

"My Mom died when me and Travis were young. Our Dad took it really hard and kind of put us on the back burner. We pretty much had to fend for ourselves. I thought that if I became a cop like him that he would be proud of me and I hoped that would make us closer."

"Did it?"

"Nope, he didn't even show up when I graduated from the academy."

"It's weird isn't it? No matter what age you are or what happened in the past, a son always seeks the approval of his Dad."

"It's true. Even Travis sought his approval for so long until he finally had enough. He felt so abandoned by our Father that he just gave up. He didn't want to be anything like him "

"That's why he became a Marine and not a cop?"

"You got it. He even changed his last name

to distance himself from our Dad as much as he could. I mean before our Mom died my Dad would spend so much time with us. We got a lot of 'training' from him on how to be a good cop. I figured why not take what I know already and use that to become an officer."

"Travis didn't feel the same way."

"No, not at all. Once he feels that someone has abandoned him or done wrong by him, then you are dead to him. He just figured he had the same 'training' I did so why not join the military."

"Why did he choose the Marines? There isn't anything wrong with that but there are many routes he could've chosen. Just curious why he chose to become a Marine."

"Because you don't mess with a Marine. You stay on their good side or you stay out of their way. They're the toughest guys there are."

"Oorah." John says in agreement.

"You were a Marine?" Bryce asks unknowingly.

"Yes, sir. Stationed at Marine Barracks in D.C. from 2018-2021 and then recruited to join Di9 which I've been doing ever since."

"I thought it was a four to six year commitment for the Marines?" Bryce asks.

"It is, but like I said, I came highly recruited and couldn't turn down this opportunity. Di9 and the Marine Corps came to some sort of agreement to let me leave."

"Which do you like better?"

"I like them both. There are pros and cons for each but I like where I am now."

"It's always a good thing to enjoy your job." Bryce says as John nods in agreement.

"So what made you want to leave the MPD and join Di9?" John asks.

"A couple different reasons. The first was that I got to work with my brother. He was recruiting me for a while and I finally decided to join him."

"What took you so long to come here if you really wanted to work with him?"

"I was on the fence about leaving, I was comfortable. I was a detective for nine years, lead detective the last four."

"So what made you leave then?"

"I found out my partner was a bad cop. Not bad in a way that he didn't do his job well. Bad in a way that he was into some stuff that would one day get him sent to prison or killed. I didn't want anything to do with that. I wasn't about to go to prison or have my son and wife live without me around."

"Why didn't you say something?"

"I talked to my partner about it. Basically told him I didn't like what was going on and that I didn't want to be a part of it. So I left."

"You didn't go to your superior?"

"It's not my style to rat somebody out. If you have a problem with someone you should talk to them about it. I'm not eight years old and have to tell my teacher."   "So what did he say?" John asks, perplexed.

"He was up front with me. He was my partner for three years and we became close. He told me that a lot of the cops were bad cops, even some of the superior officers. I don't know how many there were but I wouldn't be able to stop it by myself and I didn't want to put my family in danger. So I told him I was going to take a job with my brother."

"Aren't you worried that he's going to come after you since you know what he's into?"

"No, I gave him my word that I wouldn't say a thing about any of the stuff that is going on. I just wanted a clean break to get out of there and be a part of something good."

"He believed you?"

"Like I said, he was my partner for three years so he knows me very well. When I give my word I mean it. He's not worried about me saying anything and I'm not worried about him."

"So now you're happy here at Di9?"

"I'm not happy about the attack here a few days ago or losing my brother, but I do see many positives and I'm liking the work so far."

"I heard it's good to enjoy your job." John says, repeating what Bryce told him earlier.

"Speaking of jobs, are you ready to finish up our investigation?"

"Let's do it." John says, standing and

reaching out his hand to help Bryce up.

"Thanks." Bryce says, brushing off his pants.

"Before we head over I wanted to apologize."

"What for?" Bryce asks, confused.

"When we first met at the firing range I was a little short with you. I was having a tough time and took it out on you. I'm sorry." John says, embarrassed.

"No worries, we are all going through some stuff. It's water under the bridge."

John looks up and sees Bryce's hand extended. He nods and smiles as he shakes hands with his partner.

"Now," Bryce says, taking a deep breath. "Let's go search the area where the President was and see if we can find anything else."

CHAPTER 18

Tuesday, July 7th, 2026

Philadelphia

12:35 P.M.

Bryce and John stand in the exact spot where the stage was set up for the President to speak. The area has already been cleaned and taken care of so there won't be much for the Agents to investigate. After reading the report of what happened at the scene over 100 times it is burned into their brains. Bryce still can't fathom that his brother is gone. Staring down the street he uses the information from the report to run the scene through his head just like he did in the alleyway. He begins to visualize what exactly went on during the attacks.

"You doing that thing again where you can see what happened?" John asks.

"Hang on." Bryce says, holding his finger up.

"I don't know why you would want to

envision that."

"Because it helps me."

"Doesn't it upset you or make you mad?"

"Of course it does, but if this is what I have to do to help me find the guys that did this then that's what I'll do."

John watches his partner relive the scene over and over for a few moments before speaking up.

"Let me help." He says.

"No offense, but it's honestly just easier and faster if I visualize it myself."

"Show me how you do it. Walk me through your process. Let me help you."

Bryce glances over at John and sees the look on his face. He knows that look, it's the same one he makes when he means business.

"Okay, I assume you read the reports of what happened?"

"More than once."

"Good, let's start with Agent Florida. What did the report say?"

"That he was killed in hand to hand combat with one of the terrorists."

"Start from the beginning. There was a gun shot that alerted Florida, then another shot fired into the air, followed by a sniper who took out the two Secret Service members. Put yourself in Florida's shoes, what did he see? What did he do?"

"I would assume he scanned the crowd

with his gun drawn."

"Visualize it. What did he see?"

"He didn't see anything."

Bryce gets right next to John and they both look in the direction Agent Florida would have looked.

"Picture it. The street is filled with civilians when two gun shots are heard. What did he see?" Bryce asks.

"Panic." John answers.

"He saw chaos. Just imagine all the people running as fast as they could to escape the area. People got trampled, families were separated, and screams echoed off the buildings."

"Okay, I got it." John says, taking a few steps forward. "Florida was probably about here when all this was going on. Just in front of where the stage was."

"That's right. What happened next?"

"He spots the boy on the street crying and runs over to help him."

"Keep going." Bryce says.

"He finds the boy's mother and reunites the two but is then ambushed from behind by a terrorist."

"Right. Now watch it unfold in your mind as you recall the info from the reports."

Bryce takes a step back and stays silent while John pictures what happened.

"Alright, now what?" John asks after a few moments.

"Did you notice anything else besides what happened? Did anything seem out of place to you?"

"Not really, did you see anything?"

"Nope. That only leaves one more scenario to walk through." Bryce says, starting to tear up.

"How about I try again so you don't have to relive it." John says.

Bryce nods and the men walk to where the stage was set up. They stand where Travis would have been on the back of the stage and look out towards the street.

"Two shots to cause panic followed by two kill shots from a sniper." John says out loud. "Travis jumps off the stage to cover the President."

"He watches Florida fight to his death. Cadillac One is only a half block away, why would he watch?"

"He was hoping Florida would handle business and then help protect the President."

"So Travis is left alone with the President and a half block to get to safety."

John starts to walk in the same direction Travis did to get the President out of harms way while he recalls what happened.

"Travis kept the President low to the ground and kept taking cover." John says, standing behind a parked car on the side of the road. "But every time they took cover the man in black kept getting closer."

"There were no reports of shots fired either. Travis probably didn't want to shoot towards a crowd and the assassin didn't have a gun according to reports."

"Right, but Travis couldn't have been positive that the man in black didn't have a weapon and he still had to worry about the sniper." John interjects.

"Which is why he kept taking cover even though the man in black was gaining ground."

Bryce and John arrive where Cadillac One was parked. They turn and look back to continue their visualization.

"Travis gets the President to Cadillac One but just as he is about to get into the car the man in black grabs Travis." John says.

"Which was a mistake because my brother quickly got free and took the assassin down."

"He opens the door to Cadillac One and gets the President inside before turning to see another man in black with a gun." John says, doing what he thought Travis would have done in that situation. "He yells for the driver to go and shuts the door saving the President's life."

"Travis was then shot twice as the President drove away. He gave his life to save another." Bryce says, dropping his head.

"The President said he looked back from the car and saw the assassin fire two more shots towards Travis while he stood over him. Then the explosion happened ten seconds later."

Bryce looks at John perplexed seeing the route Cadillac One took and then looking back to where Travis was killed.

"What's wrong?" John asks.

"That's the part I don't understand." Bryce responds.

"The explosion?"

"Yeah, the explosion. Why would you detonate a bomb when you are standing right next to the bomb and your target has already fled the scene?"

"Maybe it was on a timer?" John asks.

"Then why send the assassins? If it was on a timer they could've just let it explode and they wouldn't have had to be there."

Quietly John tries to comprehend what could have happened. Bryce stands next to him looking in the opposite direction.

"You forgot to visualize one person." Bryce says.

"Who?" John asks.

"The man who killed my brother."

"How would I know what to picture?"

"Don't start from the beginning, start from this point when he's standing over my brother and Cadillac One is driving away."

John imagines the car driving away and Travis laying on the ground in front of him. He can only shake his head not knowing what Bryce is getting at.

"Don't you see it?" Bryce asks.

"I don't know what you're talking about."

"The report states that Travis said Cadillac One was a half block away from the stage. What if it wasn't quite half way?"

"What are you getting at?" John asks, befuddled.

"Look." Bryce points to the ground twenty feet away towards where the stage was. "Do you see the that?"

The two Agents walk over to where Bryce is pointing and John finally realizes what Bryce sees.

"What if the men in black wanted people to think they were dead by detonating a bomb in the middle of the city when really they escaped through the manhole cover before the bomb went off?" Bryce asks.

"Maybe you should check it out." John states.

"I think we should both go check it out."

"You go, I'll stay up here and keep a look out."

"Are you afraid of the sewers?" Bryce asks.

"No, I just don't like tight spaces."

"Maybe you should buy some bigger shirts then." Bryce says sarcastically. "You know the ninja turtles aren't real, right?"

"How about you just go down before I throw you down there."

"Alright, alright. Take it easy, Gigantor."

Bryce says, starting to climb down the ladder into the sewer.

He jumps off the second to last rung and splashes down into three inches of sewer water. The stench is unbearable and it is dark and nasty causing him to pull his shirt up over his nose. He shines his flashlight down both sides of the sewer to take a quick look.

"You see anything down there?" John yells down.

"Not yet." Bryce responds, looking at the rungs closely, followed by the area around the ladder.

Just as he is about to stop his search and leave the sewer to take a breath he spots something just a few feet away on the ground next to the wall. Quickly he walks over to it and realizes it's just a dead rat. He turns towards the ladder to head out of the sewer and then stops for a couple seconds before turning back around.

A small piece of fabric is pressed between the rat and the wall. Squeamishly he picks up the fabric and hurries back to the ladder.

"What is that?" John asks.

"I don't know yet, do you have any water left?"

John hands Bryce his water bottle so he can rinse off his hands and the piece of fabric. It is diamond shaped and completely red except for two black letters in the center. The letters are D and S.

"It looks like some sort of patch." Bryce says. "Do you have any idea what this is or could be?"

"Not a clue. We should definitely bring it back to HQ though. Where did you find it?"

"It was at the bottom of the sewer floating on a giant turd."

"Come on." John exclaims, dropping the patch to the ground and taking the water out to rinse his hands.

"I'm just kidding." Bryce says, laughing hysterically. "That was payback for you laughing at me when those pigeons stole my donuts."

"Alright, you got me." John says, picking the patch back up.

"It was under a dead rat though." Bryce says straight faced.

"Nice try, I'm not falling for that again."

Bryce looks at John and shrugs his shoulders.

"Wait, are you messing with me?" John asks.

"You should've come down with me." Bryce responds.

"Bryce, this isn't funny. Was it under a rat or no?"

"I don't remember."

"Bryce!"

"No, it wasn't under a rat. Come on, let's get back to HQ and get this stuff sorted out."

Bryce and John get back to their car and

start the three hour drive back to Washington D.C. They won't be able to bring back the fallen Agents of Di9, but they hope they've found something that might help them find the people responsible for the attack.

CHAPTER 19

Tuesday, July 7th, 2026

*Di9 Headquarters -
Washington D.C.*

5:08 P.M.

Amy walks briskly down the hallway on her way to Washington's office. It's not very often he tells her to drop what she's doing and come right away, and she doesn't want to find out what will happen if she doesn't. It didn't take long for her to rise up the ranks of Di9. Her years of hard work and skill have paid dividends. Even though Agent Texas is technically second in command, Amy has been Washington's right hand woman for the last couple years. Di9 wouldn't run as smoothly without her and Washington knows it.

She reaches Washington's office and adjusts her suit jacket, right before knocking.

"Come in." Washington says from inside the office.

Amy opens the door and sees Washington sitting at his desk with Bryce and John across from him. She closes the door behind her and anxiously walks to join them.

"Take my seat, Amy." Washington says. "I need to get a drink and stretch my legs."

"Thank you, sir." She says, noticing a couple things on the desk. "Is this the stuff you found in Philly?"

"It is. We're not sure what it is but we have a guess. I also have pictures on my phone from the scenes." John replies.

He pulls out his phone and hands it to Amy so she can connect it to the computer. They are uploaded to the screen behind the desk.

"So what do you guys think you have here?" Amy asks, turning to look at the screen.

"This metal ball we found in the ceiling of the bulkhead on the roof where Michigan was killed. We aren't sure what it is but it looked like it didn't belong." Bryce says. "John also found this metal shard on the roof of the same building by the cooling tower. When we took a closer look at the shard it appears that's what caused the concave holes in the walls. We think that somehow these tiny shards, or spears, came from that metal ball."

Amy and Washington look at the photos from John's phone as they listen to the Agents. They can see the holes in the wall that Bryce is talking about along with other pictures from the crime scenes. She picks up the round piece of metal and takes pictures of an exact area of the ball and places it back on the desk.

"What are you doing?" Washington asks.

"I'm just looking for something." Amy responds, zooming in on the picture. "There, that's what I am looking for." She says, handing the phone to Washington so he can take a look. "Do you see the symbol that I zoomed in on?"

"I do. What is it?" Washington asks, passing the phone to Bryce and John.

"That exact symbol was on the piece of metal that Bryce brought in from the explosion at Travis's house." Amy states.

Bryce looks up at Washington and Amy trying to connect the dots. He makes eye contact with his fellow Agent, inquiring if he has any insight to offer, but John just shrugs.

"What are you saying? That whoever was behind this attack was also the person who exploded my brother's house that killed my sister-in-law?"

"We're not sure, but we're going to find out." Washington says, walking over to his desk and to pick up the phone. "Send Avery in."

Within seconds there is a knock at the door.

"Come in." Washington says.

"Sir, you wanted to see me?" Avery asks.

"I need you to take this to the Professor." Washington says, handing the metal ball to him.

"Tell him to drop what he's doing and to take a look at this immediately. Call me with the results."

Avery nods and takes the metal ball from Washington and starts to leave the room.

"As quick as you can, don't delay." Washington calls out to his assistant.

"Yes, sir." Avery says and then leaves the room.

"Amy, I believe you have something for us?" Washington says.

"I do. Our intel has informed me that Tiffany Peterson is meeting with someone in Moscow at Red Square."

"Who is she meeting?" Washington asks.

"We aren't sure. We do know that it is in two days. The meeting will be at noon, Russian time."

"Do you want me to go and find out what the meeting is about?" John asks.

"Not yet. Let's wait and see what the Professor can tell us." Washington responds. "For now you can tell me what else you learned in Philadelphia."

"Besides the stuff we found?"

Washington nods as he sits on his desk.

"We learned that the men in black are very, very good and they are well trained. They knew exactly who the Di9 Agents were and where they were located. In their minds Di9 Agents had to die and they executed their mission without hesitation."

"Is that all?" Washington asks.

"No, sir. We also learned that we might have a double Agent in Di9." John says, sheepishly dropping his head.

Washington quickly gets up and walks to the door to close it. He pours himself another glass of scotch and drinks it down before heading back to the desk.

"John, if you say something like that again you make sure it is in private. I don't need anyone out there worried for their lives because someone might be a double Agent." Washington regains his composure and takes a deep breath. "What makes you believe that someone from Di9 is a double Agent."

"There are a lot of little things that add up to that possibility. For instance, only Di9 members were killed in the attacks. Believe me, I'm happy that no civilians were injured or killed, but with all the people there to see the President, not one of them was shot by a stray bullet? These guys were precise."

"Go on." Washington says.

"There were 48 concave holes in the walls. That means there were 48 little metal spears that created those holes. The assassins picked up every single one of them except for the one I found by the cooling tower. They cleaned up their tracks."

"How do you know the local police or

another agency didn't pick them up?" Amy asks.

"There was nothing in any of their reports about these. Which to me means they didn't know what they were so they didn't mention them or they weren't there to begin with so there was nothing to report." John retorts.

"Why didn't they take the metal ball?" Washington asks.

"To be honest, if it wasn't for Bryce then I don't think anyone would've found that and I don't know how he found it either. Maybe the assassins just overlooked it. Maybe there was more than one of them on the clean up crew and they assumed the other guy got it."

"That isn't a lot to go on to make an accusation of a double Agent." Washington says.

"I said the same thing when Bryce mentioned it to me. It isn't much, but when you add them all up it starts to make more sense. It is something we should look into." John replies.

"Is that all?" Washington asks.

"There is one more thing and I believe it is the biggest piece of evidence there is that someone might be a double Agent."

"What is it?" Amy asks.

"Every Agent that was killed was left where they were....except for two. Agent Maine and Agent Dakota. Sir, I believe.......I believe that....." John pauses before he can get the words out.

"Sir." Bryce says, interrupting John.

"Maine was at the sight of the bomb so there wouldn't be a body left to recover. Dakota was up on the roof just like Michigan was. Why was Michigan recovered and not Dakota?"

"So you are saying that Dakota is a double Agent?" Washington asks.

"I don't want to say that for sure, there is no evidence to support that claim. But like John said, there are a lot of little things that add up to a good possibility of that being the case."

"I'll take it under advisement." Washington says, dismissing the idea. "Is there anything else you guys found?"

"There is one more thing that I forgot I had until just now." Bryce says, pulling out the patch from his pocket and tossing it on the table landing face down. "I put it in a ziplock bag because it was pretty nasty. We found it in the sewers at the site of the explosion."

"What is it?" Amy says, grabbing the bag to see what's inside.

Immediately her face goes pale and her eyes widen like she just saw a ghost. Washington sees her reaction and walks over next to Amy to see what it is. Before he can even get close enough to pick it up he already knows what it is from the red, diamond shape. The black D and S just confirm what he already knows.

"What's wrong?" Bryce asks, watching Washington's shoulders slump as he takes a deep breath and exhales for what seems like a minute.

Amy frantically types on the keyboard to bring up a file of Russian man and puts it on the screen behind her for all to see.

"That is Dmitri Sachenkov, an ex KGB member nicknamed 'The Executioner'. Deceased in 2024 after an explosion in a warehouse building where he was stationed. His body was never found." Washington explains.

"What does a dead, ex KGB member have to do with anything?" John asks.

"A dead, ex KGB member would have nothing to do with any of this. But that patch being out there is a huge deal." Washington replies.

"Why?" Bryce asks.

"Dmitri left the KGB a few years before he was killed. He felt they needed to show their strength and superiority through more aggressive tactics and torture techniques to inflict fear and gain respect. He felt like he wasn't being listened to even though he was a high ranking member of the KGB. Every day he would bring up how he thought the KGB should be even more feared than it was. After months of not being heard he got into an argument with another member and Dmitri wound up killing him in front of many of the other agents." Washington says.

"They just let that happen?" Bryce asks.

"Dmitri was so feared that nobody wanted to confront him on it. After the argument he turned to the other agents and told them that they are either with him or with the KGB. The members who didn't want to join him were immediately killed. That night he formed what was known only as DS. I guess he wasn't clever enough to come up with something better so he just used his initials." Washington replies.

"So this patch either means that there is a copycat situation going on or that DS is still active now?" Bryce asks.

"According to our intelligence, Dmitri always said that if anything ever happened to him that the DS would no longer exist. Members were told to burn their patches immediately if that ever happened. After he died a couple years ago there was not a single thing that happened that the DS was responsible for. He was so feared and respected that even after death his men were afraid to betray him. DS would not exist without Dmitri. There would always be someone who was loyal to him that wouldn't allow it." Amy explains.

"Do you think DS could stand for something else?" Bryce asks.

"I sure hope so." Washington replies.

Just then the phone rings and Washington picks it up after only one ring.

"Professor, that was fast. Let me put you on speaker." Washington says, pressing the speaker button on the phone.

"Sir, I was able to digitally reconstruct the

piece of metal you sent down. It is an exact match to the metal that was found at Travis's house."

"What is it?" Washington asks.

"It comes from Russia. It is called черный еж which translates to Black Urchin."

"How do you know it comes from Russia?" Amy asks, hoping that the Professor is incorrect.

"There is a sickle and hammer symbol on the inside of the metal ball. It is tiny but if you zoom in enough and enhance it you can see it clear as day." The Professor responds.

"Is there anything else you can tell us about it?" Washington asks.

"The weapon is designed after the sea urchin but the spikes are on the inside instead. There is a motion sensor on the outside of the urchin. Anyone or anything that comes in sight of the sensor causes the urchin to open and shoot out little, metal spears. These were made in different sizes and most of them are rather small and house between forty and fifty spears."

Bryce and John look at each other without saying a word. They've seen the damage the urchin can cause and realize just how serious the threat is.

"This is a brilliant weapon to use. There is no risk to yourself as long as you set it and get out of there as quickly as you can. It's quite menacing to be honest, you just never know it's there until it's too late." The Professor adds.

"Thank you, Professor. That will be all." Washington says, hanging up the phone.

Washington looks at Amy and takes a deep breath. Everything seems coincidental but his gut tells him Dmitri Sachenkov is still alive. He knows there is no evidence or proof that he is behind any of this but needs to find out as quickly as he can. "I need you to go to Moscow. Find out who Tiffany is meeting with and see if there is any evidence of DS." He says, turning his back towards his Agents to stare at the picture of Dmitri on the screen.

"When do you want me to leave?" John asks.

"Not you," Washington says, looking at John. "Bryce."

"I think I should go with him, sir. He's going to need backup and two sets of eyes are better than one."

"No, every Agent here is now compromised. We don't know what other Agents they know about and I will not compromise any more men. The only reason Bryce is going is because he was just promoted and they wouldn't know him yet." Washington says before looking at everyone in the room. "I don't want anyone outside of this room except for the Professor to know that Bryce is going. Do I make myself clear?"

"Yes, sir." Bryce and Amy say in unison.

"John?" Washington asks, looking at his

peeved Agent.

"Yes, sir." John says begrudgingly.

"Good. Bryce, I need you to go see the Professor. I'll send down a message that you're coming and where you're going. He'll take it from there."

"Yes, sir." Bryce says before he and John stand.

"This is a recon mission. Report to me with everything you find. Stay out of sight and don't cause any commotion. Dismissed."

John darts out of the room leaving Bryce a couple steps behind him. His hands shake from trying to keep his composure. He's never been put on the sideline before and knows that he should go to Moscow with Bryce.

"John!" Bryce calls out.

"What?!" John stops in his tracks and turns back toward Bryce.

"You aren't mad at me, are you?"

"No. I'm pissed, but not at you."

"Why don't you just come with me then?"

"Washington told me I wasn't going. Those are his orders, as much as I disagree with them."

"You always follow orders?"

"Always."

"Even when you know I might need help."

"Without order there is chaos. I might not like what the order is but Washington is usually right. We don't need anymore chaos right now."

"I'm sorry, man."

"Don't be, it's not your fault. Call if you need anything though." John says, putting his fist out towards Bryce.

Bryce nods and gives John a fist bump. He watches his fellow Agent walk down the hall until he is out of sight before pulling out his phone and taking a deep breath. Hopefully by now Kayla is calm enough to talk.

After dialing her number he listens to the phone ring and ring causing him to get angrier with each time she doesn't answer. He just wants to talk to her to let her know what is going on and hear his son's voice before he goes to Moscow.

The call goes to voice mail and Bryce is so angry that he can't even leave a message. He knows if he did he might say something he shouldn't that would get him in even more trouble. Frustrated, he hangs up the phone and makes his way down the hall to get to the Professor in the basement. Amy watches the whole thing unfold, standing in the doorway of Washington's office.

"Do you really think he'll be okay by himself?" Amy asks, turning towards Washington.

"Close the door and have a seat." He replies. "I want you to have a look at this."

Amy sits at Washington's desk across from him as Washington pulls up the video from

Bryce's training program. "Is this from the other day?" Amy asks.

"It is. I want you to watch how he moves, how he reacts, and how quickly he thinks about every move he makes."

"It seems like he's taking his time."

"He is. I like to call it a calm urgency. His decision making is off the charts and he moves quick and precise."

"Why are you showing me this? You never show me any of the videos from the training program."

"I want you to see how good he is. Bryce scored the highest mark of any Agent that ever took the test. If it wasn't for the trick at the end he would've beaten the program."

"That's why you have so much faith in him?"

"It's one of the reasons."

"And that's why you trust him by himself? You think he'll get the job done?"

"I know he'll get the job done, he's Bryce Stone."

CHAPTER 20

Tuesday, July 7th, 2026

5:32 P.M.

Bryce stands in the basement in front of the IT department confused on where to go. He knows the Professor's office is down here somewhere. "Can you tell me where to find the Professor?" He asks an IT guy who is walking by.

"You haven't met him yet?" The man asks with a giant smirk on his face.

"I haven't. Why are you smirking?"

"You'll know why when you meet him. You see that door on the far end of the room?" The man says, pointing at the lone door away from everything.

"Is that his office? I was wondering what was in that room."

"Yeah, that's his office. Good luck in there."

"Why do you say that?"

"Some things you just have to find out for yourself." The man says, walking back to his desk.

Bryce glances at the Professor's office door and looks back at the man he was just talking to. He wonders why the man acted that way when he spoke of the Professor. Walking through the middle of the IT department he notices there are two rows of desks on each side of him and five desks in each row. With each step he sees everyone in the IT department smile at him, some even wish him good luck.

"It must be some kind of hazing for the new guy to put a little scare into him", he thinks to himself while chuckling and shrugging off the comments.

Finally he reaches the isolated office. The only reason to be over here is if you are going to see the Professor. He finds it kind of odd but maybe the Professor needs silence to think.

After opening the door and he sees a man inside working at his desk with his back to the door. The man is not very tall, maybe 5'-8" at the most and very lean. Thick glasses sit on top of his head and his shirt is covered in sweat.

"Professor?" Bryce says, knocking twice on the door and continuing into the room.

"Did I say you can come in?" The Professor rudely says.

"I'm sorry, your door was open." Bryce says, stopping in his tracks.

"If my wallet were open on the table would you take my money?"

"You're right." Bryce says, taken aback by

the interaction with the Professor so far. "What if I start over and try this again?"

He walks back to the door and stands outside the office. The Professor doesn't even turn around to acknowledge what Bryce is doing and continues to work like he was never there. He knocks three times and stands silent waiting for a response.

"What." The Professor says after five seconds.

"Professor, I'm Bryce. I was told to come down and see you. Can I come in?"

"It's may I come in, not can I come in." The Professor says, rolling his eyes. "What do you want."

"Washington told me to come down here and see you before I leave on my mission."

The Professor never looks at Bryce and takes a step to the side to start typing on his computer. "Yes, he told me."

"Your office is huge. It's very nice in here." He says, trying to create some dialogue and ease the tension.

"I know. It's the biggest office in Di9 Headquarters. The most important people usually get the biggest offices." The Professor says, talking down to Bryce. "How big is your office?"

"I don't have an office."

"You must not be very important then."

"Yeah, I guess not."

Bryce watches the Professor continue to type away at his keyboard in silence. While he waits he pulls his phone out to see if Kayla has called or texted only to angrily shake his head when he sees he has no messages.

"Am I taking too long for you?" The Professor asks.

"Not at all. I was just seeing if my wife called me back."

"You're married? We'll see how long that lasts." The Professor says, chuckling to himself.

"What do you mean by that?"

"You're an Agent."

"And?"

"All you Agents are the same. You'll do anything to stroke your ego no matter who it hurts. All you care about is yourself."

"You don't know anything about me."

"I know you're an Agent."

Bryce stands in disbelief at how the Professor is talking to him. Usually he makes a good first impression but for some reason it's not going so well right now.

"Why don't you show me what you need to show me?" He says, trying to change the subject to de-escalate the tension.

"Fine, if that will get you out of here faster." The Professor responds.

"Have I done something to offend you?" Bryce asks, wondering why the Professor is acting the way he is.

"You mean other than barging in here like you own the place? No, nothing at all."

"I told you I was sorry. That won't happen again."

"We'll see. Follow me over here and don't touch anything." The Professor says sternly.

Bryce follows the Professor all the way to the back of his office. Along the back wall sits a table with a dozen guns all personalized for different Agents in Di9. The Professor walks to the third gun from the right and stops.

"The Glock 19 with laser sight customized just for you." The Professor says, standing in front of the side arm. "Each magazine holds fifteen rounds of 9mm ammo."

He picks up the Glock and pulls out a loaded magazine from his pocket. He looks at Bryce and quickly loads the clip, aims the gun at his chest, and pulls the trigger.

"What are you doing?!" Bryce yells angrily.

"The gun has a finger and palm reader on the handle. You are the only one who will be able to fire the weapon." The Professor says, grabbing the gun by the barrel and holding it out for Bryce to take. "It's a safety mechanism in case you ever lose your weapon in a fight. Go ahead, try it out."

Bryce watches the Professor press a button opening up a sliding window in the wall behind the table. He sees a dummy with a kevlar vest on standing in the middle of the room when he looks through the window. Glancing at the Professor he takes aim at the dummy and fires.

POP. POP. POP.

Three shots are fired into the vest on the dummy before the Professor takes the gun from him and attempts to fire.

"See, you are the only one who can fire the gun. Your finger and palm prints are the only things that will unlock the safety." He says, handing the gun back to Bryce who holsters it.

"I like that only I can fire the weapon. That's a great idea, thank you." Bryce says.

"Come with me."

The Professor quickly walks to the far end of the table and opens a door. In the next room there is a row of vehicles from cars to snowmobiles and bikes.

"I don't know why you are getting this car but yours is right around the corner." The Professor says.

"What is it?" Bryce asks.

"I'm going to show you, hang on." The Professor replies impatiently.

The two men walk around the corner and Bryce stops in his tracks after he sees the only car sitting there. His jaw drops from the shear beauty of the vehicle.

"This is a 2019 Ford Mustang GT Shelby Super Snake. It has an 825 horsepower supercharged V8 engine and can go 0-60 in 3.5 seconds." The Professor says while Bryce circles the car.

"I had a 2019 Mustang before my son was born. I had to give it up when we found out my wife was pregnant for something a little more useful with a kid. It was my favorite car and wish I didn't have to get rid of it. Now I get to drive it again. I'm loving the black too, it's like I got my own version of the Batmobile."

"The car is fully bulletproof, the tires will never go flat, and of course it has rocket launchers behind the headlights and machine guns in the front and back of the car." The Professor continues, ignoring Bryce's comment.

"You can't even tell that you put those modifications in there. You did an amazing job."

"Yes, I can see that." The Professor says arrogantly. "Now for the part I'm most proud of."

The Professor opens the driver side door and holds his hand out inviting indicating Bryce to get inside. Without saying a word he quickly walks over to hop in.

"This car has a cloaking device. Once activated, the car will go invisible for thirty seconds before reappearing. It takes a lot of energy for the car to do that and takes about an hour for the capability to recharge, so use it wisely."

"Can I try it?" Bryce asks.

"Fine." The Professor says with a sigh. "Lift the latch on the top of the gear shifter and press the red button inside."

Bryce does just that and watches the car go invisible in less than three seconds. He looks through the windshield and sees the front of the car isn't visible but that he can still see everything around the car.

"Won't I be visible if I'm inside the car?" Bryce asks.

"As long as all the doors and windows are closed you won't be able to see anything inside the car but you'll still be able to see everything that's going on around you."

"Does it have satellite radio too?" Bryce asks jokingly.

The Professor looks at Bryce and acts like that question was never asked. He walks over to the driver side door and bends down so he can see inside the car better.

"There is one more thing this car has that I need to show you." The Professor says as the car becomes visible again and he presses a button underneath the steering wheel. "This button will drop down the face of the steering wheel revealing a gaming controller. Press the green button to launch the C4 drone that is under the car. The drone is on four wheels and you can make it go where you want control where it goes with the controller. There are eight cameras on the drone so you can see in every direction."

"What are these other two buttons for on the controller? Green launches the drone but what do the yellow and red buttons do?"

"Green launches, yellow will shoot the C4 straight up in the air, and the red...."

"Red means stop?"

"Red detonates. Red is dead."

"That makes sense."

"The C4 has a powerful magnet on the top. So if you shoot it up against something metal it will stick to it no problem."

"That could come in useful."

"Yeah, maybe. Now follow me so I can show you the tech."

Bryce gets out of the car and follows the Professor back to the main part of his office where he was working before he came in.

"How do you get that car out of here? Do you have to take it apart piece by piece and then reassemble it once you get it outside?" Bryce asks.

The Professor just looks at Bryce and shakes his head before turning his attention to the tech he is about to give Bryce.

"This is your phone." The Professor says, handing Bryce the latest version of the iPhone. "Do not lose it. I've spent a long time customizing that phone and everything you would ever need is on it. Don't let anything happen to it. I would rather you get hurt than the phone."

"Gee, thanks." Bryce says sarcastically. "What makes this so important?"

"It has a facial recognition app on it. Not only will it give you the name of anyone you take a picture of but it will also give you their entire file. Any bit of information you want to know will be in the palm of your hand. All you need to do is take a picture through the app and it will tell you everything."

"No more privacy, huh?"

"Not with this phone."

"Anything else I need to know?"

"There is also a decoding program on the phone. If you come across any door or safe that has a digital lock you can hold the phone up to it and it will figure out the code and unlock it for you."

"So I can rob a bank and retire?" Bryce says with a huge, playful smile.

"You aren't very funny." The Professor says, straight faced.

"It appears not."

"There are two more apps you might need. You'll need this for the first app." The Professor picks up a computer chip the size of a dime and holds it in the palm of his hand. "This chip has nano technology. Any picture you have on your phone you can run through the app that tells the chip to create a mask that fits around your entire head."

The Professor peels a small piece of tape off the back of the computer chip and sticks it to his forehead. He holds his phone up and takes a picture of Bryce and uploads it through the app. Within seconds the chip starts to grow and form around his head. Only a few more moments go by and the chip has now entirely covered him from the top of his head to the base of his neck.

"I'm stunned." Bryce says in disbelief. "Just ten seconds ago I was looking at the Professor, now it's like I'm looking in a mirror."

"This mask will stay on until you end the program in the app. It will never end on it's own. If you lose your phone or forget it somewhere after you put on a mask then you'll look like this for a long time until you come back here for me to fix it."

"Why don't you sound like me?"

"How would the computer chip know what you sound like? This is only used to blend in. If you need to speak then you better be good with accents and disguising your voice."

"That's pretty cool. I'm going to need a few of them."

The Professor ends the program on his phone causing the mask to loosen and fall apart right off of his head.

"There is one more thing that I'll show you and then you can go. This device also uses an app on your phone."

"I better not lose that phone, huh?" Bryce asks jokingly.

"I think that's pretty obvious."

The Professor opens a different app and presses the center of the screen. Bryce watches the phone's screen turn into what looks like a video game. He can't quite make out what he's looking at but it seems as though the Professor is controlling something that looks like it's flying. It's not until he sees himself on the phone that he figures out what he's looking at.

"This is the house fly drone." The Professor says. "It is the world's smallest drone and is flown through the controls on the app. The fly has a camera and a mic and is great for eaves dropping and snooping."

"How do you come up with this stuff?"

"Some men can fire a gun and fight. Others use their brains and make all the cool stuff that the meatheads use in the field."

Before Bryce can respond to the snarky comment, the door swings open to the Professor's office as Agent Delaware bursts in. He's wearing a tight, black t-shirt and has tattoos all over his arms and neck. Bryce notices Delaware's nose ring and the long, pointy beard first and then the ripped muscles.

"Where is my gun?! Do I need to smack you around until you finish?" Agent Delaware barks, walking towards the Professor.

"Hey!" Bryce yells, getting in the way of Delaware before he can get any closer to the Professor. "I don't know who you think you're talking to like that, but it stops now."

"Do you know who I am?" Delaware asks, getting right in Bryce's face.

"I don't care, but if you keep speaking

to him like that then we're going to have a problem." Bryce says judgmentally, not moving an inch. "I love fixing problems."

"Who are you, his bodyguard?"

Bryce looks at the Professor and then back at Agent Delaware.

"I guess I am. Let me tell you something, if you ever talk to him like that again or give him any problems then you aren't going to like what happens next. I can promise you that."

Agent Delaware can see the look on Bryce's face and knows that he isn't messing around. He slowly backs up and keeps his eyes on him.

"Just get my weapon finished! I'm getting ready to leave for my mission!" Delaware says, turning his back to walk away.

"How big is your office?" Bryce asks.

"What?" Delaware says, stopping in his tracks to turn back around.

"How big is your office?" Bryce asks again.

"I don't need an office."

"That's too bad." Bryce says before pausing and looking at the Professor. "They usually give the biggest offices to the most important people."

"Whatever." Delaware says, leaving the room and slamming the door behind him.

"You okay?" Bryce asks the Professor.

"Yes."

"Are we all done here?"

"Yes. Take your phone and gun.

Everything else will be waiting for you at the safe house in Moscow."

"Thanks." Bryce says about to leave the room. "You never told me your real name." He says, stopping right in front of the door.

"I'm the Professor."

"Fair enough."

Bryce leaves the office and walks back towards the IT department. He sees the man that told him good luck before he met with Professor and walks up to him.

"Hey, is the Professor having a bad day or something?" He asks.

"Nope, that's just how he is." The man says, chuckling.

"Is everything okay with him?"

"He's good, he just doesn't like Agents. Most of them give him a hard time and pick on him and try to bully him. He doesn't ever stand up for himself so they just keep giving him crap."

"Well maybe it's time for someone to stand up for him. Someone who will stand up for those who can't stand up for themselves."

Bryce walks through the door to head back upstairs while the man watches from his desk. He looks across the room and notices the Professor standing in his doorway watching him leave the basement. As soon as he's out of sight the Professor goes back into his office and closes the door. The man can only wonder what happened before getting back to work.

Now back upstairs Bryce walks down the hallway towards his desk. On the way he spots Agent Delaware complaining to another Agent about what just happened.

"That's the guy!" He can hear Delaware say from the hallway.

"Him? That's Bryce Stone, he's Agent Maine." The other Agent says.

Delaware looks over and makes eye contact with him and then quickly drops his head and walks away. Bryce can only smile as he grabs his bag and heads towards the door. He'll be all alone in the field on his very first mission in a foreign country. He still has a few things to take care of when he gets home, but for now, it's on to Moscow.

CHAPTER 21

Red Square, Moscow

Thursday, July 9th, 2026

11:50 A.M.

Bryce does his best to blend in as he waits for Tiffany's meeting to start. He's wearing his t-shirt, blue jeans, white sneakers, and a light windbreaker, following closely behind a group of tourists.

He uses the facial recognition on his phone while pretending to 'take pictures' and can't help but notice the beauty of the area. The Kremlin covers almost seventy acres and is surrounded by a giant, red brick wall with 20 towers. The palaces and cathedrals stand well above the wall and add to the picturesque view with their bright and colorful domes. To the right of the Kremlin wall stands the Lenin Mausoleum and just past that is the GUM department store. GUM is a three story building with many shops, a few restaurants and a theater. He would love to check it out and see if they sell any types of pastries but first he has a job to do.

Already at Red Square for two hours studying the area, his body is becoming fatigued. He's not adjusted to the time change yet but luckily for him this is just a recon mission and there is only ten minutes until the meeting.

With his phone held high above the tourists he scans the faces of the crowd hoping to find Tiffany or anyone that would send an alert to him. Suddenly he is bumped into from behind causing him to drop his phone. He sticks his foot out to break its fall and to save it from shattering. It lands on his foot and bounces off to gently land on the ground face down.

He gives the man who bumped him a glare as he bends down to pick up his phone. The man stares back for a few seconds and then turns and continues on his way. A slight bump isn't enough to cause Bryce to ruin his mission and confront the man, but he could've have at least said excuse me.

After standing back up and checking to make sure his phone is okay, he flips it over to look at the front and sees that it has sent an alert. A facial recognition flashes on the screen with a 100% match of Tiffany Peterson.

Looking at the photo, he sees her pulling an oxygen tank with the tubes connected to her nose. Knowing she won't be hard to spot since not too many people are carrying around big, metallic cylinder he quickly finds her and begins to follow. While watching every step she takes from a distance he can't help but notice the two men walking closely behind her in stereotypical black suits.

When he takes a closer look at the men he realizes that one of them is the man who bumped into him earlier.

"*Of course.*" He thinks to himself.

He starts to follow them, making sure to keep his distance, knowing that the man got a good look at his face. Now is not the time for aggression, and he knows he has to be extra careful. Continuing to blend in he decides the best thing to do is to use the 'fly drone' that the Professor gave him.

He pulls a small box out of his coat pocket and opens it revealing the 'fly'. Placing the drone on his shoulder he puts in his ear piece to hear what the drone picks up and then opens the app he needs to control it.

The drone takes off and flies ten feet high to avoid crashing into anything on its way towards Tiffany. He watches her walk along the south wall that surrounds the Kremlin towards the corner.

Once there he watches her say something to her two body guards before they immediately turn around and keep a watch to make sure nobody comes around the corner. She continues on by herself with her oxygen tank in hand.

Needing to get a closer look he drops the drone lower to approach the corner. He has to find out who Tiffany is meeting and why. By the time the drone turns the corner he can see she is already talking with two men. Both are wearing baggy sweatshirts with the hoods over their head. They are loose and cover most of their recognizable features and both men keep their heads down the entire time to make sure nobody sees them. The drone is lowered to about a foot above the meeting to be able to hear what is being said.....

-SCREEEEEEEE-

Bryce winces and gets a sharp pain in his ear caused by the screech and rips the ear piece out from the noise. One of the men must have some sort of device that causes interference, and he won't be able to hear what is being said. At least he still has the camera and knows he needs to find out who Tiffany is meeting.

The drone is lowered to eye level with the men but all Bryce can see are shadows on their faces from their hoods. He knows he has to get closer. Dropping the drone even lower he gets a closer view to their faces. The drone flies back and forth between the two men trying to get a facial recognition of at least one of them, but has no luck. Without any other options he gets the drone as close as he can. He hovers the drone at chest level right in front of the man on the right.

Slowly the drone moves closer and closer to his face. In an instant, the man swats the drone, causing it to crash into the ground and stop working. The screen goes black on Bryce's phone causing him to drop his shoulders and head in disgust.

All he had to do was figure out who Tiffany was meeting with and why but he couldn't even do that. It was a simple recon mission and he got absolutely no information that could help at all. He begins to wonder why Washington sent him here and not any other Agent if it was just a recon mission. Just then his phone starts beeping with an alert. Bryce looks at the phone and it says there is a facial recognition of 100%. He opens the app to see who it is and it shows the last image the drone saw before it stopped working. The face of the man who smacked it out of the air is in full view and he taps on the picture to reveal the name of the man on his screen.

The phone flashes in red:

FACIAL RECOGNITION
100%
DMITRI SACHENKOV

CHAPTER 22

Thursday, July 9th, 2026

12:08 P.M.

Bryce is dismayed at the sight of Dmitri's name. He places the phone in his pocket and covers his head with the hood from his windbreaker. Losing the fly drone has cost him the ability to view from afar. Now, he'll have to rely on his own eyes. Keeping an eye on Tiffany's guards he walks towards the corner where the meeting is being held. With the Kremlin wall on his right, he can barely see the guards through the crowd.

All of a sudden the guards turn around and Tiffany walks between them saying something when she passes. He realizes the meeting must be over when she slowly walks his way with the two guards close behind her.

Bryce waits for them to get closer and then bends down to tie his shoes. The guards look down at him when they pass and continue on their way before he stands, keeps his hood on, and begins to follow. He keeps his head down, trying to stay close enough to see them but far enough behind to avoid being noticed.

It doesn't take long for to realize how slow Tiffany gets from one place to another. Frustrated, he notices how much harder it is to follow her than someone sprinting at full speed. He keeps his distance watching her approach St. Basil's Cathedral ahead on the right before turning the corner and disappearing out of sight.

Needing to stay close enough to not lose them, he jogs towards the cathedral but quickly stops in his tracks. The same guard who bumped into him a short while ago has turned to check to see if anyone is following. The two men make eye contact for a couple seconds until the guard turns the corner and walks away. Continuing to jog, Bryce approaches the corner and then slows down when he gets to the area where the guard just was. His heart drops when he peeks his head around the corner. Not only has he lost sight of both guards but Tiffany is also nowhere to be seen.

Frantically he looks around to see if he can spot them but has no luck. He starts to jog in the direction he thinks they were headed and still there are no signs of Tiffany or her guards. Picking up the pace he runs towards the GUM department store and knows he needs to find where they went and any information he can about their meeting.

Now running at three quarters speed, not

quite a sprint but faster than a jog, he passes in front of GUM looking to his right then to his left. Still not able to find anyone he has a feeling someone is now watching him. He looks straight ahead and spots the guard who made eye contact with him at the cathedral, standing twenty feet away. The guard opens his jacket to show his gun, before concealing it again.

Without the gun the guard would be intimidating. He is a head taller than most of the civilians in the area and although he wouldn't win any body building awards he is still a big guy. Bryce can only assume he is about 6'6" tall and about two hundred and eighty pounds. It also looks like he knows where all the best places to eat are located. Normally he would not be too upset about a situation like this, he's defended himself many times, today is just not the day to do that. He needs to get whatever intel he can and disappear without causing a scene or being found out.

Slowly he turns, keeping his eyes on the guard as long as he can. He takes two steps in the opposite direction of him and stops again. The second guard has just walked right in his line of sight. He isn't as tall or as big as the first guard but this one looks to be in much better shape.

Taking a deep breath he lets out a sigh knowing he's trapped in between two men that could cause a lot of pain. He points at the second guard, opens his jacket and points inside to where a gun would be kept, and then raises both hands with his palms up almost asking if the guard also has a gun. The guard smiles widely and opens his jacket revealing his weapon.

Bryce nods with pursed lips and internally assesses the situation. *"If he fights, he may win and survive, but at what cost? Will he be arrested or found out? Would Tiffany and Dmitri be alerted that someone is on to them? If he loses he would likely be tortured or killed and the mission would be a failure."*

His nerves are getting the better of him knowing what he has to do. He looks at one guard and then turns towards the other seeing them start to slowly converge towards him but then stop. Raising his hand with one finger pointed up, almost asking them to wait for a second, he begins to throw up where he stands. The guards look at each other with furrowed brows and are disgusted at what they see.

His body is hunched over vomiting in front of GUM while people look at him judgmentally. He stands up straight and wipes his mouth with the back of his hand before spitting on the ground. The guards look on confused when he holds up his other hand to each of them while nodding his head. Then like a bat out of hell Bryce takes off towards GUM. Most likely he can lose them in there and get away without being caught. The guards quickly follow and he notices how much faster they are than he thought they would be.

Bryce dodges people on his way to GUM while the guards just run them over trying to get their man. Getting closer he can see that there is a security checkpoint you must go through before entering the department store. Knowing he doesn't have time to stand there and get checked out while the two guards are close on his heels he makes a quick decision he won't feel right about but is something that needs to be done.

"I'm sorry!" Bryce yells towards the security checkpoint, only feet away.

The man at the security checkpoint hears the yell and looks up just in time to feel Bryce crash into him causing both men to fall to the ground. Quickly, Bryce gets back to his feet and rushes through the door. The guards hop over the man seconds after the collision, their guns set off the metal detector but they don't care. They want to know why they were being followed and will stop at nothing to find out.

With the alarm blaring he looks behind him while he runs to see the guards not far away. It won't be long until he'll have more than just the guards after him either. He needs to get out of here quickly and without being found out. Given the predicament he's in, he'll need a miracle to get out of this.

CHAPTER 23

Thursday, July 9th, 2026

GUM Department Store

12:23 P.M.

The alarm is almost deafening throughout GUM, as civilians stop to look around to see what is going on. Whatever chance Bryce had of trying to hide and blend in is now gone since he is the only person running and being chased. To make matters worse, three GUM security members come out of a room up ahead and they are dressed with helmets and bullet proof vests with batons in hand.

Knowing he needs to create space if he has any chance of getting away, a plan needs to be quickly thought up. With Tiffany's guards hot on his heels and the GUM security now joining the chase he sees and escalator up ahead coming down from the second floor. It won't be as easy to run up this escalator as it would be one that is moving up towards the second floor, but it won't be easy for the guards either.

Looking back at the security team he sees four more members have come out to join the original three. "Crap." He says, almost at the escalator.

Now being chased by nine people at once he knows he needs to get off this floor. The security team moves quickly as Bryce starts to run up the 'down' escalator to the second floor. Two of the security follow him and the guards up towards the second floor while the other five run in the same direction on the first floor.

"Move! двигаться! двигаться!" Bryce yells in English and Russian, running up the escalator stairs two at a time weaving around civilians before finally reaching the top.

Tiffany's guards are half way up the escalator pushing people out of the way trying to capture their target. Most people get bumped hard and become angry, while others get pushed over, making them fall and tumble down the stairs.

Bryce looks behind him and grimaces, watching the civilians pile up at the bottom of the escalator. He lets out a sigh of relief watching the GUM security delay their pursuit to help the civilians in need.

The guards have fallen back some, but not much. Bryce needs to keep moving and figure out how to get away. Another escalator is just ahead leading to the third floor, and again, this one is heading down. He finds it odd that the escalator is right next to the rail of the second floor but he assumes they did it that way to save space since GUM isn't very wide. However, It will let him see the floor below him when runs up.

Just as he gets to the bottom of the second escalator the guards have gotten to the top of the first. Bryce doesn't stop and continues to run up the escalator faster than he did on the first one. His heart is racing from the combination of being chased and the physical exertion. Sweat runs down his back and drips off his brow. He continues to sprint next to the rail on the third level and checks the floors below to see where security is.

Quickly glancing behind him while he runs he sees he's created a little more space between himself and the guards but there are two problems. Only one guard is still behind him and he is quickly running out of real estate. He spots a crossing coming up to get from one side of GUM to the other and another escalator on the far side of the crossing. Security is still in pursuit but still on the first floor, if he can get to the escalator he might have a chance to head back in the opposite direction without them seeing him.

Finally getting to the crossing he heads to the other side before abruptly stopping. The guard that he lost track of has just come up the escalator from the second floor and is blocking the path. Bryce turns around just in time to see the other guard slow down his run to stop behind him. He looks at each guard and then over the railing to see that security is just getting up to the second floor. He doesn't have much time before they are here so he knows he needs to make this quick.

"I don't know why you guys are chasing me. I don't want any trouble, but I'll defend myself if I have to." Bryce tells the guards.

"There are two of us and he is all by himself." One guard says to the other in Russian.

"That's good, it will even up the fight a little bit then." Bryce says, replying in Russian while staring at the guard.

"I was in a Russian prison for five years and had to fight off some of the worst criminals in the world!"

"Did you eat the rest of the time you were in there?" Bryce says, pointing to the guards stomach.

The guard grits his teeth and snarls. Right as he is about to approach Bryce he feels a tap on his shoulder.

"Can you let me by?" A little, old woman asks sternly. "You're standing in front of the escalator."

The guard looks at his partner and shrugs as the woman squeezes by. Bryce looks over the rail and notices GUM security getting closer and closer.

"Why don't you have a seat, ma'am. Take

a rest and enjoy the show." Bryce says with a smile, leading her to a table sitting right in front of the railing. "Do you mind if I borrow this for a second?" He says, grabbing her cane before walking back to the middle of the crossing.

"We are about to have company, this is your last chance to walk away." Bryce says, switching his attention to the guards.

The men laugh and crack their knuckles and neck. Each of them take off their jackets and throw them down on the tables that line the railing.

"Don't say I didn't warn you, Shamu." Bryce says to the guard right in front of him.

"Shamu?" The guard says with a furrowed brow.

"I figured I would call you Shamu, like the whale." Bryce says, turning to the other guard standing behind him. "You can be lemonade."

"Why Shamu and lemonade?" The guard asks.

"Because he's fat like a whale and I'm probably going to make you pee your pants by the time we're done here. So he's Shamu and you're lemonade."

Before the guards can even react to his statement, Bryce walks briskly towards Shamu with the cane in his right hand. The guard stands perplexed before he raises his fists. Usually he is the one who approaches someone and is surprised that he's not the aggressor.

With his eyes locked onto the guards eyes, he walks towards him waiting for him to make the first move. Just as he gets within striking distance, Shamu becomes the aggressor which is exactly what Bryce hoped for. He raises his right leg and kicks Shamu in the stomach with a front kick. The guard bends over from the pain and wheezes from the loss of breath. Bryce drops the cane to the floor, cups his hands, and smacks Shamu in both ears causing the guard to stumble backwards.

Lemonade snarls and runs to help his partner. Unfazed by another approaching attacker, Bryce sticks his foot under the cane and flips it up to himself and catches it, quickly turning sideways to spear Lemonade in the gut with the cane. Facing the hunched over guard, Bryce puts the handle of the cane behind his foot and lifts his leg, causing the guard to fly into the air. Swiftly he lands another punch to the chest causing Lemonade to hit the ground with much more force.

Bryce turns and sees Shamu is back on his feet getting his bearings. The two men run at each other as Lemonade struggles to roll over and get back to his feet. Before Shamu can get within striking distance, Bryce lightly tosses the cane towards him distracting him just enough to attack. He throws a left jab followed by a quick, right cross landing both square in the nose.

Lemonade gets back to his feet and lets

out a yell before sprinting ready to attack. Bryce stays calm and under control as Lemonade throws a flurry of punches. He leans back avoiding the first punch towards his face and ducks under a right hook. The third punch is a left cross that is easily dodged. Before Lemonade can throw another punch Bryce opens his hand and strikes the guards throat with a chop sending him back a couple steps struggling for air.

He looks back at Shamu and sees the cane laying on the ground in front of him. Shamu tries to clear his vision, but Bryce quickly bends down and grabs the cane. He places the handle of the cane inside the collar of Shamu's shirt and forcefully pulls him towards Lemonade. The two guards clonk heads knocking them both out cold. Lemonade falls to the floor belly up, with Shamu hitting the deck right next to him face down.

"I told you both to walk away." Bryce says to the unconscious guards, standing over them.

He watches for a couple seconds and chuckles before finally turning away. "Lemonade." He says to himself looking back one more time to see the guard's pants drenched in urine.

The fight took enough time that the GUM security is closing in fast from all directions. In the matter of seconds he will be totally surrounded. They are approaching from the second floor to the escalator he is standing at the top of. Quickly he looks for an exit on the third floor but they are coming from both directions towards the crossing as well.

Realizing it's much too high to jump over the railing and only seconds before he is surrounded he looks at the cane in his hand and then the escalator. The security team on the second floor is now half way up to the third floor and the crossing is almost full of them.

He sprints towards the railing just as security gets to the crossing and jumps off the third floor catty corner towards the escalator. He reaches the cane out and the handle latches onto the handrail of the escalator. Holding on to the bottom of the cane he slides all the way down the handrail until his feet land firmly on the second floor.

He leaves the cane on the handrail and sprints along the second level back towards the front of GUM. The security quickly change direction and continue the chase. The old woman wonders what is going on watching her cane still attached to the handrail come up the escalator as she gets up from the table. It reaches the top at the same time she does and she reaches out to grab it. Standing at the railing she watches Bryce run for his life with security hot on his trail.

CHAPTER 24

12:32 P.M.

Sweat drips down Bryce's forehead and his muscles start to tighten. He's been running and fighting and climbing stairs for almost ten minutes straight. His body is drained and weakened but he knows he can't stop, security is persistently gaining ground on him. They are a well oiled machine running as a unit but breaking off individually at each possible escape route making it impossible for him to turn back. He knows he has to get out of GUM, the longer he is inside the fewer chances there are for him to escape, and hopefully, the building is not surrounded too.

It is impossible to exit the building from the second floor, and he is running out of real estate. Sprinting along the railing he sees a red and white striped umbrella covering a shoe kiosk on the first floor just ahead. He gets just above the kiosk and looks over the side with security closing in on him fast. Looking back at them and then at the umbrella again, he places both hands on the railing. Kicking his feet out to the side, he jumps off the second floor onto the umbrella.

The people around the area are startled and confused. They see him rip through the umbrella and crash into the kiosk, smashing it and breaking it into pieces.

"Why couldn't this be a pillow kiosk?" He asks himself, lying on the ground and looking at the shoes scattered all over the floor.

Security watches him grab his shoulder to try to reduce the pain from the fall before rolling over to slowly get to his hands and knees. Quickly they run towards the end of GUM to the closest escalator.

Bryce grabs a pair of shoes off the ground and slips them under his hurt arm inside his jacket, stands, and starts to run. It takes a few seconds after the fall for his body to loosen up enough to run without limping but the pain in his shoulder makes him clutch it on his way to the bathroom in the hallway across from the kiosk.

"You got to be kidding me." He says to himself, noticing it costs money to get into the bathroom.

Taking a step back, he forcefully kicks the door open before closing it behind him to look for another way to escape. The window on the far wall is not big enough to fit through but he notices a vent above the second stall that might work.

He runs into the stall and stands on the

toilet to bend the cover of the vent back before pausing. Without knowing where the vent leads, he knows it would be much easier to just walk out the front door. After a quick change of plans, he pulls the stolen shoes out and swaps them with the ones he's wearing. He leaves his jacket on top of the toilet and throws the shoes he just took off into the vent.

On his way to the sink he can hear security running down the hallway closing in on his location. Now standing in front of the mirror he pulls a nanobyte mask out of his pocket to put it on his forehead and quickly pulls up a photo that he took of a Russian man at Red Square.

Security finally reaches the bathroom and is just outside the door. Bryce watches the mask form around his head to the exact likeness of the man in the picture. He turns on the water and starts to wash his hands, just as the door is flung open by security. Acting startled, he looks up and raises his hand when security comes in with their guns drawn.

"Turn around! Put your hands on the sink!" They yell in Russian.

Bryce does as he's told and tries not to grimace from the pain in his shoulder when the security team grabs him to pat him down. He watches two members keep their guns aimed at him in the mirror while the rest of the team checks the stalls.

"Did you see an American?" The head

security asks Bryce, motioning for the others to lower their weapons.

He doesn't say a word but looks towards the stalls and points to the vent. The head of security turns around just as the other members come out of the stalls, holding Bryce's jacket.

"Check the vent." The head of security barks.

"The cover is bent and I see a pair of shoes inside." Another security member says.

"You can go." The head of security tells Bryce, turning to his security team. "Someone find out where that vent goes!"

Bryce nods thankfully and lowers his hands to casually leave the bathroom. As quickly as he wants to get out of there he makes sure to take his time walking through GUM towards the exit. Occasionally he stops and pretends to look at something at a kiosk so he can see if anyone is following him and every time he realizes he doesn't have a tail. It's hard to hide the huge smile on his face knowing security is still running around looking for him and he is right in front of them hiding in plain sight.

With only a few stores left before the end of GUM, he can see the sunlight shining through the exit doors and lets out a sigh of relief. Taking one last look around he feels like he can relax when security is nowhere to be seen. To make things even better he sees a bakery near the exit and decides to go in to get something to eat.

Almost immediately he spots something that looks delicious.

"What is this?" Bryce asks a worker at the bakery.

"That is waffle cake." She responds.

"Is it just wafer filled with chocolate?"

"That one is filled with nutella and caramel. We do have a chocolate and walnut one over here though."

"They look really good. Can I get two of each?"

"Of course." The woman says with a smile as she begins to bag them up.

"Could you give me two bags? One of each flavor in each bag?"

"Anything else?"

"That will be it. Thank you."

Bryce pays the woman and leaves the bakery to head out of the department store with his bags of waffle cake in hand. Once outside he sees the man at the security checkpoint he ran over on the way into GUM.

"I saw what happened to you earlier when the American ran you over." He says in Russian. "I got you this. I thought it would make your day a little better."

The man turns around and sees Bryce holding out one of the bags from the bakery. He looks inside to see the waffle cakes and looks up with a big smile.

"Thank you." He says, holding his hand

out.

Bryce nods and shakes the man's hand before he makes his way through Red Square all the way back to his car. Once inside, he makes sure nobody is looking and takes off the nanobyte mask.

"I can not wait to eat you later." He says, looking inside the bag of waffle cakes.

He puts them on the seat next to him and starts the car. The radio connects to his phone and picks up where he left off with *Island of Fools* by his favorite band, Alter Bridge. Just as he is about to drive off he looks across the street and sees Shamu helping Tiffany into her car. Once she's in he closes the door and looks up to spot Bryce staring at him.

The two make eye contact for a couple of seconds before Shamu knocks on the passenger window telling Lemonade to get out. Bryce watches both guards talk to each other and angrily pointing at him. They are bloodied, battered, and bruised and they don't look like they want to let go what he did to them. The last thing he wanted to see was the guards tell the driver to get Tiffany out of there just before they pull their guns and walk towards his car.

CHAPTER 25

12:50 P.M.

Bryce knows his car is bullet proof, but it's not something he wants to test out right now. Nobody likes getting shot at, and he doesn't want any more attention on him than he already has. This was supposed to be a recon mission, but it has turned into a big scene that everyone has noticed. What he's gotten himself into is far from quiet and unnoticeable. If he gets shot at in public it will only add to the chaos.

He watches the guards walk to the edge of the street and get in their shooting stance to prepare to fire at him. With their guns aimed at the driver's side window he notices a delivery truck in his side mirror driving up the street behind him. Just before they fire, he peels out right in front of the truck causing the driver to lay on the horn and slam on the breaks. Two rounds hit the side of his car as he speeds off with the truck blocking the path of the guards. He can only hope the sound of the loud horn drowned out the noise of the gunfire.

Quickly, the guards run behind the

delivery truck and stop the next car that comes their way. They waste very little time pulling a man out and throwing him on the ground. Now in the hijacked car, they drive around the delivery truck and watch Bryce turn left at the first road, leading to the highway.

"Bolshoi Theater." Bryce says to the car's GPS system, just before passing the Kremlin on his right hand side. Heading towards the Moskva River he speeds up when he sees the entrance to the highway not too far ahead.

The directions and map come up on the screen showing him the way. It should only take about six minutes and he figures it is a good place to hide and blend in to lose the guards.

The Bolshoi is a world-famous, historical theater and opera company that gives performances of ballet and opera. There are always many tourists around taking pictures and looking at the building even when there isn't a performance. Not having caused any kind of commotion there will make it easier to hide.

He turns onto the highway which immediately turns into a bridge going over the Moskva River. Looking in his rear view mirror he sees a car getting closer and closer to him. When he changes lanes so does the other car, when he goes back to the original lane the other car follows. After a few moments the car is close enough behind for him to realize it is Tiffany's guards. He tries to speed up to pull away but the car in front of him is going the same speed as the car on his side boxing him in.

"Come on." He says impatiently, honking and flashing his high beams. "Why are you going so slow in the passing lane? Are you from Pennsylvania?"

The driver in front of him refuses to speed up and won't move over. He knows he has to get around these cars to have any chance to get away from the guards. Looking ahead at the road he notices a gap coming up. Although not the best idea, desperate times call for desperate measures. He drives into the oncoming traffic and speeds past the driver in front of him and without hesitation the guards follow right behind.

Swerving in and out of the oncoming vehicles makes him think it will create some separation between himself and the guards but to his surprise they remain right on his tail. With a bus barreling down on him he decides to make his move. The bus gets closer and closer before he steps on the gas at the very last second. He swerves his car right in front of the car he was riding next to as the bus zooms by barely missing him.

The guards slam on the breaks and try to get back into their lane. They just miss the car that Bryce swerved in front of but the bus clips the back end of their car causing them to spin out and crash into another vehicle in the middle lane before skidding all the way to the shoulder. Smoke comes from the engine after it finally comes to a complete stop.

Bryce watches this all unfold in his rearview and slows down to blend back in with traffic. He takes one more look in the mirror to see the guards get out of their car and pull their guns. They walk into the first lane and aim their weapons at the first car that comes along.

The sound of tires squealing against the pavement can be heard by everyone in the area. Smoke surrounds the back of the car as the guards approach the vehicle. The woman driver inside is terrified when the guards approach her car and walk to the driver's side window.

"Get out of the car!" The guards yell to the woman with their guns pointed at her.

Frozen from fear, the woman doesn't move a muscle. Only her hands shake and tears roll down her face.

Angrily, the guard takes a step closer and smashes the window with his gun. He reaches inside to unlock the car before opening the door. The woman has her hands up and pleads for her life, but the guard doesn't listen to a word she says. He forcefully pulls her from the car by her arm and throws her to the ground. They quickly get in their second highjacked car and continue with the chase.

Already off the highway and thinking the pursuit is over Bryce drives slow to look around at the scenery on a side street. There are people walking on the sidewalk with their loved ones or pets. Families play in the park on his right side making him think of Kayla and Michael and how he'd love to be home with them both. Then without warning he is jostled when a car hits him from behind. Looking in the rearview he sees a big, black SUV right on his bumper with Tiffany's guards in the front seat.

The collision forces him to steer right into the park he was just looking at with all the families inside. With no other choice he decides to go with it and try his best to avoid everyone. People scatter when they hear the car's horn warning them that he is coming fast. Parents grab their children and dive away from picnic tables as he speeds towards them. He swerves around the tables but watches the guards crash right through them with no regard to the people in the area. He knows he has to get out of the park as quickly as he can so nobody will get injured or killed by him or the guards who seemingly don't care who they hurt.

On the far end of the park he can see a water fountain with an exit that looks big enough to fit his car through. It's not the best idea but it will have to do. Now approaching the end of the park he goes left around the fountain hoping to slow down his chasers before turning right to head towards the exit.

"That's not good." He says to himself,

seeing a police officer standing on the back side of the fountain keeping a watch over the park. The officer takes out his walkie talkie most likely calling for backup.

Speeding towards the exit he can see there are too many people in the area. To his left is a row of bushes running parallel to a road just on the other side. Hoping nobody is coming his way on the sidewalk he yanks the wheel to his left and heads towards the shrubs. He plows through the greenery and lands on the sidewalk. Liberated that the area was clear of civilians he quickly pulls the hand break, turns the wheel to the right, and gets back on the street before speeding off.

The guards follow suit and take the same path. Just as they get back on the road they side bash another vehicle causing it to pull over but they couldn't care any less. Without slowing down for a second they continue their pursuit and will stop at nothing to get their man.

Not much space is between the two cars after turning on a three lane, one way road. Bryce looks in his rearview mirror when he hears sirens from the four police cars now in on the chase and closing fast. He watches the guards hit everything in sight to delay the police, but their efforts are unsuccessful in slowing them down. The move to the right lane and hit the right rear of the car in front of them making it spin out. It collided with a police car pinning it to the side railing on the shoulder of the road.

"Shoot them!" The guard driving the car says to his partner in the passenger seat.

With sirens blasting and lights flashing behind them from the police cars now in a triangle formation the guard rolls his window down and sticks his head outside to start firing. The first five rounds hit the grill of the of car before the sixth finally hits the tire on the front right. He watches the tire explode making the car get out of control before flipping multiple times down the road. A huge smile comes across his face when the car finally stops after landing on one of the other police vehicles blocking the road behind them.

Bryce knows he has to stop the chase soon. The guards will do anything they can to catch him and they don't care what they do or who they hurt. He presses a button under the steering wheel, causing its face of it to open. The display screen on the dash changes from GPS to the cameras of the C4 drone under his car. Remembering what the Professor told him about the drone, he wonders if it would be easier to continue on and try to navigate the drone backwards or drive in reverse to make it easier to control the drone.

After a quick thought, he pulls the hand break and whips the car around 180 degrees before releasing the break to put the car in reverse. Now speeding down the middle lane of the highway in the wrong direction, the small rearview mirror is all he can use to see where he's going.

With no traffic on the road because of the pileup, now would be the perfect time to act so nobody else will be hurt. Looking through the windshield he sees the smug look on the guards faces only two car lengths away. He wonders if they are curious why he's driving backwards but decides it would just be easier to show them why.

The C4 drone slowly lowers from the bottom of the car after he presses the green button in the middle of the steering wheel. The tires start to spin furiously just before touching down to get released from the car.

Doing his best to stay in control while driving two things at once, he starts to get dizzy and discombobulated. With his hands on the gaming controller to drive the drone and his knees on the steering wheel to navigate the car, he gets more nauseous with each moment as his eyes shift from the screen to the rearview.

The guards begin to fire at his vehicle. Bryce can see the confused look on their faces when there isn't even a scratch on it after they unload their clips. They are so focused on shooting him, they don't even notice the drone going under their own car.

They look at each other when they reload their guns. Before they start to fire again, they see Bryce looking at them and holding up three fingers. Trying to figure out when it means they furrow their brows before sticking their weapons out the window.

Bryce lowers one of his fingers, leaving only two showing, while another round of bullets hits his bulletproof car. He hits the yellow button on the steering wheel, launching the C4 straight up onto the guards car, which stays in place with its magnet.

The guards hear the thud underneath their car from the C4 and look back at Bryce and see he only has one finger up. They quickly put two and two together and slam on the breaks to try to get out of the car.

Continuing to drive and far enough away Bryce presses the red button just before the guard's car comes to a complete stop. The C4 explodes causing the SUV to shoot up into the air, flip over, and land on its roof with flames engulfing its body.

He completes another 180-degree turn and comes to a stop, then checks his rearview mirror to ensure the guards are incapacitated. Within seconds the gas tank explodes from the flames confirming their death. Sitting and watching the car burn and trying to stop his head from spinning he notices flashing lights coming down the road towards him from behind the burning car. He puts the car in gear and peels out towards the Bolshoi Theater making the gaming controller go back into the steering wheel and the display screen turn from drone camera back to GPS.

The Bolshoi is just ahead on the left past Theater Square. The GPS shows there are only one way roads in the area and most of them are alleyways with buildings on both sides.

He makes the left past Theater Square and drives to the end of the road to stop. The police follow him down the same road and see him sitting idle at the end of the street. There are three possible exits, back where he came from towards the police, the wrong way down a one way road to his right, or make a left down another alley.

The police slowly drive towards him side by side to block the road in case he tries to get past them. Their lights are flashing but their sirens are off. Checking the GPS he sees another alley around the corner on the right.

With the car in neutral he does a burnout filling the area with white smoke blocking the police sight lines. As the smoke clears the police realize Bryce is gone. They speed up to the end of the road and make the same turn to find him. Before they even get to the end of the road, Bryce has already turned down the second alley and pulled over to the side. Hopefully his plan works because he can see the alley is blocked at the other end.

He opens the latch on the gear shift and presses the button to make his car invisible. The timing has to be perfect because he only has 30 seconds before his car will be visible again.

The police cars approach the alley and stop to take a look. Only fifteen more seconds until he is a sitting duck in a blocked alley.

With only eight seconds left before the police will be able to see him, he breathes a sigh of relief when they realize the alley is blocked on the far end with no other way out and leave the area to continue on their way with only a few seconds to spare.

Almost instantly after the thirty seconds elapse, the car becomes visible again. He looks around to make sure nobody saw him and the police are gone before backing out of the alley.

His body is worn out and tired and he needs to rest. He knows he has to get to the Di9 safe house. Hopefully he'll have better luck on the highway this trip. It can't get much worse than what just happened.

CHAPTER 26

Thursday, July 9th, 2026

Moscow

DS Warehouse

8:08 P.M.

Four DS members hustle into a dark, damp room in the basement of their warehouse, each carrying a black duffle bag. Victor, second in command, follows right behind. "Put the bags on the table." He tells the members.

They do as he says and line the bags up on the table from smallest to largest. They quickly walk to the same door they entered through and line up, two on each side. Each of them knows who is coming when they hear the footsteps slowly walk down the hall towards the room.

With their hands down by their sides, they stay as silent as they can, watching Dmitri enter the room in his white tank top and cargo shorts. He rubs his stubble beard and takes one last drag of his cigarette, before putting it out with his shoe.

"Wake him up." Dmitri says, pointing to a man at the far end of the room.

The man is tied up and passed out. His hands are bound to both ends of a rope that wraps around the support beam in the ceiling. His body is covered with bruises and he looks drained.

The members approach him and smack his face making his head sway from one side to the other but he remains unconscious and continues to slouch. Finally one of the members holds up the man from behind for another member to punch him in the stomach.

The force of the blow and loss of air from the punch make him cough and wheeze but does little to rouse him. It's not until a member throws a cup of cold water on his face that the man is fully awake and alert although disoriented and weak.

"That's enough!" Dmitri says, walking over to the man with a towel in his hand. The members stop abusing the man and walk to the door to wait for the next orders from their leader.

"Alexi, let me dry you off." Dmitri says to the man.

"Dmitri, why am I here?" Alexi asks, struggling to speak.

"I think you know why." Dmitri says, wiping off Alexi's face. "There are two reasons, can you guess what they are?"

"Please, Dmitri. I did everything you've asked."

"Then why didn't the bomb go off in Philadelphia?"

"There was a malfunction. I pressed the button many times, it didn't go off."

"But I put you in charge to make sure that it did."

Alexi can see the anger on Dmitri's face. He looks at the other members in the room then at the table to his left. The four duffle bags sit there waiting to be opened and he knows exactly what is inside. His eyes quickly move back to Dmitri before he drops his head to his chin and begins to softly cry. "Please, don't kill me. This will never happen again." He pleads.

"You think I should give you another chance?" Dmitri asks.

"Yes, I promise I won't let you down again."

Dmitri gets right in Alexi's face, calm but growing more and more irritated. "I do not tolerate failure." He whispers sternly.

"Please, it was a technical problem. There was nothing I could do."

"Perhaps you're right." Dmitri says standing back up and taking a few steps back. "That was your only mistake that day, right?"

"Of course, I did everything like you."

"Then tell me, why didn't you come back

with your DS patch?"

Alexi didn't know he had returned without his patch, and if he did, he would've just killed himself. To most people, a patch may seem insignificant, but to Dmitri, that DS emblem represents loyalty and respect. Let anything happen to it then it's an act of treason in his eyes.

"Victor." Dmitri says, nodding to his second in command.

Victor walks over to Alexi, with a wooden chair in hand, and places it next to him. "I'm sorry, Alexi. I always liked you." He says, ashamed.

Without warning he punches Alexi in the gut with his right hand followed by the left, then a backhanded smack across the face causes his nose to start bleeding. Victor cuts the ropes from Alexi's arms and sits him in the chair. His legs are tied to the front of the chair and his arms are bound to the armrests.

"I know that you know what's coming. I'm going to give you a shot of my special serum to help you through what happens next. It's not going to take away any pain, you'll feel everything. But it will make sure you don't pass out and will stay awake the entire time. I call it 'Hell's Fury'." Victor says, pulling a syringe from his pocket and injecting it into Alexi's arm.

"Is he ready?" Dmitri asks Victor.

"He's ready." He replies.

"Bring her in!" Dmitri yells.

Alexi's wife is forced into the room by two members. She has no idea where she is or why and her fear turns to horror when she sees her husband across the room tied to a chair, bloodied and bruised.

"Alexi!" She yells before running over to him. She puts her arms around his neck and hugs him tight. Tears run down her face as she tries to untie her husband.

"I wouldn't do that if I were you." Dmitri says, cocking his gun and pointing it at her.

"Why are you doing this? What did he do?" She asks through her tears.

"He failed me. He betrayed me. Now he must pay."

"Are you going to kill him?"

"No, I'm not going to kill him." Dmitri says with a straight face. "You are."

"I will never kill my husband!"

"We'll see." Dmitri says with a grin before turning his head to the DS members. "Bring in the apparatus."

The four members exit the room and quickly return with the apparatus. Dmitri watches them slowly roll it into place and lock the wheels. Alexi's wife wonders what this could be used for since it's in the center of the room and nowhere near her husband.

"Strap her in." Dmitri says.

Alexi's wife screams and tries to break free of the member's hold on her as they drag her towards the apparatus. They lift her up onto the platform and hold her against the side wall. It takes three members to hold her still, one on each leg and the other on her arms, as the fourth straps her legs to the wall one at a time. After her legs are fastened to the wall the two members holding her legs let go and take a hold of her arms. They lean her to the side onto a padded area and fasten her body so she can't move. She is slightly bent at the waist and leaning to her right.

At the front of the apparatus a gun is connected to the wall. The members tie her left hand to the underside of the pad and slide her right arm through a strap in the wall of the apparatus.

"Grab the gun." Dmitri tells her.

She wraps her fingers around the gun so the members can strap her hand to it. The only things she is able to move are the fingers on her right hand and her head. Dmitri turns on Tchaikovsky's Nutcracker to fill the room with the beautiful sounds of the orchestra. He closes his eyes to listen and get in the mood before walking over to the woman.

"Before we begin I wanted to let you know what's going to happen." He says, standing right in front of her and looking her in the eyes. "I'm going to torture your husband right in front of you. Do you see those black duffle bags on the table there?" He asks pointing to the table.

The woman nods and begins to cry from the thought of her husband being tortured.

"Each of those bags are filled with my 'tools' that I use for torture. The first bag is the starter bag. After each bag I will give you an opportunity to end the torture by shooting your husband and ending his life. Each time you don't shoot him I will open up the next bag and use it. Believe me, each bag gets worse and causes more and more pain." He says as he walks in front of Alexi, turning around to face the woman again. "The gun will be safetied while I work. That way you can't shoot me or any of the other members. When I'm done with a bag, we will take the safety off and you will have a chance to end it. You will not be able to change your mind in the middle of a bag. Once I start I won't stop until the bag is empty. Do you understand?"

The woman's eyes are blurry from the tears that she can't wipe away. She sobs uncontrollably at the thought of what's about to happen.

"I take from your sadness that you understand." He says, walking up to the woman again. "So let me ask you, would you like to end the torture before it even begins?"

"I will not kill my husband, you monster!" The woman screams.

"As you wish. Let's begin." He safeties the gun on the apparatus and walks to the table to open the first duffle bag. "Oh, I forgot to mention one thing. We gave your husband a shot of our special serum. It's going to help him stay awake and alert the whole time. I didn't think it would be right for him to miss anything."

He pulls out a pair of brass knuckles from the first duffle bag and slides them on his right hand before waking up to the tied up DS member. Alexi is silent while he looks at Dmitri standing right in front of him and then turns his head to see his wife. Dmitri glances back at the woman and again at Alexi before unloading a fury of punches to his face, ribs, and torso.

Blood flies out of Alexi's nose and mouth with every strike to the face. The members cringe every time they hear a rib break from the force of the punches. He hits Alexi fifteen times in total causing massive swelling and bruising. His skin is ripped and oozing blood and he screams in agony. One final punch lands on Alexi's mouth causing three teeth to fly out onto the floor. Dmitri then grabs Alexi's right hand and places the pointer and middle finger in his right hand and the ring and pinky in his left. With all his might he pulls the fingers apart causing the skin to rip between Alexi's middle and ring fingers and all four fingers to break.

He looks back at the screaming, sobbing wife then walks over to the other hand to repeat the process. Alexi's screams are almost deafening to everyone in the room, everyone except Dmitri.

The brass knuckles are placed back in the duffel bag and a roll of duct tape and a box cutter is pulled out next. Walking behind Alexi he pulls his head back against the head rest of the chair and duct tapes it in place.

Looking back at the woman he tosses the duct tape on the ground and takes the box cutter. His face looks angry and excited at the same time holding Alexi's head still with one hand and using the box cutter in the other to cut the top of his right eye lid. He watches as blood runs directly into Alexi's eye causing that eye to go blind.

The screams get louder while Dmitri walks to the table to put the box cutter back in the duffle bag. He looks at the members and nods wiping his face and hands with a towel. They take the safety off of the woman's gun and back away. Dmitri approaches her from the side continuing to wipe away his sweat and Alexi's blood from his body.

"I'm all done with the first bag, that wasn't so bad, was it? Before I move on to the next bag, would you like to end the torture?" He asks the woman.

"No." She says, crying uncontrollably. "I can't kill my husband."

"I'm very impressed. I thought you were going to put him out of his misery after the first bag. Let's see what the second bag has to offer, shall we?" Dmitri nods to the members and walks over to the table. They safety the gun on the apparatus and return to their post against the wall. "Just so you know, I've never made it to the fourth bag. If I had to guess, I would say you'll kill him after this bag." He says, almost daring her not to kill Alexi. "Let's continue."

The unzipping of the second bag causes Alexi to cringe and sweat. A hunting knife with a four inch long blade is pulled out and placed on the table followed by a pair of pliers.

"It's not about how big the bag is or how many tools are inside." Dmitri says to the woman walking over to Alexi, with the knife and pliers in hand. "It's about how I'm going to use them and how much more they'll hurt than the tools in the last bag."

He puts the pliers in his pocket and tells Victor to hold Alexi's head still. Now behind Alexi he grabs his left ear to pull it away from his head. The screams are so loud it makes a couple of the members cover their ears. They turn their heads away as Dmitri slices through Alexi's ear with the knife until it is severed completely. Blood pours out and runs down the side of his head and Dmitri walks to the front of Alexi to face him with his ear still in his hand.

"It's lighter than I thought it would be." Dmitri says, surprised.

"I thought it would flop around a little too." Victor says jokingly.

"How about you, Alexi. Did you think it

would be flopping around like a fish too?"

Still in agonizing pain he doesn't answer, he isn't really aware of what's going on around him anymore. His ear is gone, he can only see out of one eye, and he's lost a lot of blood.

"Can you not hear me?" Dmitri asks, holding Alexi's ear closer to his mouth. "I didn't want to have to do this to you. Why didn't you just set off the bomb?" Alexi doesn't answer as his body starts to go into shock. "Answer me!" Dmitri screams angrily.

He walks up to Alexi and places the ear on his own hand that is still tied to the arm rest of the chair. Victor watches Dmitri slam the knife through Alexi's ear and hand so hard that the arm rest splinters.

"No!" The woman yells.

"Shut up! You had your chance to end this." Dmitri responds.

He pulls the pliers out of his pocket and grabs Alexi's septum and squeezes tight. The shear pressure on the nose causes Alexi to scream once again. The septum is pulled clean off but still has pieces of cartilage and bone attached. The screams become louder as he begins to cry.

Noticeably angered he pulls his knife out of Alexi's hand causing his ear to fall to the floor. One of the members leaves the room to throw up when Dmitri grabs Alexi's nipple and slices it off with the knife. He tosses the knife on the floor and sticks the nipple on Alexi's forehead. He looks at the members still in the room and nods. One of them walks to the apparatus and takes the safety off the gun. Dmitri walks to the side of the woman and wipes the tears from her face.

"You've made it through two bags. I promise you it's going to get worse from here. I'm giving you another opportunity to end this right now. All you have to do is shoot your husband and kill him. You can aim for the bullseye on his forehead."

The woman looks at her husband who is obviously near death already. The two make eye contact causing the woman to cry again.

"I can't do it. As much as I don't want him to hurt anymore, I can't shoot him." She says after making the tough decision.

"So be it." Dmitri says, safetying the gun himself before walking to the table to open the third duffle bag.

Three things are pulled from the bag and placed on the table for Alexi and his wife to see. A sledgehammer, a nail gun, and an electric drill. Dmitri tosses the bag aside and picks up the sledgehammer and walks up to Alexi.

"Please, Dmitri." He says with what little energy and strength he has left.

Dmitri smiles and without hesitation takes the sledgehammer and swings it like a baseball bat. It strikes Alexi's left shin shattering the bone. Before anyone can react to what just happened he takes the sledgehammer and swings it again, this time striking the right shin. Victor winces during this part of the torture, as hard as it is to watch someone's legs being shattered by a sledgehammer, the sound that the bones make when they are struck is not something anyone wants to hear.

"Please stop! I'll do it!" The woman says, sobbing uncontrollably.

"What was that?" Dmitri asks.

"I'll do it."

"Normally I would make you wait until I was done with the bag, but you have guts to make it this far. I didn't think you would."

"Please stop torturing him. I'll do whatever you want."

Dmitri walks up to the woman and takes the safety off the gun. "I want you to kill him."

Alexi and his wife look at each other one last time before she pulls the trigger.

"I'm sorry, Alexi." She says.

"It's okay. I love you." He replies.

"I love you too."

The woman closes her eyes tightly, her hand trembling as she pulls the trigger.

POP!

The bullet goes right into Alexi's head, killing him instantly. Alexi's wife opens her eyes and sees her husband bleeding from almost every part of his body. She can only focus on the bullet hole in her husbands head caused by her and begins to sob.

"Get her down." Dmitri tells the members as he walks back to the table to put the sledgehammer away.

The members unstrap the woman from the apparatus and help her down off the platform. They take the apparatus out of the room as the woman stands there sobbing and staring at her dead husband.

"You did a great job hanging in there." Dmitri says, approaching the woman.

"Am I supposed to thank you? You killed my husband!" She screams.

"No I didn't. I was just punishing him for failing me. You killed your husband."

The woman looks over at Alexi's dead, limp body replaying the scene over and over in her head. It's not something she will ever forget but it's also not something she wants to remember either.

"You know, I owe my friend ten rubles now." Dmitri says, pointing at Victor. "You lasted much longer today than I thought you would. I didn't think you would make it past the first duffle bag." Dmitri says to the woman who looks at him in disgust. "But you did just kill a DS member and we can't have that can we?"

Dmitri quickly pulls a gun from the back of his pants and points it at the woman.

POP!

The woman drops after the bullet goes

into her head causing it to fling back and blood to fly out and splatter everywhere.

"Clean this mess up. I need to check on the bomb." Dmitri says, putting the gun in the back of his pants and grabbing a towel on his way out of the room.

CHAPTER 27

Thursday, July 9th, 2026

Moscow

DS Warehouse

8:42 P.M.

Roman Bovanovski wipes sweat from his forehead with his left sleeve and continues to work. He has been working around the clock for days with little to no sleep, and just enough food and water to keep his body functioning. The room is dark and damp, with very little ventilation, and it is hot and muggy. Not the typical situation for the country's best nuclear physicist, but he does not have much of a choice. Dmitri wants a nuclear weapon and he wants it now.

A DS member stands guard by the door, watching every move Roman makes. Every four hours, a new member comes in and replaces the member already in the room. There is no clock in the room and no window. The only way he has any idea of the time is through the changing of the members every four hours on the dot. He has been stuck in the room long enough to get a feel for when the four-hour mark is about to come. When the door suddenly opens earlier than expected he is not only surprised but terrified.

Dmitri strolls in with fresh blood on his shirt and wiping sweat from his face with a towel. Roman watches him tell the DS member to leave the room and his limbs tremble knowing he will be the only person in the room with him.

As the member leaves the room Roman sees Alexi and his wife's bodies being carried away by other DS members just before the door closes. He looks at Dmitri in fear, not knowing if he is going to be next.

"How much longer?" Dmitri asks, continuing to wipe blood off of himself.

"I don't know, maybe a week?" Roman responds.

"That's not good enough. I need this done faster than that. You have the plutonium you need, now finish the bomb!"

"I'm working by myself. This isn't the best environment for this type of work."

"Excuses!" Dmitri yells in anger.

"I'm sorry, I'm working as hard as I can."

"Perhaps you need some motivation?" Roman is perplexed at the statement until he pulls his phone out of his pocket. "I think you know who this is." He states, flipping the phone around to show Roman a picture of his wife. "She's very pretty. She works at the grocery store not too far from here, isn't that right?"

"Dmitri, please."

"And how about this little guy? What is he, five, six years old?" He asks, scrolling to the next picture showing Roman a picture of his son. "I'd really hate for anything to happen to him."

"Please don't hurt them. I'll do whatever you ask." Roman pleads with Dmitri.

"That's good to hear." Dmitri responds, placing his phone on the table in front of Roman. "But if you don't finish this bomb in two days, your wife dies. If you don't finish in three days, your son dies too. Do you understand?"

"I do, please don't hurt them, I'll get it done."

"Good." Dmitri says, patting Roman on the cheek.

Just then, the door swings open, and a DS member comes in. "Dmitri, there's been an explosion on the highway near the Bolshoi." He says urgently.

"So what." Dmitri responds.

"The American says it looks like a Di9 car. He says he knows where their safe house is. Come take a look."

Dmitri leaves his phone on the table and heads towards the door in a hurry to see the news on the television and talk to the American.

"Watch him." He tells the DS member on his way out of the room.

Roman continues to work on the bomb after Dmitri exits the room. He knows he shouldn't be making the bomb nuclear but knows if he doesn't that his family's life is in danger. While he works and contemplates what to do he notices Dmitri's phone on the table. Peeking up at the DS member standing at the door and sees the member won't take his eyes off him. Purposefully he drops a tool on the ground while the guard watches. In one motion he bends down, slides the phone into his pocket, picks up the tool and places it back on the table.

Knowing there is no way he will be able to call or text anyone with someone watching his every move he knows he still has to find a way. Even though he has no idea who or what Di9 is, the way the DS member was talking about them makes it seem like they might be able to help.

"I have to go to the bathroom." Roman tells the DS member.

The member waves him over and opens the door. He follows Roman down the hallway and into the bathroom before pointing to the urinal while he stands by the door. Roman stares at the member and sheepishly holds up two fingers. The DS member nods and points to the stall allowing him to enter. After getting in the stall he pulls out Dmitri's phone and holds it while he pulls his pants down.

The DS member takes a deep breath now that he can finally relax for just a minute and walks to the sink to splash some water on his face. Roman knows he doesn't have much time, if he can send a quick email to his wife, and Di9 is who he thinks they are, they should be able to hack the email and get the information they need to put an end to Dmitri's plan before it even starts.

Roman types:

Stefaniya,

I don't have time to tell you what happened. Just know that I love you and that I'm okay. I am in the Kuzminskoye Cemetery in the Kuzminki District. I am being forced to do something against my will so you and our son can be safe. Please do not come to look for me or call the police. I will be home soon.

You won't understand what I'm about to say, but if things work out the way I hope they do then the correct people will get a hold of this email and come to help. I'm doing work for Dmitri Sachenkov and he wants to set off a nuclear bomb on American soil. I don't want that to happen because it won't end at just one bomb. There will be retaliation, and then another strike, and then another. I don't want any people to die.

Stefaniya, please know that I love you very much. Tell our son that I love him too. I promise I will see you soon.

Roman Bovanovski

P.S. There is a double Agent here from Di9 that has info on where your safe house is in Moscow. It sounds like they are about to go check it out. Please hurry, you don't have much time.

"Let's go in there!" The DS member shouts into the stall.

Quickly Roman sends the email and deletes it from the phone. He pulls his pants up, exits the stall, and walks to the sink to wash his hands. Without saying a word he walks back to the bomb and continues to work knowing what he just got away with.

A couple minutes pass and he is deeply focused on the task at hand. Suddenly the door swings open and Dmitri walks in. He starts to walk over towards the bomb, but stops to say something to the DS member at the door. Instantly Roman remembers he has Dmitri's phone in his pocket still. He nonchalantly takes it out and places it on the table and gets back to work. Dmitri approaches the bomb and notices his phone in a different spot than where he left it. Without saying a word to Roman he grabs him by the throat and slams him against the wall.

"Why is my phone not where I left it?" Dmitri asks, squeezing Roman's neck.

"I...I moved it....out of the way." Roman

replies, gasping for air.

"Why don't I believe you?"

"It's the truth."

Dmitri lets go of Roman's throat and throws him to the ground.

"Get over here!" Dmitri yells to the DS member at the door. The member comes running over and stands next to Dmitri. "Were you watching him the whole time?"

"Yes, Dmitri. He was working the whole time. He only took a break to go to the bathroom. I was with him the entire time though." The member replies.

Dmitri looks at the member then at Roman before picking up his phone from the table. "If I see one thing on here that proves you did anything on my phone then I will kill you and then your family." He threatens, starting to look through his phone.

Roman can only look on, hoping he erased everything he did on the phone. The seconds seem like an eternity for him. Even though he knows he deleted all proof that he was on the phone, there is a moment of nervousness that maybe he forgot something. Finally he sees Dmitri put the phone back in his pocket and he can breathe a sigh of relief.

"Get back to work." Dmitri tells Roman. "Don't let him out of your sight for a second. If he does anything suspicious, shoot him." He tells the DS member.

Dmitri leaves the room and lets Roman get back to work on the bomb. On the way out, Roman can hear him say, "Victor, grab six members and come with me. Let's go to the Di9 safe house."

Roman hopes Di9 intercepted the email he sent to his wife. He did all he could to include enough words and names that would get flagged by Di9. Now, he can only pray they are as good as he hopes.

CHAPTER 28

Thursday, July 9th, 2026

Moscow

Di9 Safe House

9:45 P.M.

Bryce sits with his eyes closed on a recliner in the middle of the living room. He isn't asleep, just resting his body. His gun and the wafer cake he got from GUM are on the end table next to the chair. Knowing he should be on Moscow time to better prepare his body, he knows he should go to bed even though it is only 2:45 in the afternoon at home but he's had a long day and who knows what tomorrow will bring.

Before he falls asleep he pulls his phone out of his pocket to check in with Washington. He dials the number for Di9 and waits to be connected.

"Calvary." A voice answers on the other end.

"I'd like to speak to a manager." Bryce states.

"Sign in for voice recognition."

"Agent Maine. 1101422581."

"Please hold."

It isn't long before he hears Washington's voice on the other end.

"Agent Maine, we got the intel you sent us, good work." Washington says with a brief pause. "But it was a recon mission. You were supposed to be in and out without being seen. Not only were you spotted outside of GUM, but you also caused an explosion on the highway and had the Russian Police involved in a car chase. I don't know about you, but to me that doesn't sound like something that would happen to an Agent at Di9. When you are supposed to be invisible, you're invisible. When you're supposed to gather intel and not let anyone spot you then that's what you do."

"You're right, sir. I'm sorry. It won't happen again." Bryce says, disappointed with himself.

"I'm beginning to wonder if I put you in the field too soon. I let the failure of Philadelphia cloud my judgment."

"Are you going to bring me in?"

Before Washington can answer, the door swings open to his office and Amy comes rushing in.

"Sir, I'm sorry to interrupt, but we just

intercepted an email Roman Bovanovski sent to his wife." She says.

"Who is Roman Bovanovski, and why should I care about an email to his wife?" Washington asks.

"Roman is the best nuclear physicist in Russia. He is working for Dmitri Sachenkov against his will to make a nuclear bomb set to go off on American soil."

"How do we know this is for real and not a trap or a misdirection?"

"He wrote the email to his wife but he wanted us to find it. He said there is a Di9 double Agent working with Dmitri who knows where our safe house is in Moscow. They are on their way there now."

Washington's look of panic startles Amy but he tries to stay calm before speaking to Bryce again.

"Agent Maine, you need to get out of there now. The safe house is compromised. Grab whatever you can and leave. DS will be there any minute."

Immediately Bryce stands and hangs up the phone before placing it in his pocket. He runs to the closet by the front door and grabs a duffle bag full of weapons and gadgets he always has ready to go in case of situations like this. As he closes the door to the closet he can hear a car pulling up the driveway to the safe house. He peeks out of the window through the shades and sees two cars coming down the driveway. Each car has four people in it and Bryce can see Dmitri in the passenger seat of the first car.

He waits and watches to see what DS is planning. The four people in the second car all get out along with the two members in the back seat of the first car. All of them are dressed in black with semi-automatic weapons and night vision goggles. Five of the six DS members stand around behind the cars as the sixth member walks half way between the cars and the Di9 safe house and holds something up that resembles a gun.

Before Bryce can figure out what it is, the power to the entire house goes out making it pitch black inside and impossible to see anything. Quickly he puts the duffle bag over his shoulder and walks eight steps back to his chair in the middle of the room to grab his gun and holsters it. He turns 90 degrees to his right, takes five steps, and turns 90 degrees to his left to take another four steps putting him at the base of the stairs.

After running up the first six steps to the landing he drops to one knee. It doesn't take long for him to locate the latch six inches off the ground in the center of the landing wall. He opens the latch and grabs the metal wire pulling it across the landing and attaching it to the opposite wall. Just as he finishes attaching the wire he hears the lock on the front door being picked. Scampering up the final six stairs he turns the corner heading to the room at the end of the hall.

The DS members finally get the front door opened and come into the house in groups of two. The first set of two goes left into the kitchen, the second set goes right into the bedroom, and the last set checks the living room. Each set does a thorough check of the room before they say it is clear. Every door and cabinet is checked as well as behind furniture and any place that could have a hidden compartment. Once each room is clear the members all meet at the bottom of the stairs. The third set of two head up slowly in a staggered formation while the other members keep watch for any attacks from behind.

Even with the night vision goggles on, the first member up doesn't notice the metal wire stretching across the stairs. He gets to the landing and steps on the wire and before he or any other member can realize what is going on, a six inch diameter metal rod the width of the stairs comes swinging out of the ceiling connected by chains on each end. Four inch spikes cover the metal rod and point in all directions. In an instant the rod hits the first member causing one of the spikes to go through his eye and into his brain. His body immediately goes limp and swings with the rod until it drops and tumbles down the stairs.

The members look at each other in

disbelief and horror. They wonder what other traps could be set around the house for them. The second set of members decides to follow up the member on the stairs while the third set stays at the bottom. Cautiously they continue, taking each step slowly and carefully making their way up. They finally reach the top and realize there is only one way to go. The hallway turns left and has a single door at the far end.

Inside the door Bryce patiently waits for them to arrive. He has already grabbed an urchin, multiple magazines for his Glock, another fly drone, some knives, and an explosive and placed them in a second duffle bag. Crouching just inside the door with a knife in hand knowing the members have night vision goggles on, he sets up a battery powered flood light on a table on the far side of the room pointed at the door. It is connected to a pressure switch which is activated by the door being opened.

The members set up ready to enter the room. There is one member on each side of the door with the last laying on his stomach at the top of the stairs. The door is kicked open causing the flood light to shine brightly down the hall. Each member closes their eyes and reacts to the extremely bright light coming through their night vision goggles. Before they can take them off and adjust to the light Bryce has already stabbed the first member in the throat with his knife and shot the second one in the head.

Bryce retreats into the room, grabs both duffle bags, and gets in the closet to open a hidden door to walk through. The door is connected to a tunnel that leads from the house to the woods about one hundred yards away from the safe house. After closing the door behind him he punches a code into a keypad just inside the tunnel. A clock next to the door reads one minute and begins counting down, the self destruct sequence has just been initiated.

He climbs down a ladder leading him back to ground level and sprints down the tunnel towards the exit. Every twenty yards he stops to close a safety door behind him. The door acts as a buffer to keep the blast and flames from coming down the tunnel and giving away the secret exit.

Back inside the third member upstairs in the hallway shoots the flood light causing it to power off and puts his night vision goggles back on. He makes his way inside the room but can't find Bryce anywhere. "Dmitri, I lost him. I don't know where he went." He says looking around the room some more.

"Does anyone know where he is?" Dmitri asks everyone in the safe house.

"He went upstairs, we haven't seen him come down yet." The set of members say at the bottom of the stairs.

"He has to be somewhere. Find him!" Dmitri orders.

"He vanished. There has to be a hidden

room somewhere up here." The member upstairs says.

"We sent in six DS members to get one guy who didn't know we were coming and they fail? Get the rocket launcher out of the trunk." Dmitri tells Victor, frustrated and angry.

"You want me to blow up the house?" Victor asks.

Dmitri nods in approval.

"If I blow up the house we will lose our men." Victor informs Dmitri.

"I know, but we'll kill the Di9 Agent too."

Victor slowly nods before getting out of the car to open the trunk and take out the rocket launcher. Ten seconds remain on the self destruct timer as Victor takes a knee and aims the rocket launcher at the gas line heading into the house. He looks at Dmitri and back at the house and with two seconds remaining on the timer he fires the rocket launcher. Both men watch the rocket fly through the night air and hit the gas line just as the timer hits zero. The explosion annihilates the house and disintegrates into dust. Victor puts the rocket launcher away and gets back in the car upset that he had to kill his own men.

"Good job, Victor." Dmitri says, patting him on the back.

"We killed our own men. We should've let them find him and finish the job." Victor responds.

"We don't have time to be here all night. Who knows where he went? Maybe he would've escaped and come back with even more men."

"Or maybe our men would've done their jobs and killed him themselves."

"Sometimes people have to die to accomplish your mission."

"Your own people?"

"If it helps the cause."

"Would you give your own life to 'help the cause'?"

"I would sacrifice you and myself to finish the job. But why sacrifice ourselves when we have other people to sacrifice first?"

Victor stays silent and looks out of the window. He wonders if and when the time will come when Dmitri will sacrifice him to help his cause.

"Lets get back to the warehouse. We have work to do." Dmitri says, starting the car and driving off.

CHAPTER 29

Thursday, July 9th, 2026

10:08 P.M.

Bryce stands in the middle of the woods watching what's left of the Di9 safe house burning to the ground. Watching Dmitri and Victor drive off he can only wonder how much they know about Di9. *'If they can locate the safe house that easily, just how safe are my wife and son'.* He pulls out his phone and texts 9-1-1 to Kayla, knowing that no matter how bad of a fight they are in or whatever is going on, if either of them texts 9-1-1 to the other they know to call. Only a few moments pass before his phone starts to ring.

"Hey, Kayla." Bryce says quietly into his phone.

"Bryce, is everything okay?" Kayla asks, nervously.

"Yeah, I'm good. I just needed to talk to you, I'm not sure I'll get another chance."

"What do you mean by that?"

"I'm in a tough spot. I'm in Moscow

all alone trying to take down a terrorist organization. They were able to locate our safe house which I was in. I escaped, but if they could find a place that is supposed to be safe then I'm not sure if I'll be able to survive."

"Bryce...."

"Let me finish." Bryce says, cutting off his wife. "I just wanted to call and apologize. I love you and Michael so much and I never meant for any of this to happen. If I'm able to get through this mission and make it home then I'll quit Di9 if you want. I'll do anything to make this right."

"Bryce, I knew what you were getting into when you got the job at Di9. I kind of figured you would become an Agent at some point too. I'm seriously fine with all of that. What I didn't like and what pissed me off the most was that you didn't think of me and Michael first. You were so worried about what you wanted to do that you didn't even think of us."

"I did think of you."

"You did? Then why didn't you talk to me first like I asked before you became an Agent?"

"I assumed you were fine with it. So I told you after I became one."

"I am fine with you becoming an Agent. But I wanted to be involved and thought of before you made the decision, not after. I'm your wife, we're a team. Your decisions affect me just as much as they affect you."

"You're right. I understand that and I

won't let that happen again. I'm so sorry, would you forgive me?"

"You know I will, I just need a little time to move past this."

"I get it. Do you want me to quit Di9?"

"Of course not, this is your dream. I want you to use your instincts and training. Remember what the tattoo on your arm says and come home when you're done your mission."

"Yes, ma'am." Bryce says, smiling. "Hey, did you read the note I left you on the bureau before I left?"

"Yes I did. Did you mean what you said?"

"Every word."

"So you're sorry enough that you will take me to the ballet once a month for a whole year?"

"That's right."

"But you hate the ballet."

"That's very true. But I love you, and I need you to know that."

"I do. Finish your mission and come home. We miss you."

"I will." Bryce says before pausing. "I need you to do something for me though. It's very important."

"What is it?"

"I need you to pack a bag for you and Michael and go to Di9 headquarters tonight. I need you to stay for a couple days or until I get home."

"What? Why do we need to do that?"

"I need to know you both are safe. If they can find me here at our safe house then that means that somebody helping them knows about Di9 too. They might know who the Agents are and where they live. I need to know you will be okay. I don't want what happened at Travis's house to happen at ours with you inside."

"So I just show up and they'll let me in to live there for a couple days?"

"I'm going to call them as soon as I'm done talking with you. I'll tell them you're coming. Please just do it and go as quickly as you can. Don't wait until tomorrow."

"Okay, I'll do it."

"Thank you."

"Bryce?"

"Yeah."

"Come home safe."

"I will. I love you. Tell Michael I love him too."

"I love you too. I will."

Bryce hangs up the phone and breathes a sigh of relief. As happy as he is to talk to his wife again the joy must come to an end so he can get back to work. He takes a deep breath and makes another call. "I'd like to speak to a manager." He says.

"Please sign in for voice recognition." The voice on the other end replies.

"Agent Maine. 1101422581."

"Please hold."

Again, Bryce doesn't have to wait more than a couple seconds before Washington answers the phone.

"Agent Maine, I'm glad you're okay." Washington says.

"Me too. Thanks for the heads up. If it wasn't for the warning then I'd most likely be dead right now." Bryce responds.

"Were you able to grab anything on your way out?"

"I got everything I need."

"Good. According to the email we received, Dmitri is in a building in the Kuzminskoye Cemetery. We don't know which building, that will be up to you to find."

"I thought you weren't sure if it was too soon to have me in the field?"

"Well we don't have much time. By the time we send another Agent it might be too late."

"Don't have much time for what?"

"We were able to hack into Tiffany Peterson's phone. She has a meeting tomorrow at noon, Moscow time."

"They love their noon meetings, don't they?"

"It would appear so. I need you to go to the meeting. She is going to check on the progress of the bomb they are making and to give the final payment to Dmitri. I need you to find them and put an end to it by any means necessary."

"Yes, sir."

"How's the safe house?"

"It's gone, sir. I used the self destruct sequence."

"That's unfortunate. Do you still have your car?"

"I do."

"Then you've got it made."

"Yes, sir." Bryce says, chuckling.

"One more thing: don't kill Roman Bovanovski. He's the man who sent the email warning us about the attack on the safe house. I'll send you a picture of him. Do what you can to save him and get him out of there. He helped us, so let's help him get back to his family."

"Yes, sir. I'll get it done."

"Make sure you do." Washington says, sternly.

"Sir?"

"Yes?"

"I need to tell you something. I know it's against protocol but I had no other choice."

"What is it?"

"I told Kayla everything. I told her about Di9, I told her where I was, and I told her to pack a bag for her and our son and go to Di9 headquarters."

"Why would you do that?"

"I thought it would be the safest place for them to be right now. If DS can find our safe house because of a double Agent and they knew where Travis lived and blew up his house with my sister-in-law inside then how can I believe that my wife and son will be safe at home?"

"Alright, we will make sure they are safe and comfortable here but we're going to have a chat about this when you get back."

"Yes, sir. Thank you, sir."

"Get some rest, you're going to have a lot to do tomorrow. Check in with me after your mission."

"Yes, sir."

Washington hangs up and Bryce slides his phone back in his pocket. He looks around the area of where the safe house was to see if anyone is still around and then walks back to it when he sees it is clear. Luckily the car was parked far enough away from the house that there is no damage to it and is still usable. He climbs inside and puts the duffle bags on the passenger seat. Taking one more look around outside to make sure it is clear he opens up the first duffle bag and looks inside before pushing it aside. Frantically he opens the second bag to look through. He lifts up both bags to see that there is nothing underneath. Putting them back down on the passenger seat, he retraces his steps. It doesn't take long to realize what he did.

"I left the wafer cake on the end table in the living room." He says to himself, disgusted.

He lets out a scream and smacks the headrest on the passenger seat and then the steering wheel twice. Angrily he drives off to an apartment complex just a few miles from the safe house and parks all alone away from the building before climbing in the back seat.

All he can think about while he sets his alarm for 8:00 a.m. is the wafer cake he could be eating right now. He looks at a picture on his phone of him and his family turning his anger into happiness. After closing his eyes he thinks about seeing them soon, but first he needs to get through tomorrow.

CHAPTER 30

Friday, July 10th, 2026

Kuzminskoye Cemetery

11:26 A.M.

It isn't hard to figure out what building Dmitri is in. The many DS members armed with semi-automatic weapons guarding the building are the giveaway. Bryce can see two members on the roof, three by the front door, and one on each side and back of the building.

The three members in front of the building stand close to each other smoking while they chat. He can almost sense their impatience as they long for some action. The men on the roof aren't even holding their weapons while they lean against the chimney not even paying attention to anything going on below.

What worries him the most is the members on the sides and back of the building. They are concentrated and focused, pacing from one corner to the other and back. Neither of them stop to chat or smoke and all of them keep their eyes peeled for anything out of the ordinary.

The one good thing he has spotted so far is that the building is in the back of the cemetery and far enough away that nobody else should know what is going on if things get out of hand. The two story building sits at the bottom of a hill that wraps almost completely around. The only way to get there is down a single path that leads to the front door.

As he sits on the elevated hill surrounded by trees and bushes, he starts to think of a way to get into the building. The front and back door are the only way in without climbing through a window and there are too many members to just walk up and start shooting. With only a half an hour until the meeting, he takes a 'fly drone' out of his bag and powers it on. He flies the drone to the building to confirm there are eight total members around and on the building.

There is no way of knowing how many members are inside, but that doesn't matter if he can't get past the eight that are outside first. He brings the drone up to the roof and hovers over the two members to listen to them speak.

"Why do we need so many men out here to wait for one woman who can barely walk?" The member says, lighting a cigarette.

"I don't know but I'm not going to question Dmitri, are you?" The other member answers.

"Nope. I don't want to end up like Alexi."

"Me neither."

"Maybe Dmitri just doesn't trust anyone but Victor." The smoker says before inhaling again.

"You shouldn't trust anyone that has that much money."

"Agreed. I think Dmitri just wants to make sure everything goes smoothly with no problems. I heard him saying that the physicist will be done in two days which means the bomb will be nuclear."

"Which also means Dmitri will have no use for the physicist anymore so he's as good as dead."

"Along with millions of Americans." The smoker says, laughing.

Bryce flies the drone back to himself and shuts it down. He has heard enough and knows he has to get into the building to put an end to this. Before he can load his weapons he notices a car driving towards the building. The three members near the door approach the car when it parks in front of the building. They spread out in a triangle formation with the lead member in front of the car and the other two behind and on either side of him.

The two members on the roof grab their guns and aim them at the car before kneeling to take cover. Even the three members on each side of the building that were once pacing are focused entirely on the car. Two large men get out of the front of the car on either side. The members keep their guns aimed at them until they see the driver open the back door to help Tiffany get out. Every gun is lowered as she and her guards slowly make their way into the building.

Bryce is amazed at how every single member watched the car approach and wonder who was inside. Not one of them looked at anything other than the car. If he can just cause a distraction in the front of the building long enough for him to get to the back he should be able to take out the members one by one without being seen.

He remembers a case he worked a few years ago when he was a detective. A man was driving home one night after a long day of work, it was dark out already and the rural roads were almost empty when all of a sudden the driver was shot and killed.

Although there was no evidence except for the dead body and bullet holes in the car, the death was ruled a homicide. The more he thought about the case the more he knew something didn't add up so he began to investigate.

He saw what everyone else saw; the missing driver's side window, a few bullet holes in the dash and front seats, and that the car was parked but there was nothing missing from the man or the car.

The more he investigated the more he

realized something wasn't right. He continued to search the rest of the car until he finally came across a bullet hole just underneath the back seat. The placement of the hole and the entry angle made it impossible for it to be there from someone shooting from outside the vehicle, especially since the windshield was still in one piece with no blemishes.

The shot had to have come from someone inside the car while sitting in the front seat. He wondered how that could be since there was no signs of struggle, nothing stolen, and no signs of self defense from the driver.

After walking to the front of the car he looks through the windshield trying to figure out what happened. Nothing seems out of the ordinary on the roof or the grill of the car. He does notice a small imperfection on the hood though. It's not a dent or a hole, but there is a small raise.

He pops the hood and sees a hand gun sitting on the engine that for some reason didn't have a heat shield. The gun has a magazine loaded but there is no ammo inside. Finally he realizes that the engine got so hot that it caused the gun to fire. The driver was just unlucky enough that he was hit by a stray bullet which killed him.

Bryce walks directly to his car and opens the hood to take the heat shield off. He pulls out two magazines for his Glock and uses electrical tape to fasten them to each side of the engine. After closing the hood he lines himself up with the side of the building opposite the driveway.

Looking at the members he knows it's now or never. The only hope of stopping whatever Dmitri has planned lies with him and if he doesn't get the job done millions of people will suffer and die because of it.

The fear of failure starts to creep into his head. The thought of never seeing his wife and son again makes him lose control of his guts and he throws up all over the ground. "Come on, Bryce. Get it together." He says to himself taking out his phone one last time to look at his wife and son. Looking back at the building he sees the members are all relaxed again and going about their own business. "Okay, let's do it." He says starting the car with his phone and revving the engine twice to make it heat up faster.

The car navigates through the trees toward the main road that leads to the building. While navigating with his phone he can see exactly where he is going through the hidden cameras attached to the front of the vehicle.

The members see the car coming towards the building and react the same way they did when the last car came towards them. Bryce stops the car ten feet behind Tiffany's car but keeps the engine running. He watches the members slowly approach with their guns drawn, and he can hear them yelling from his position. The rotating members make their way to the corner of the wall they are guarding closest to the front of the building to see what is going on. They are befuddled when they hear the engine rev twice.

Bryce slyly smiles when he sees the members closest to the car start to surround it, still yelling. Nothing feels better to him when he's in the field than when a plan works. Suddenly, one of the magazines attached to the car's engine starts firing, signaling it's time to make his move. He immediately stands up and starts to sprint towards the building screwing on the silencer of his Glock as he watches the DS members unload their guns at his car. His heart races faster with each stride towards the building.

To the member's surprise, the car is unharmed; the bullets just deflected without even leaving a scratch. They quickly reload their weapons and slowly move even closer to the car.

Finally reaching the building, Bryce hears the second magazine attached to the engine start to fire. Again, the members shoot at the car, causing enough of a distraction for him to make his move. He shoots the guard on the side of the building in the head, killing him instantly. Then, he walks towards the newly killed member to pick up his semi-automatic weapon.

He walks around to the front of the building towards the three members firing at the car and quickly takes them out and drops the weapon before they even realized what was going on. The last two members see what just happened and immediately take cover from Bryce. One runs to the back of the building, just around the corner. The other runs to the opposite side of the building. The two members on the roof see what Bryce did but by the time they grab their weapons they lose sight of him.

Bryce sprints towards the back of the building and pulls out his Glock to fire two shots to make the member take cover fully around the corner. Immediately he drops to the ground and lies on his stomach with his Glock pointed towards the corner. The member fires a couple of shots without looking and Bryce doesn't move a muscle. The member peeks his head out to see why he hasn't heard any shots or seen Bryce getting to him yet and the last thing he sees is a 9mm round go right into his eye and through his head. Bryce gets back up and sprints towards the back of the building and picks up the semi-automatic weapon that the member had and knows there is only one more member outside with him, besides the two on the roof.

At the corner he slowly peeks around and sees that the last member left is not where he thought he'd be. He jogs towards the far corner of the building with the semi-automatic weapon drawn and gets about half way when he sees the back door to the building underneath a balcony. He stops and looks both ways and tries to open the door but it is locked. Without knowing what is behind the door he knows he might need to find a different way into the building.

POP!

A piece of the wall shatters right next to the door from a bullet. Bryce looks to his left and sees the last member outside has run all the way around the building to flank him. Before the member can even take another shot Bryce fires a couple of rounds from the semi-automatic weapon and dives behind a headstone just feet from the door. The member takes cover around the corner of the building but keeps an eye on Bryce who is pinned down. The two men on the roof run to that side of the building when they see where their fellow member is shooting, and take aim.

Bryce notices the motion on the roof with his peripheral vision and fires his weapon in that direction to slow down the members. He then fires a few more rounds at the corner of the building and then some more towards the roof. With only a few seconds before the men on the roof peek back over and start shooting at him, he sets up the semi-automatic weapon beside the headstone facing towards the corner of the building. He quickly lays flat on his back directly behind the headstone and keeps his eyes on the roof.

Almost immediately he can hear the sound of the members semi-automatic weapon firing multiple rounds from the corner of the building. He winces when he hears the bullets hit the headstone directly behind his head. Finally the shooting stops and he doesn't hesitate to roll onto his stomach away from the gun he laid down and fires two shots.

He jumps to his feet and watches the member drop to the ground and lose his grip from his gun. After firing some more rounds towards the roof he sprints to the fallen member. The man is still alive, he's only been shot in the shoulder, but he's writhing in pain. Kicking the member's gun away, he grabs the arm of the wounded shoulder and pulls the man towards the balcony with one arm and shoots towards the roof with the other.

"We don't have much time." Bryce says to the member in Russian, finally under the balcony and out of sight of the two men on the roof. "Where's Dmitri?" The member looks at him and laughs through his pain. "This will go a lot smoother if you cooperate." He says, sternly.

"You don't want to meet Dmitri." The member says.

"Oh no? Why is that?"

"Nobody wants to meet Dmitri. He is the most feared man in all of Russia."

"Lucky for me I'm not from Russia. Now tell me where he is or I will make your other shoulder look just like this one."

The member stays silent and smiles while staring him in the eye. Shaking his head in disappointment he shoots the member in the other shoulder.

"Are you going to tell me where Dmitri is now or should I shoot one of your knees next?" Bryce pauses to wait for an answer. "Tell me where Dmitri is." He sternly says over the agonizing screams of the member.

"He'll kill me if I tell you."

"And what do you think I'm going to do if you don't." Bryce says with a cocky look, holding his gun in the face of the member.

The member lowers his eyes in shame, knowing he has to betray Dmitri. "He's meeting the woman." He says quietly.

"Where is the meeting?" Bryce asks.

"In the basement."

"Is that where the bomb is too?"

The member doesn't answer but shakes his head to let Bryce know he is right.

"How do I get to the basement?"

"The door to the basement is in the back of the building. It's the only way down."

"How many more men are inside?"

"I don't know."

"Maybe this will help you remember." Bryce says, putting his foot on the members gunshot wound on his shoulder applying pressure.

"Okay, okay. There are maybe ten men besides Dmitri and Victor, a dozen tops."

Bryce takes his foot off the member and

holsters his weapon.

"Thank you. That wasn't so hard was it? Now can I trust you to leave the area and not come back?"

The member looks up at Bryce and shakes his head surprised that he is going to be let go.

"You know what?" He says, right before he lets the member go. "You're a member of DS, I can't trust you." In the blink of an eye he pulls his Glock out and shoots the man in the head. "Hey! You two up there!" He yells up to the roof while still under the balcony. "I don't really have a lot of time. If you both surrender and throw your guns over the side I will let you leave the area and walk away without killing you."

He can hear them laughing on the roof as he reloads his gun checking how much ammo he has left.

"We have the advantage!" One of the men yells down as the other still laughs. "We're in an elevated position, there is no way for you to come up here without either one of us killing you."

"Challenge accepted," he says to himself while nodding his head, before yelling up to the men on the roof. "I'm going to go around to the front of the building. I'll be right up."

CHAPTER 31

DS Warehouse

Kuzminskoye Cemetery

12:08 P.M.

Bryce makes his way to the front of the building and is just a few steps from the door. The two men on the roof know he's coming in that way so he has to be cautious and have some sort of plan. He looks around for another way in but cannot see a plausible solution. There is no way he could get in one of the windows without being seen immediately and killed on sight. Continuing to scan the area he spots one of the members he killed in the front of the house when he first approached.

He grabs the body of the fallen member and puts his own hat on him. He then takes his t-shirt off and puts it over the members blood soaked shirt hoping that the blood will not soak through his own before he carries out his plan.

Now standing in a tank top and pants, he

holds up the dead member by the front door. Holding the back of the member's shirt he leans him against the door before slowly turning the handle. A barrage of bullets fly towards him before he can even poke the member's head inside.

He lets go of the member and makes sure he falls forward through the door. The shooting stops when the members see Bryce's hat and shirt on the motionless body. While they laugh and joke about killing a Di9 Agent, Bryce peeks in the window with his mirror and sees the two men from the roof are the ones inside laughing. They stand next to each other overlooking the railing on the second floor with their guns down by their side. The front door bursts open and before the members can realize what is going on he fires a bullet into each one of their heads with marksman like shooting and then crouches by the front door and stays silent to check his ammo.

While he waits to see if anyone else is coming he scans the building to get a layout. There are two sets of stairs leading to the second floor. One on each side of the room against the front wall that go half way up, have a landing and turn ninety degrees, and then go up the rest of the way. Four closed doors stare at him on the second floor behind the railing that the two snipers are now laying next to.

Bryce can see from the front door all the

way to the back of the building through the narrow hallway running right down the middle of the room. Each side of the hallway has four glass wall offices that are empty. He stands and walks towards the offices taking his time to thoroughly check each one making sure nobody is hiding and about to attack. After he sees the offices are clear he walks back to the middle of the front room between the two staircases and reaches into his bag to pull out a black urchin. After setting it up, he runs down the hallway towards the back of the building.

To his surprise he hasn't run into or seen any other members besides the two snipers he killed when he first got inside. He starts to wonder if that's a good thing or if he should be worried about an ambush. Either way, he has to find the door to the basement. He goes left into the big room in the back with his gun in his right hand to slowly open each door with his left. The mundane repetition starts to get annoying for him as he makes his way around the left side of the room. So far, each door has either been a closet, a bathroom, or the kitchen.

As he walks along the back wall, he comes to the door leading outside. He stops and opens it to look outside to make sure nobody is around out back either. After confirming the outside is clear, he closes the door behind him but leaves it unlocked for a quick getaway. After opening the next door he pauses, it isn't the way to the basement but it does look like their surveillance room. There are six televisions on the wall each showing a different part of the building. The front door and where the cars are parked, just inside the front door, the big room in the back, the hallway upstairs that show the four closed doors, a random room with some sort of apparatus and a bunch of tables with bags lined up on them, and the basement.

"That's what I'm looking for right there." He says to himself, seeing Dmitri and some members, Tiffany and her goons, and Roman Bovanovski. "What are they saying?"

A lone computer sits on a table on the far end of the room, most likely controlling the televisions in the area. He holsters his weapon before going over to the computer to see if he can turn on the volume on the TV showing the basement. It doesn't take long to find it for the correct television and he watches the people in the room while slowly turning up the volume just loud enough to hear them speak. Just as he begins to make out what Dmitri is talking to Tiffany about, a voice comes over the speaker in the room.

"It isn't polite to eavesdrop." The voice says.

Bryce quickly pulls his Glock and whips his body around to see the room is still empty and the door shutting automatically. He runs over to the door and tries to open it but it is locked.

"You won't be able to get out unless I let you out." The voice says again through the speaker.

Disregarding what he hears on the speaker Bryce empties his magazine into the handle of the door but it causes almost no damage. He then tries to kick the door down with no success.

"I told you that you can't get out. The door is impenetrable unless you know the code. It is made of composite metal foam with titanium on both sides. You should save your energy, you're going to need it." The voice says.

"I know this isn't Dmitri, I can see him on the screen. Who am I talking to?" Bryce asks.

"My name is Victor."

"Dmitri's right hand man."

"You know about me I assume?"

"I know all about DS. Mostly about Dmitri since he's the only important one to know about." Bryce says, trying to get under Victor's skin.

"A pitiful attempt to draw my ire."

"You knew I was coming didn't you?" Bryce asks.

"Of course we knew. The men outside were just a test to see how good you were. I must say, you passed with flying colors."

"How did you know I was coming?"

"We'll get to that later."

"You want me here for some reason. That's why there were no more men inside waiting for me."

"You're a quick one. It's too bad you aren't working for us."

"It's too bad you aren't in here with me right now." Bryce says, almost daring Victor to come in.

"Another time perhaps." Victor says as gas starts to fill the room from the vents.

"Are you going to kill me with gas like a coward?"

"No, no, no. We wouldn't do that. Where would be the fun in that?"

"Then what are you doing?" Bryce says, covering his mouth and nose with his shirt.

"Be patient, American. You'll find out soon enough."

Bryce does whatever he can to get out of the room. He tries the door again with no luck, he tries to get up into the wooden ceiling but won't be able to before the gas fills the room, and he tries to break through the wall but his body is beginning to weaken. He takes his gun and starts firing rounds at the door. Each bullet just bounces off without causing any damage.

His weakened legs start to lose strength, causing him to stumble around the room. With enough energy for one more attempt to flee he tries to break through the wall one last time but his body just can't stand anymore and it crashes onto the desk causing the computer to fly onto the floor.

"You are killing me, aren't you." Bryce mutters.

"I told you the gas won't kill you." Victor says just before Bryce blacks out. The last words he remembers hearing after his eyes slowly close and he passes out are: "Dmitri would like to have a word with you."

CHAPTER 32

DS Warehouse

12:40 P.M.

Slowly Bryce regains consciousness and opens his eyes. He's in a different room and tied up with his arms restrained above his head. The cold of the concrete floor absorbs into his bare feet while he stands in his pants and tank top. Looking around the room he notices his bag next to his gun sitting on a table to his left. To his right sits a bigger table with knives, some tools, and a few weapons. Doing everything he can to trick his mind into thinking they are for something different doesn't help, he knows all too well that the items on that table are used for torture.

His energy and strength are renewed now that the gas is completely gone from his body and he tries to pull his arms free but they are secured tightly. Above his head is a titanium latch holding the rope connected to his wrists. The latch is connected to a pole going from the floor to the ceiling and equally distanced between the walls to either side and the wall behind him. With all his might he tries to get free from the restraints by placing his feet on the pole that he is tied to and pushing while he pulls down with his arms but neither the pole nor the latch budge an inch.

He turns his head as far as he can to take a look at the pole and notices two DS members standing behind him against the wall on either side of a closed door. "Hey, I didn't even know you guys were back there. You wouldn't want to untie me, would you?" He asks.

The members don't say a word. They stare straight ahead without even looking at Bryce.

"What kind of gun is that?" He asks again, trying to loosen up the members and again neither of them makes a sound. "I wasn't snoring earlier when I was knocked out, was I? My wife says I snore in my sleep." He says.

Finally one of the members looks at him, but before he can say anything, the door across the room from them opens. Victor enters followed by a DS member, then Tiffany Peterson and her two goons, and Roman Bovanovski who is battered with a black eye and swollen lip. Finally Dmitri comes into the room and closes the door behind himself. Slowly he walks towards Bryce eyeing him up and evaluating him with each step he takes. Everyone else in the room stays silent, standing along the side of the room.

"Do you know who I am?" Dmitri asks,

now inches away from Bryce's face.

For the first time since his son was born, he feels scared. He doesn't show it and doesn't panic, he is just starting to accept the fact of what's going to happen.

"Dmitri Sachenkov." He answers. "Ex KGB, bomb maker, and presumed dead. Also known as 'The Executioner'."

"That's right." Dmitri replies with a sly smile. "I know who you are too, Bryce Stone. So, Mr. Stone, who else is here with you?" Bryce looks Dmitri in the eyes and then at the other people in the room. He stays absolutely silent, looking back at Dmitri "Answer me!" He yells before punching him in the stomach with his left fist, followed by a right cross to his head.

Hunched over as far as he can, he wheezes trying to catch his breath and spits out blood. He takes a deep breath, regains his composure, and stands tall to look Dmitri in the eyes without saying a word.

"I like this one." Dmitri says to Victor with a smirk. "He knows he is about to die but he still has some fight in him."

"Untie me." Bryce says, making Dmitri turn back to face him. "I'll show you how much fight I have."

Dmitri smiles and turns to the table to grab a hunting knife. He holds it up to Bryce's face and gently rubs the point on his cheek. "Tell me what you know first." He demands.

"I know you're making a nuclear bomb and that you want to detonate it on American soil. And she is providing the money for you to make that happen." Bryce says, using his head to point to Tiffany.

"Anything else?" Dmitri asks.

"Yeah, you hit like a woman."

Everyone's eyebrows raise when they hear those words. Dmitri has never been talked to like that before and his face shows how angered he is. He turns to Victor and puts the knife in it's sheath, then looks back at Bryce and smiles. In the blink of an eye he lands two massive blows to his left side just below the ribs.

"Thank you for proving my point." Bryce says, coughing violently and struggling to catch his breath.

Dmitri slowly walks around Bryce thinking of the best way to make him say what he knows. Just as he gets back in front of Bryce he notices the tattoo on his arm.

"Who is Jeremiah, is that your son?" He asks maniacally.

"It's a Bible verse. Jeremiah 17:7." Bryce struggles to speak, still catching his breath.

"A man of God? Tell me what this verse says."

"Blessed is the one who trusts in the Lord, whose confidence is in Him."

"Interesting. Do you believe what that says?"

"Every word."

"How is that working for you now?" Dmitri asks while staring Bryce in the face before pausing. "How did you know where to find us?"

Bryce again stays silent and takes a deep breath.

"How did you know where to find us!" Dmitri yells before punching Bryce square in the nose.

Immediately Bryce's eyes water and blood fills both nostrils before running down his lip towards his mouth. "I am a member of Di9." He says proudly.

"Di9?" Dmitri asks before letting out a loud laugh. "Isn't that the same organization that we just slaughtered?" Bryce tries to get free angrily, tightening every muscle and bulging his veins as he attempts to pull himself free from the rope. "That was so easy, it was very fun. Were those your top Agents or was it their first day?" He asks, trying to antagonize Bryce even more.

"My brother was one of those Agents." Bryce says with a snarl.

"That's too bad. It must be tough for you knowing how he died and the man responsible is standing right in front of you." Bryce does all he can to try to get free one more time, and again, the results are the same leaving him frustrated and angry. "You keep trying to get free. What do you think would happen if you got free?" Dmitri asks.

"I would kill you." Bryce responds.

"You would kill me?" He says, almost falling over from laughter. "You're just an analyst and I'm 'The Executioner'. Give me your analysis on how that fight would go."

"How did you know I'm an analyst?"

"Just like you, I also have intel." Dmitri walks over to the table to take a drink of water and then returns to Bryce. "Do you know why I want to detonate a nuclear weapon in America?"

"Well, I don't see you being a guy who gives an ultimatum, so you don't want money. I don't think you've been wronged by my government or country, so it can't be revenge. So I guess the reason you're doing this is because you're afraid."

"You think I'm afraid?" Dmitri says, chuckling. "I'm not afraid of anything."

"No? You started your own terrorist organization. You want so badly to rule the world that you'll stop at nothing to make that happen." He pauses to get a read on Dmitri's reaction. "The only problem is that you're afraid of the United States. If you take us out then your biggest adversary is gone. So again, I think you're doing this out of fear." Bryce watches Dmitri pace back and forth getting angrier and angrier by the second. "I have a question for you now." Bryce states.

"What is it?" Dmitri barks.

"If you kill everyone with a nuclear bomb,

then who will be left to rule?"

"I don't want to kill everyone, just Americans. She thinks the same way." Dmitri says, pointing at Tiffany.

"And what do you think will happen if you detonate a nuclear bomb?"

"You'll die."

"Many will die, but we'll retaliate. Then you'll retaliate. Then other countries will get involved and before you know it the world will burn from nuclear war. So again, what good is it to rule the world if there is nobody left to rule." Bryce waits for an answer, but Dmitri stays silent not knowing how to answer the question. "I don't agree with what you're doing at all, but at least you want power. She is doing this for revenge for something she knows nothing about. To be honest, I think it's a pretty stupid reason."

"A stupid reason?" Tiffany interjects. "Do you know what happened to my family?"

"You mean when you were deported or when you had your parents plane go down in the alps?"

"How dare you say that!" Tiffany says, stunned. "I would never kill my own parents, I loved them!"

"You loved them or you still love them?" Tiffany looks confused by the question and stays silent, looking around at the other people in the room. "Never mind, we'll get into that another time and you'll pay for what you did. I mean, with all the evidence and coincidences of the crash, it's what a prosecutor would call a slam dunk."

"You don't know what you're talking about." Tiffany says defensively.

"Maybe you're right, but I do know the reason you were deported with your family. That's why I know your reason to attack the U.S. is just plain stupid."

"Nobody knows why we were deported, we weren't even told." Tiffany says, getting right in Bryce's face.

"I know why."

"Then tell me. Since you are the only person who knows, please tell me." Tiffany says sarcastically.

"You were deported because of your father."

"Gee, thanks for the breaking news. I know that my father had a disagreement with the President and he deported us all."

"No, the President had you all deported because your father had an affair with the First Lady."

"You're a liar!" Tiffany yells before slapping Bryce across the face. The yelling and screaming and physical exertion causes Tiffany to drop to one knee in pain. Her body just can't take that much stress.

"It's up to you if you want to believe me or not, but I'm not a liar." Bryce says.

Tiffany's goons run over to her, help her back to her feet, and stand next to her to help her stay upright. "How do you know that when nobody else does?" She asks after taking a few breaths from her oxygen tank.

"I made a call to the President, the same man that deported your family. I told him that I needed to know and that it would never get out. I now owe him a favor."

"If that's true, then why deport us all? Why not just fire my father?"

"I asked the President that same question. He told me that every time he saw your father after the affair that he wanted to kill him. So instead of letting you grow up without a father he decided to deport you all instead."

"Even if that's true, America still needs to pay."

"So you want to kill millions of Americans for something your father is responsible for? That makes a lot of sense." Bryce says sarcastically. "Seems to me that you already got your revenge when your parents plane went down in the alps because of you." Bryce, now getting angrier, turns his attention to Dmitri. "So I know you're doing this out of fear, but what is the reason you tell yourself for wanting to kill Americans?"

"You mean the spoiled, bratty egotists? Paying other people to clean your mansions, mow your lawns, and drive you around in your fancy cars? Americans think the world revolves around them. You hate foreigners and minorities and anything else that is different than you. Now it's time for me to put an end to it all. Don't worry though, you won't be around much longer so you won't have to live through it." Dmitri tells Bryce.

"What are you waiting for then? Why haven't you killed me yet?"

"I will kill you, don't worry. There is just one more person who wants to talk to you." Dmitri nods to the two DS members in the back of the room behind Bryce.

The members turn towards the door and open it up. Bryce can't see what's going on behind him but he can hear slow moving footsteps coming towards him. A man starts to talk in a Russian accent as the footsteps become closer and closer. "It hurts, doesn't it? Your hopes dashed, your dreams down the toilet, and your fate is sitting right beside you."

It takes a second for Bryce to realize that what he just heard is a line from one of his favorite movies, *Rounders.* He looks at Dmitri and then Victor who are both smiling, then the realization starts to set in.

"Travis?" Bryce asks, hoping he's wrong while trying to look over his shoulder. His eyes widen and his jaw drops as confusion sets in.

"Hello, Bryce. It's good to see you again."

CHAPTER 33

1:06 P.M.

"What's wrong, Bryce? It looks like you've seen a ghost." Travis says with a smile.

"I thought you were dead." Bryce replies, trying to comprehend what is happening.

"I'm sorry to disappoint you."

"You know what I mean. I thought you were killed in the attacks in Philadelphia."

"Obviously not."

"The President said you were shot protecting him. Then he watched from his car as an assassin shot you two more times point blank."

"That's true, I was shot in the arm and shoulder right in front of him. A sacrifice I was willing to make so the whole thing would be more believable."

"What about the explosion?"

"That was the perfect cover to wipe away any evidence I was still alive and escaped in the sewers."

"Travis, why are you doing this?" Bryce asks, befuddled.

"Remember when I was in the Army? Four years ago we were stationed in Turkey. We were doing a routine training exercise one night when we were ambushed by a militant group from Syria. They slaughtered almost all of us. I was one of the 'lucky' ones who they kept alive."

"What does that have to do with you being involved in this?"

"I'm getting to that. While I was held captive they would beat and torture me. Every single day for weeks they would come in and abuse me. They would cut me just enough so I wouldn't bleed out. They would beat me within an inch of my life. I was electrocuted, suffocated, and they even urinated on me. Every scar I have on my body is from them." Travis pauses to lift his shirt and show Bryce the scars all over his upper body. "They wanted to use the few of us left as trade bait for twenty Syrian prisoners in custody with the U.S. They figured if they beat us that bad that the President would have to make the trade to save his people."

"I'm sorry you had to go through that. Why didn't you ever talk to me about it?"

"It's not something that I wanted to relive."

"At least you made it home eventually. I assume the President made the deal? It still doesn't explain what you are doing here with DS."

"That's the thing, the President never

made the trade. He said twenty Syrians is too much to give up for only six Americans. 'Only six' he said. We were expendable to him and he abandoned us there in control of the Syrians. He left us to die."

"Then how did you escape?"

"With the help of that man right there." Travis says, pointing to Dmitri. "He was part of that same militant group that captured me. He used to tell me how much he liked the fight in me and how loyal I was to my country. Then one day he came all by himself to see me. He told me who he was and that he didn't want to be thought of as a Syrian. He wanted to go back to Russia to continue with DS. He then made me an offer and I accepted."

"And what was that? Betray your country and forget everything you believe in?"

"No, it was a hope of survival. It was all I had left. He told me that if I would help him take down the Syrians that he would help me escape and get back at the Americans for leaving me there to die."

"But there was a catch. You had to join DS."

"That's right."

"That's a pretty steep price to pay. So you shot your way out and came to Russia?"

"Right again. We immediately started working on our plan which we are carrying out as we speak. I then went home to retire from the Army. They tried to get me to stay because of my skills. Once they realized they weren't going to talk me out of retiring they got me in contact with Di9. Me and Dmitri thought it was a good idea for me to work there so we could know everything that is going on."

"So that's how the attacks were so precise. You knew exactly what we would do and where we would be."

"Makes it easier to attack when you know every single detail about your enemy." Travis says before pausing for a second. "Did you like my misdirection? You probably thought that Dakota was the double Agent didn't you. I thought that was a pretty smart move, You could call me a genius if you want."

"A genius? I would call you a traitor." Bryce states.

"I'm a traitor? The President left me to be tortured. He left me to die. There was never a rescue attempt or a deal made to bring me home. He betrayed me! We all know that the penalty for treason is death. I can't wait to give him his sentence."

Bryce shakes his head in disbelief and disappointment. "Why wait? Why didn't you just kill him in Philadelphia if you want him dead? Why did you save him?"

"There is no point in killing someone before getting what you want. Plus I had to save him to make it look like I wasn't involved."

"What is it that you want from him?"

"Fifty billion dollars in cash and fifty billion dollars in gold."

"And if he doesn't give it to you?"

"Then he will receive his sentence, in the form of a nice, big mushroom cloud over Washington D.C."

"What if he does give you what you want? What will you do then?"

"There will still be a mushroom cloud, I will just be far away with Emma living on an island where nobody will find us."

Bryce looks at Dmitri who is smirking, and realizes that Dmitri hasn't told Travis what they did to Emma. "Travis, Emma is dead." He says.

"No she's not, you're lying!" Travis yells in disbelief.

"Look at me. You know I don't lie."

Travis looks at his brother and realizes he's telling the truth, "What did you do?" He asks, turning to ask Dmitri.

"I did what had to be done. There can be no loose ends." Dmitri reminds Travis.

"I told you she can be trusted. She wouldn't have said a word!"

"And now we know that for a fact."

Now enraged, Travis grits his teeth and clenches his fist. He wants so badly to go after Dmitri but would never make it out of the room with all the DS members there. He then watches Dmitri slowly walks towards Travis with his hand out. Just before he gets to him, a DS member hands Dmitri a gun. He takes the magazine out but leaves one bullet in the chamber and hands the gun to Travis.

"What do you want me to do with this?" Travis asks.

"Kill your brother." Dmitri responds.

"What if I don't want to?"

"That's okay, I will kill him, but then I will kill you too."

"How about I just shoot you instead?" Travis asks, pointing the gun at Dmitri's head.

"You can if you want, I can't stop you. Just remember that there is only one bullet in that gun. If you shoot me then you are basically just killing yourself."

"No, I'd be killing you."

"And then every DS member in here will shoot you."

"You know I'm getting awfully tired of all these tests. I've done everything you've asked of me."

"Then kill your brother, it will be your last test. Then I will trust you fully and you will be a true member of DS."

Travis lowers the gun and looks at Bryce, who stands silent. Thoughts of his childhood run through his head as he remembers playing in the backyard with him, playing video games, defending him at school when he got bullied, and protecting him from dad when he would come home drunk. The thing he remembers most is how often he would tell Bryce that he is his big brother and that he'll always have his back.

"I'm waiting." Dmitri says impatiently.

Slowly Travis raises the gun and aims it directly at his brother's head. He sees Bryce nod to let him know it's ok and that he forgives him. Travis pulls the hammer of the gun back and stands tall and steady. He places his other hand on the gun to hold it still and then winks before he shoots.

Bryce can only drop his head and close his eyes waiting for the gun to fire. He squeezes his hands tight and tenses his muscles thinking one last time about Kayla and Michael.

POP!

Bryce's arms drop and he opens his eyes to see the smoking gun pointed above his head. He looks up to see that Travis shot the rope keeping him restrained.

"I'll always have your back." Travis tells Bryce.

POP! POP!

Travis's body falls limp and gives a thud as it hits the ground.

"No!" Bryce screams, watching his brother's body quickly lose blood from the two bullet holes that Dmitri just put in him. Water fills his eyes seeing the motionless body lay on the concrete floor with blood oozing out of him faster than an overflowing toilet.

"It's hard to have someone's back when you are laying on yours." Dmitri says, arrogantly.

Bryce's face turns red and he clenches his fists as his body shakes with anger. He's always been able to control his emotions, but he's never felt this way before.

"I'm going to make you feel pain, I'm going to make you bleed, and then I'm going to kill you with my bare hands." Bryce grumbles to Dmitri.

"How do you plan on doing that? You are unarmed and surrounded by DS members with their guns pointed at you. Tell me, where is your God now?"

Bryce takes two steps towards Dmitri but stops in his tracks when every member of DS pull the hammer back on their gun.

"Hiding behind your goons like a coward. You took my brother from me." Bryce yells.

Dmitri raises his gun and points it at Bryce with a big smile on his face. "Well, you are about to be reunited."

CHAPTER 34

1:15 P.M.

Bryce is at peace and is surprisingly calm even though he knows what is about to happen. The last few seconds before someone knows they are about to die seem to last forever, but it feels that everything is moving in slow motion and time has stopped as Dmitri pulls the hammer back on his gun and takes aim.

"I've killed hundreds of people. I've never felt any certain way about it, it was always just business." Dmitri says. "But this feels different. I think I'm going to enjoy this very much."

Calmly Bryce looks up and stays silent. He doesn't beg for his life, nor does he shake with fear. His eyes stare blankly at Dmitri but all he sees is Kayla and Michael.

"Nothing to say? No final words? You aren't going to plead for your life?" Dmitri asks stunned. "I guess there's only one thing left to do then. Say hello to your brother for me." He says, raising his gun.

Bryce closes his eyes and crosses his arms behind his back before he drops his chin to his chest.

KABOOM!

He flinches and is met with a blast of heat in front of him. Surprised he's still alive, he opens his eyes to see the door blasted off its hinges from an explosion just outside the room. The DS members who were by the door are now sprawled out and lifeless on the floor. Dmitri now lays on the ground just outside his reach trying to regain his composure and stand back up while Victor lies unconscious in the corner and covered by shrapnel.

POP! POP!

The two DS members behind him fall to the floor and he looks around the room and sees that it didn't come from anyone in there with him. Looking up at the doorway through the flames and smoke he sees a large silhouette walking towards him with a gun in his right hand.

"I thought you could use my help." A deep, masculine voice says.

Bryce smiles and breathes a sigh of relief when he sees who that voice belongs to. "John! Am I glad to see you. I guess Washington sent you to help me after all?" He asks.

"Washington doesn't know I'm here." John says, tossing Bryce his Glock that was sitting on the table.

"I thought you always follow orders. I remember him telling you not to come here to help."

"Some orders need to be ignored to do what is right."

John hears someone moving in the corner behind him and whips around with his gun raised.

"John, wait!" Bryce yells. "That's Roman Bovanovski."

"Who?" He asks with his gun still pointed at Roman.

"He's the guy whose email we cracked to find out where DS is. He's helping us."

"I thought Tiffany Peterson would be here too." John says, finally lowering his weapon and holstering it.

"She was here." Bryce says, looking around the room at the bodies on the floor. "She had two of her goons with her."

"I don't see her here."

Bryce walks over to where Tiffany and her goons were standing and feels a light breeze. "We're in the basement, I shouldn't be feeling a draft through the wall." He says, perplexed, while feeling around the area where the air is coming from before giving a little push on the wall. A secret door opens slightly revealing an escape tunnel inside. "I can hear movement. They must have gone this way." He says after sticking his head through the doorway.

"Then let's finish up here and go after her." John replies.

"No, I'll finish up in here, you go after her. If she escapes now we won't know when we'll get a chance to get her again. Failure doesn't stop terrorists, they just consider that practice for the next time."

"Are you sure?" John asks.

"I got this. I need to get Roman out of here anyway, he's my responsibility."

"Alright, be careful with him." John says, pointing to Dmitri. "If I were you I'd just put a bullet in him now and call it a day." He says before taking a step into the tunnel and pulling out his gun and flashlight.

"John." Bryce says, making him stop and turn around. "Thanks."

John nods and continues into the tunnel. He has some ground to make up and has no idea where the tunnel leads.

Bryce turns around and sees Dmitri starting to move around on the ground, groaning in pain. With every other DS member dead or still unconscious he slowly walks towards him with his gun drawn and watches as he rolls over to his back. Their eyes lock and he circles around until he is standing above Dmitri's head with his gun pointed directly at his face.

"Would you rather see it coming or would you rather turn around like a coward?" Bryce asks.

"I thought you said you wouldn't need a gun." Dmitri replies.

Bryce thinks for a second and takes a couple steps back. He thinks of all the movies he's watched and wonders why the person with the gun would never just shoot the other person instead of going off on a long monologue. Normally he would do what he needed to do to finish the job, and what Dmitri just said wouldn't bother him either. But this is different, this just became personal, and he is about to become one of the people from the movies. "Stand up." He tells Dmitri, looking over at his dead brother's body.

Dmitri stands and stares angrily with his muscles trembling, just wishing he could get hold of Bryce.

"I should just shoot you now, but this is for my brother." Bryce says, lowering his gun.

Without taking his eyes off of Dmitri he takes the magazine out of his gun and tosses it aside and then retracts the slide to remove the round in the chamber. It pops out and lands on the floor just in front of him. He kicks it away before dropping his gun to the ground.

"Stupid, arrogant American." Dmitri says with a big grin on his face. "You could've ended this, but your ego just cost you your life." He watches Bryce cracking his neck and loosening his arms while standing perfectly still waiting to square off. "I really do like the fight in you. Your brother had that same fight, it's a shame I had to kill him." He says, chuckling.

Immediately Bryce charges and runs into Dmitri and pushes him back until both men slam into the wall. His left hand pushes against Dmitri's right shoulder and his right arm is under Dmitri's chin pinning and choking him. He lands two quick punches to the side and then throws a quick, right cross but Dmitri's tremendous speed and reflexes help him duck under the punch and in one motion grabs Bryce and takes him to the ground. He winces in pain from the thud against the floor; landing squarely on his back has knocked the wind out of him, but he is still able to wrap his legs around Dmitri to be in a defensive position.

Dmitri throws a barrage of punches, landing two quick right hands to Bryce's face followed by a left elbow. The pummeling already has his nose bloody and his eyes swollen and blurry.

Finally Bryce is able to wrap up Dmitri's arms and hold them close to his body to at least delay the attack. The men wrestle and struggle for an advantage over the other as they both sweat and groan in pain.

POP! POP! POP!

Bryce turns his head towards the tunnel hoping that the three shots he just heard were coming from John's gun and not going towards him. In the second it takes for him to look towards the tunnel he loses focus just long enough for Dmitri to get an arm free...

CHAPTER 35

Escape Tunnel

1:34 P.M.

The dark tunnel is long and winding. A single lightbulb hangs from a chain in the middle of the walkway every forty feet or so. It's not until John passes the third lightbulb that he sees what looks to be a flashlight and movement up ahead. If he can take out at least one of the men before they know they are being followed...

POP! POP! POP!

"Dang it!" He says in disgust, seeing that he missed his target.

Tiffany's goons stop to look at her and then at each other when they hear the gunshots echo through the tunnel. "Get her out of here." The second goon says to the lead goon, "I'll hold him off."

The lead goon picks Tiffany up and puts her over his shoulder, grabs her oxygen tank in his other hand, and continues down the tunnel as quickly as he can. The second goon slowly walks back towards the DS warehouse, staying as close to the walls and out of sight as he can. Every time he hears a noise or sees any sort of movement, he fires a shot in that direction. If he hits whoever is following him then that's great, but his objective is to just slow him down and every time he fires his weapon John has to take cover.

Sweat drips from John's brow and his heart races in the hot tunnel. Advance too quickly then he runs the risk of being shot or killed, go too slowly and he might lose Tiffany. He can see the goon up ahead taking cover just around one of the bends of the tunnel across from an electrical panel. John takes cover behind a wooden beam that supports the tunnel from collapsing, and has to come up with a plan.

He shoots the lightbulb above him, causing it to go dark in his area, and then begins shooting at the electrical panel right across from the goon. The goon takes cover behind a support beam and doesn't notice the shots are aimed at the panel and not at him. John's third shot hits the panel perfectly causing sparks and flames to shoot out. He sees the goon cover his eyes and shield his face from the sparks giving him just enough time to run through the tunnel to get close enough to shoot the goon in the knee. The goon screams in agony, drops to the ground, and loses his grip on his gun.

"Tell me where they're going." John demands while approaching with his weapon drawn, kicking the loose gun away.

Other than the screams of agony from the hole in his knee, the goon doesn't say a word and is more focused on the writhing pain he's in.

"Where?!" John yells, stepping on the goons bloody knee.

"The airport." The goon moans through the pain. "We were leaving the country on her private jet."

"That wasn't so hard, was it?" John asks, lowering his weapon. "Look, I don't have time to tie you up or take you in because I need to go catch your boss. Do you promise to stay here and not do anything stupid?"

The goon nods in agreement.

"Good, because I hate surprises. You aren't going to surprise me and keep coming after me, are you?"

The goon shakes his head no and is relieved that he is going to live.

"I know you won't."

John raises his gun and aims it at the goons head.

POP!

CHAPTER 36

DS Warehouse

1:42 P.M.

Bryce struggles to defend himself as Dmitri rains down punches to his head and face. Most of his energy is spent defending himself while he waits for the perfect moment to counter attack, but this opponent is not like any other person he has fought or sparred with. He notices the look on Dmitri's face as his arms and head take the brunt of the blows. Not only does he want to win the fight, but he wants to annihilate his opponent. The fight has only been going on for a couple minutes but it seems like hours already.

Dmitri is not getting tired and shows no signs of letting up. He throws punches like a machine one after another nonstop. Every time Bryce seems to tie up one of his arms the other one slips free.

Most of his energy has been used on the defensive side, and he knows he doesn't have much strength left. As Dmitri raises his fist overhead looking to land a knockout blow, Bryce manages to get his hand free. In one swift motion he swats the punch to his side causing it to barely miss his head and hit the concrete floor. The knuckles shatter on impact and the sound of agonizing screams echo off the cinder block walls in the the room. Quickly Bryce throws his legs around either side of Dmitri's arm and puts him in an arm bar.

It doesn't take long for his arm to snap and he lets out another scream as Bryce rolls over and stands up. He watches Dmitri try to roll over with one arm and get to his hands and knees. Before he can even attempt to stand Bryce kicks him in the ribs, breaking two of them. "Stay down!" He yells. So angry and focused, he doesn't notice Victor start to move under the shrapnel in the corner.

Victor's eyes spring open from the screams and moaning of Dmitri. He regains his senses and rolls over to see his leader try to get up again just before Bryce knees him in the head, knocking him out cold.

After taking a deep breath, he wipes blood from his nose and lip, and stands over a motionless Dmitri. Through his almost swollen shut left eye he can see that the DS boss is still alive and breathing. He looks over to the side and sees Roman laying on the floor trying to hide behind the table. "Get up." He says, grabbing his gun off the same table.

"Are you going to kill me?" Roman asks.

"No, but I need you to do whatever it is you do to make that bomb useless. Denuclearize it, de-weaponize it, make it a giant paper weight for all I care."

"What are you going to do?"

"I'm going to finish what I started."

He loads his gun and walks towards Dmitri, while Roman starts to move towards the room that houses the bomb.

Just before he gets to Dmitri, Victor quietly stands and charges him. Before he realizes what's going on, Victor rams his shoulder into his back causing him to fire a round into the floor just missing Dmitri. The force of the attack makes him drop his weapon out of reach as he and the gun both fall to the floor.

Roman gasps when he sees Victor get behind Bryce and put him in a choke hold.

CHAPTER 37

Escape Tunnel

1:52 P.M.

John continues his pursuit down the tunnel keeping an eye out for Tiffany and her goon. He assumes the tunnel is man-made, most likely by DS because of the variances in its size. It gets wider in some areas but then almost too narrow to walk through in others. There are also areas where he has to duck his head to get under a support beam. Just as he starts to wonder how long the tunnel is he comes to a dead end and Tiffany and her goon are nowhere to be seen. He knows people don't just disappear; they have to be somewhere.

Looking to the left and right for any other branches of the tunnel that lead in another direction reveals nothing. Frustratedly he backtracks a little to see if there are any hidden doors or passages that he might have passed without noticing but the area is clear of any secret exits so he makes his way back to the end of the tunnel.

"There has to be something here." He says to himself, continuing to look around.

Knowing the tunnel wouldn't just end without an exit he knows he must be missing something but doesn't have time to investigate. He can't let Tiffany get away so he decides to head back to the DS warehouse to get back outside. Just before he turns to run back down the tunnel, he feels the slightest breeze coming from the wall. He follows the draft with his hand which leads him to a crack where the air is coming from.

He holsters his weapon to place both hands on the wall and begins to push. His muscles bulge as he uses every ounce of energy to try to get through but as big as he is, it won't budge. Taking a breather he feels around some more and finally realizes that the crack in the wall is not really a crack. It's the edge of a sliding door and the breeze is coming from outside. He slides it open and realizes that the tunnel leads into a sarcophagus.

After climbing out of the sarcophagus he sees he's in the middle of the cemetery and takes a look around to figure out where he is and to see if he can see Tiffany. "Gotcha." He says to himself when he spots her and her goon almost at a chapel about a football field away.

He starts to run and in just a couple of steps he is in a full sprint trying to catch up before they can get away. The goon breaks the drivers side window of a car to unlock it before putting Tiffany in the back seat and climbing in himself to drive. Now, thirty yards away he can only watch as they start to drive off. The smug look and smile on Tiffany's face makes John's blood boil. He stops and takes out his gun to shoot at the car but can't pull the trigger. There are just too many people around and not worth the risk, he'll have to continue the chase.

He restarts his sprint, approaches the chapel, and sees a 2009 Lada Priora in the parking lot. After arriving at the car he looks around to make sure nobody is watching before he breaks in and drives off. "Now that's what I'm talking about." He says out loud spotting a 2020 Portofino Ferrari on the other side of the parking lot. He makes a bee line over to the Ferrari, picks the lock, and hot wires the car to peel off towards Tiffany.

CHAPTER 38

DS Warehouse

1:58 P.M.

Bryce is doing all he can to break the choke hold that Victor has him in but is struggling to do so. He pulls down on Victor's arm and throws a couple of elbows, but he just feels the grip tighten around his throat even more. He can tell the weak landing blows to his side were easily absorbed. With each second that passes he grows weaker and weaker. His vision slowly fades as everything begins to go dark. The life is literally being squeezed out of him and he begins to twitch and struggle for just one more breath.

Victor can feel Bryce's body start to go limp and just before he dies of asphyxiation he sees Roman running towards him with a piece of block wall in his hand from the explosion. He lets go of Bryce and dodges Roman's attack and takes him to the ground in one motion. After standing back up and looking at Bryce lying motionless and barely breathing, he turns his attention to Roman who is whimpering on the ground, and grabs him by the shirt to lift him up.

He smacks him across the face and pushes him back against the wall. Roman shakes with fear, his heart races and blood flies from his mouth when a hard right cross connects with his jaw. Victor walks to the table to grab a knife and begins walking back to Roman.

"Wait." Dmitri says, struggling to his feet. "Tie him up."

Victor grabs Roman and ties him to the same pole Bryce was tied to. He stands aside, waiting for Dmitri to slowly walk over. Dmitri's broken arm hangs by his side, his shattered hand against his chest. One at a time, Dmitri and Victor take turns punching or kicking Roman. They both laugh when he starts to cry and begs them to stop but they both know it won't end until Roman is dead.

Bryce begins to regain his bearings and shakes the cobwebs from his head. His vision is still a little blurry but he will have to manage. Quietly he stands, gains his balance, and then runs directly at Victor. He lowers his shoulder and hits him in the small of his back. The force of the blow causes Victor to fling his head back while he flies forward. Dmitri can only watch in shock as Victor goes head first into the wall in front of them. His head snaps back and his neck breaks from the impact.

Dmitri tries to run to the table to get his gun, but before he can take his second step, Bryce kicks him in the knee, dropping him to the floor. He punches him across the face causing him to fall flat on his back. After picking up his gun from the ground he walks to Victor and shoots him in the head before returning to Dmitri to stand above him with his gun aimed at his chest, staring in silence.

"I'm sure you feel like a big man now?" Dmitri asks.

"I feel no different than I did yesterday." Bryce responds.

"What are you waiting for?" Dmitri asks with Bryce standing silent over him. "You can't do it, can you?"

"You act like I'm not going to shoot you, but I was just wondering about something." Bryce replies.

"What were you wondering?"

"If you had any last words."

"You know, you and I aren't so different." Dmitri says with a grin.

"No? What would you do to me if I was laying where you are right now?"

"I would torture you. I would make you scream and bleed. Then just before you die from loss of blood I would shoot you and kill you."

"I would say we are very different then." Bryce says, lowering his gun.

"Are you going to tie me up and bring me in?" Dmitri asks while laughing.

"No, I'm just not going to torture you."

Bryce quickly raises his gun and fires two shots.

POP! POP!

Both bullets hit Dmitri in the chest and Bryce watches through the smoke of the gun as Dmitri exhales one last time. Blood runs out of the bullet holes and Dmitri's mouth as his body lays lifeless on the floor.

Bryce lowers his Glock, and walks over to Roman at the pole. "I don't know why you did what you did, but thank you." He says, untying Roman.

"What do you mean?" Roman asks.

"You sent that email to warn Di9 about the attack at our safe house and you got Victor to release his grip from my neck just before he choked me out. You saved my life twice, so again, thank you."

"I just didn't want a nuclear war to happen. I didn't want anything to happen to my wife or son."

"I feel the same way for the same reasons. My son is six years old."

"As is mine."

"Maybe one day the two of them will meet." Bryce says, extending his hand.

"Maybe." Roman says, shaking hands with Bryce. "So what now, can I see my family?"

"Not yet, I need you to do one more thing for me."

"What is it?"

"I need you to take care of that bomb." Bryce says, pointing to the room containing the nuclear weapon.

"What will you do?"

"I'm going to go help my partner." Bryce states, gathering his clothes to get dressed before grabbing his gear and guns. "I'll be back to get you. You do your job, and I'll do mine." He says, stepping into the escape tunnel. "Oh yeah, don't leave this room. I will be back, you have my word."

Roman watches Bryce walk into the tunnel and out of sight and then turns to the bomb and begins to work knowing it won't take long. Finally, he can take a deep breath, knowing Bryce will be back to bring him to his family.

CHAPTER 39

Bryce can smell the scent of fired weapons as he runs through the tunnel with his gun in his right hand and a flashlight in his left. It is eerily quiet and he slows his pace when he sees the dead body on the ground ahead of him. Happy the body isn't John's, he jumps over the goon and continues down the tunnel.

Finally at the end he sees light coming through the crack in the wall. John left the door open just enough to make it easier for him to figure out how to open it quickly. He slides it open, checks to see if the area is clear before climbing out, and exits the tunnel into the sarcophagus and closes the door behind him.

Now outside, he looks around and sees the cemetery, the DS warehouse, and the chapel down the hill connected to the walkway he's on now. Immediately, he starts to sprint towards the chapel and holsters his gun on the way. There are people gathered in the parking lot and once there he sees glass on the ground in two separate parking spaces. He looks across the lot and sees a man standing by a motorcycle all by himself.

"What happened here?" He asks the civilian in Russian, acting like he doesn't know.

"We were all inside, heard some glass break, and a car alarm going off. A couple of us came outside to see a man driving off with my friend's car."

"Was there a woman in the back?"

"There was, how did you know that?"

"Anything else happen?" Bryce asks, ignoring the civilian's question.

"A big guy came shortly after, broke into a car and drove off after the first car."

"What car did the big guy take?"

"A Ferrari."

"And the color?"

"Black." The civilian says, confused. "What's going on?"

"Just trying to track down a couple of thieves." Bryce says, looking at the motorcycle behind the civilian. "Is this your bike by any chance?"

"No, it's my brother-in-law's bike." He says, turning to look at it. "Do you ride?"

"I used to. What is that, a Harley?"

"Harley Davidson XG Street 750. I only know because he brags about it constantly."

Bryce smiles looking at the bike and then back at the civilian. "You seem like a nice guy, and I'm sorry about this, but I'm going to need to take that bike."

"What?"

"The big guy you saw come through and steal the car is a friend of mine. He needs my help and I need to get to him as quickly as I can."

"And if I refuse?"

"Then I'll have to come up with another way to get the bike." Bryce says, lifting his shirt up just enough to show the civilian his Glock.

"You'll shoot me?"

"I don't wan't to, but I need to get to my friend. You either get me the keys or I take care of you and then hot wire the bike. Neither option will take much time." Bryce stares at the civilian waiting for his answer. He begins to grow more and more impatient with each second without a response. "I don't have time for this." He says frustrated, reaching for his gun.

"Wait." The civilian says, putting his hand out telling Bryce to stop. "He keeps the keys hidden in a compartment under the seat."

"Thank you." He says, pulling his shirt down to cover his Glock.

He walks past the man to the motorcycle and looks in the compartment under the seat. Just like the civilian said, the keys are in there along with a pair of sunglasses. After hopping on the Harley, he starts it up and revs the engine a couple times, puts on the sunglasses, then turns on his phone. He puts a Blue Tooth in his ear and nods to the civilian before driving off towards the cemetery's exit.

CHAPTER 40

2:47 P.M.

The motorcycle roars and rumbles as Bryce drives down the only road in the cemetery towards the exit. He presses the button on his Bluetooth and waits for the prompt. "Call the Professor." The phone rings twice before he hears a voice on the other end.

"What." He answers, rudely.

"Professor, I need your help."

"Who is this?"

"It's Bryce."

"I don't know anyone named Bryce."

"It's Agent Maine." He says, frustrated.

"I'm very busy right now, call back later. Better yet, call someone else."

"Professor! Agent Utah needs my help but I don't know where he is. I need you to locate him and lead me to him as quick as you can."

"First of all, do you know how difficult it would be to find him? It's nearly impossible to do it quickly."

"That's why I didn't call anyone else." Bryce says, reaching the entrance to the cemetery and pulling over, still not knowing which way to go.

"Secondly," Professor says after a pause, ignoring Bryce's answer. "I don't help Agents. You're all arrogant and act like you're better than everyone else."

"I saw how Agent Delaware spoke to you when I got my tech from you. Is that how all Agents act?"

The Professor stays silent and thinks back to that day, he remembers how Agent Delaware spoke to him that day and how it made him feel. Most importantly he remembers Bryce sticking up for him even though he didn't have to.

"Almost every single one of them." The Professor finally answers. "Hold on a second."

Bryce can hear the Professor typing away on his keyboard as both men stay silent. He has no idea if he is ignoring him and going about his own business, all he can do is hope that he is helping.

"Got him." The Professor says. "You're about ten miles away and getting farther. He's going about seventy miles per hour on the highway. It will be tough to catch him if you follow his route, but I think I see a way to get to him faster if you're willing to take some risks and listen to what I say."

"I'm all ears."

"Go right out of the cemetery and get on the highway. You're going to take the first exit.

Make a left and head towards the train station."

Bryce takes off like a bullet out of the barrel of a gun and makes the right to head towards the highway. Swerving in and out of traffic and narrowly avoiding cars he can see the highway coming up. "Highway, first exit, left, train station." He confirms, entering the highway at sixty miles per hour. "You still with me?"

"I'm here, I'm just watching you both on the computer. You're going to have to pick up the pace if you want to catch him. If they're going where I think they might be going then this way will cut off five miles of pursuit."

Bryce exits the highway and makes the first left just like the Professor told him to. He sees signs that say the train station is two miles away and picks up the speed again. Whatever he can do to get to the station as quickly as possible is what he'll do which is why he is cutting off cars and driving on the shoulder before speeding through a red light.

"The tracks run parallel to the road you're on now." The Professor says. "Keep going the same direction, but you need to get on the tracks."

"Wait, what?" Bryce asks, thinking he misheard.

"You need to get on the tracks. They run through a tunnel that is a straight shot to where you need to go. If you stay on the road it will lead the wrong direction. Trust me."

"You're the boss."

Bryce turns into the parking lot at the train station and heads towards the tracks but as he approaches he realizes he has a dilemma. The tracks are fenced off and the motorcycle won't fit through the turnstiles. He stops in the middle of the parking lot and scans the area for any spot where he can get through the fence but doesn't see any.

"Why aren't you moving?" The Professor asks.

"I have a problem."

"What is it?"

"Fence."

Continuing to look around he finally sees something that might help him. A flatbed truck is off to the side of the parking lot and near the fence. Without any other options he turns the motorcycle around and drives to the opposite side of the parking lot from the truck. He can hear the train's horn meaning it's beginning to move so he knows he has to hurry.

"You're going the wrong way, is there an opening that way?" The Professor asks.

"Nope, just backing up to get some speed."

"For what?"

"To jump the fence."

CHAPTER 41

3:05 P.M.

Bryce revs the engine and watches the train begin to move towards the tunnel. Smoke fills the air when he does a burnout causing the tires to get a better grip of the pavement. Civilians jump out of the way and scream at him as he peels out and narrowly misses them driving towards the truck. The throttle is rotated back as far as it can go so he can get as much speed as he can in the little amount of space he has. He gets to the central standing positions and hits the ramp of the truck.

As soon as he leaves the ramp, he backs off the throttle to keep the motorcycle level, and leans just enough to get himself and the bike over the fence before returning to a standing position. Just before he lands he goes full throttle and absorbs the impact of the ground with his legs. He sits back down and continues on his way riding parallel to the tracks.

"You need to get ahead of the train." The Professor says.

"Why?"

"There's a tunnel coming up in three miles."

"I won't use the tunnel then, I'll just go around."

"Not an option. Unless you want to back track and waste time I suggest you use the tunnel."

"Can't I just stay behind the train?"

"Not if you want to catch up to Agent Utah. There is a stop inside the tunnel, if you stay behind the train you might as well end the chase. You'll never catch up."

"How far to the tunnel?"

"A little over two miles."

Bryce shifts gears and speeds up. Normally he doesn't like going this fast on a motorcycle, but he has to get ahead of the train to catch up to his friend. Now even with the last car he looks at his speedometer and sees he's going sixty-five miles per hour on grass. He needs to get ahead of the train and doesn't want to go any faster but doesn't have a choice.

"A little over a mile to go, what are you waiting for? Get ahead of the train!" The Professor tells Bryce.

As scared as he is, it's now or never. He cranks down on the throttle and gets to seventy miles per hour. People inside the train start to notice him and begin to panic wondering what is going on and if he'll be safe. Now going seventy-five he can see only two more train cars to pass but the tunnel is coming up very quickly.

"One quarter mile to the tunnel." The Professor says anxiously.

Now even with the lead car of the train it's do or die time. Go for it and risk wiping out or give up and hit the breaks ending the chase all together. With the tunnel bearing down on him he decides to make his move. He speeds up just a little more and feels the corner of the wall graze his arm just as he gets in front of the train and into the tunnel. As much as he would love to let out a sigh of relief he knows it's not the time, he needs to stay focused. One slip up and he would be raw meat on the tracks.

"Okay good, you made it. There is a stop coming up in a little bit. After you pass the stop the tunnel will go on for another two miles and then you'll be out in the open again." The Professor says. "Let me know when you pass the stop."

"Will do." Bryce replies, speeding down the tunnel in front of the train not wanting to go any faster than he already is. He isn't putting any distance between himself and the train, but he isn't losing any distance either.

Ahead on the right he can see the lights of the platform and some people waiting to board. He hears the breaks of the train and looks in his mirror to see the gap between himself and locomotive start to widen. "Where do I need to go when I get out of the tunnel? He asks the

Professor.

"There is a road that runs parallel to the train tracks on the right hand side. You need to get on that road the first chance you get."

"Got it."

"And just so you know, it started raining."

"What? When I went in the tunnel it was clear. How long was I in here?" Bryce asks sarcastically.

"Four minutes." The Professor answers, missing the sarcasm.

"Thanks." Bryce says, shaking his head.

"Do you really not remember how long you were in there?"

"It was a joke."

"I don't get it."

"Never mind. I see the light at the end of the tunnel coming up. How far am I from John?"

"Three miles and closing."

Bryce smiles when he hears the news and exits the tunnel to see the Professor was right. "Hey, did you know it's raining out here?" He asks, messing around with him.

"Very funny." The Professor replies, acknowledging the joke.

Although there is just a light drizzle falling from the sky, it is enough to make the roads a little slick for a motorcycle. Bryce veers onto the road on the right side of the tracks as the rain hits his body like tiny pebbles at this speed. He remembers when he was learning to ride his motorcycle that for every ten miles per hour you increase in speed causes the temperature to drop two degrees and now it's raining. His limbs start to stiffen and go numb from the cold and his core temperature drops from riding in just a t-shirt but he has to continue no matter what.

"There is an overpass in one mile. There will be a fork in the road immediately after the overpass. Take the road to the right." The Professor states.

"First right after the overpass." Bryce responds, acknowledging what he just heard.

"If Agent Utah doesn't make any turns then this road will lead you right to him."

He does as he's instructed and makes the turn onto the road that will hopefully lead to John. The road has two lanes, one in each direction and is lined by trees on both sides just off the shoulder. There isn't much traffic which is good, not as many cars to swerve around on a slick road. The scenery reminds him of some of the roads near his hometown, long country roads with little to no traffic. He starts to daydream about his wife and son and unknowingly starts to slow down.

"Agent Maine, Utah is a mile in front of you on this road." The Professor says.

Bryce snaps out of the trance he's in and regains focus. He speeds back up and can see two cars going pretty fast up ahead. "Black Ferrari." He says out loud.

"What?" The Professor asks confused.

"Nothing, I can see him up ahead. Thanks, Professor. I owe you."

"Yes, you do. Please don't interrupt me again, I'm very busy." The Professor says and stays silent for a couple seconds before speaking again. "Good luck, Bryce."

Bryce smiles and hears the Professor disconnect. Now with Agent Utah in sight he refocuses his attention on helping his friend. "I'm on my way, John."

CHAPTER 42

3:18 P.M.

With help from the Professor, only half a mile separates the two Di9 Agents. Bryce keeps his eyes on the black Ferrari until it drives over a hill and out of sight. Already gaining ground quickly, he speeds up even more to get to the top of the hill to regain sight of his friend. Once there, he notices a speeding car coming down a side street and it's not slowing down. He looks at John's car, then back at the car on the side street, and then back at John.

"Oh no." He says to himself, seeing the two cars are on a collision course.

Tiffany's car passes the side street just before the speeding car comes bursting out onto the main road and slams into the back, right side of John's car. The Ferrari spins out of control and off the road and a cloud of dirt and dust kick up before slamming into a tree.

"John!" Bryce screams, continuing to drive.

The back, left of the car just behind the tire is demolished from the collision. The engine is smoking while it sits idle and slightly wrapped around the tree.

Tiffany's car doesn't even slow down and continues down the road to escape. The damage on the car from the side street is no better than the black Ferrari. The front end is smashed and the engine smokes while it sits in the middle of the road. Bryce watches three doors open on the car and three goons get out. Each of them are dressed exactly the same as the men that were with Tiffany at the meeting with Dmitri. He can only assume that they work for Tiffany and were called to get John off their tail. All three goons pull out their pistols and spread out walking towards the Ferrari.

Bryce can see his friend slouched over in the front seat and not moving. He looks at Tiffany's car and then back at the goons getting closer to John and wonders if he should stop Tiffany or save his friend. Frustratedly he watches her car make a turn and go out of sight. He knows he should go after her but he has to save his friend and has to do something about it fast.

Two of the goons slowly approach John's car from either side with their guns drawn, while the third stays behind near their car. Bryce notices a car to his right start to slow down and immediately has an idea as he pulls up next to it. He lines up his motorcycle with the goon by his car and swings his left leg over the motorcycle.

With just enough strength he jumps off the bike and onto the car riding next to him.

With everything going on, the driver of the car didn't even notice Bryce next to him until he hears a loud thud on the roof. The driver slows enough to make him slide down the windshield and onto the hood of the car, causing the driver to slam on the breaks. Bryce rolls off the car, lands on his feet, and pulls his Glock in one motion.

POP! POP!

Bryce takes down both goons with two shots just before they open the door to John's car. Before the third goon can realize what is going on, he turns to look back just in time to see the sliding motorcycle coming right at him. It breaks both legs on impact and then drags him underneath it before slamming him into his own car, pinning him and killing him.

Bryce turns and nods at the driver of the car he just rolled off of and continues to walk towards John, his gun still aimed and on high alert. He gets to the car and sees the goons are definitely dead, their blood and brains ooze out of their heads onto the ground. Holstering his weapon, he sees the airbags of the Ferrari have deployed, and John is still slouched over and unconscious. He's badly bruised and very bloody, but he's alive.

"John!" He yells before opening the door to shake his fellow Agent, trying to wake him up.

He pauses for a second before shaking him again. In the blink of an eye John wakes up, grabs his gun, and points it at Bryce.

"John, it's me! It's Bryce!" He says, smacking the gun aside and grabbing John's arm.

"What are you doing here?" He asks, trying to shake off the cobwebs.

"I came to help you. It's a good thing I did, you look pretty bad."

"I look bad? John asks before pausing. "I was just in an accident, what's your excuse?"

"I was fighting the Executioner while you were out joy riding." Bryce says sarcastically, helping John out of the car.

"Where is he now?"

"Executed."

"Where's Tiffany?"

"She got away. That car that hit you was her goons. I saw it happen."

"You saw it happen and you let her get away?"

"I was down the road when it happened, but I was able to see it. There's no way I could've saved you and gotten her too. It was you or her."

John stretches his back and arms and looks at the Ferrari. He then notices the two goons shot in the head by his car and the third lying under a motorcycle. "Thank you for making the choice you did." He says, putting his hand on Bryce's shoulder. "How did you find me anyway?"

"I called the Professor." Bryce answers.

"And he helped you?" John asks, perplexed.

"I'm here, aren't I? Why do you ask as if he wouldn't help?"

"He doesn't like Agents. He only does the bare minimum because that's his job, and Washington makes him when it comes to helping us. He won't even call Agents by their real name."

"Interesting." Bryce says, remembering the last thing the Professor said to him before he hung up. "Maybe Washington was standing next to him when I called."

"So what now?" John asks, grabbing his shoulder which is in pain from the crash.

"I need to go back to the DS Warehouse."

"What for?"

"I left Roman there to dismantle the bomb and I need to go back and get him. I can also look for any other information about DS or any other terrorists groups associated with them that I can get. I figured it would be easier to do that while I'm not getting shot at."

"Need back up?" John asks, extending his fist.

"Yup." Bryce replies as he bumps fists with John.

Both men walk to the goons' car and drive off towards the DS Warehouse.

CHAPTER 43

DS Warehouse

4:15 P.M.

Roman Bovanovski keeps looking up to see if Bryce has come back for him yet. It is eerily quiet and the smell and sight of dead bodies freak him out. Finally, after a lot of hard work, he is finished, and the bomb is nothing more than scrap metal. He stands and stretches his back and cracks his neck before heading into the room where he saved Bryce's life.

The stench is almost too much to handle and he walks towards the door. He passes Victor's dead body crunched up agains the wall and then approaches Dmitri on the way out. Even though he's dead, he still terrifies him.

After getting past Dmitri he grabs his phone from the table and sees it's a quarter after four and Bryce still hasn't returned. He walks to the escape tunnel to take a peek inside and wonders if he is ever going to come back at all. Although Bryce told him to stay in the room, he needs a change of scenery. Nobody likes being confined in a room with a bunch of dead bodies, and his nose could use a break with some fresh air.

He walks into the hall and finally takes a deep breath without feeling the urge to gag and looks through his phone. Badly he wants to contact his wife to tell her he's okay but knows he can't call her without her getting manic. Instead of calling he decides to email her instead, then she can know what's going on and that he's okay and hopefully he'll be home before she even sees it.

Stefaniya,

I'm sorry I haven't contacted you, but I've been held against my will by Dmitri Sachenkov, the leader of DS. It's a long story that I will tell you when I come home.

An American agency called Di9 came to stop what DS was doing, and a man named Bryce Stone rescued me. I am waiting for him to return so he can bring me home to you and Alexei.

Don't worry about me, Bryce is a good person and he will keep me safe until I am home holding you in my arms. I love you so much and I can't wait to see you both!

Roman

Roman puts the phone in his pocket and walks back into the room where all the dead bodies are. Now that he's had the fresh air in his lungs the smell in the room is even worse and he can't take it anymore. He knows Bryce told him to stay put, but he leaves again and decides to head outside for some real fresh air.

He walks down the hallway towards the front door and nobody is around. The exit is in his sight; just a few more steps and he'll be outside, hopefully seeing his family soon. Now, almost at the front door, he is startled by what sounds like something opening, followed by a Beep. Beep. Beep Beep Beep Beep……

CHAPTER 44

DS Warehouse

4:32 P.M.

Bryce and John pull up to the DS Warehouse, the only members around are the ones that are dead and lying on the ground. There are no signs of movement and it is quiet and calm. They stay on high alert as they exit the car with their guns in hand looking around the building. Both men have no idea if there are any other DS members around, and they don't want to find out the hard way.

"All clear." John says.

"Then let's head inside." Bryce replies. John nods and takes the lead, starting to walk towards the front door. "Not that way."

"Why not?"

"I set up a black urchin inside the front door. We should go around back."

"Good idea."

Bryce takes the lead and heads towards the back of the building with John close behind. They move like a well oiled machine and cover each other with each step along the way passing multiple dead DS bodies.

"You took out all these guys yourself?" John asks, continuing to scan the area.

"Just got lucky I guess." Bryce answers humbly.

"Taking out this many guys all by yourself is not lucky. Doing it in an unknown environment with no idea what is around each corner makes you a legend. I see why Washington wanted you in the field so bad."

"And yet, I wouldn't be here now if you hadn't come along when you did."

"Every Agent needs help at some point. Most Agents wouldn't even have made it inside the building in this situation."

Embarrassed and humbled by the compliment, Bryce doesn't quite know how to respond, so he changes the subject. "How did you know where to find me?"

"We knew that Dmitri was in the cemetery somewhere, I just had to hack the Di9 mainframe to get your exact location."

"You know how to hack stuff? You'll have to show me how to do that sometime." Bryce says before stopping. "We're at the back door." He grabs the handle and waits for John to let him know he's ready. With his gun in his hand, John gives a nod to Bryce, who quickly opens the door. The area is clear, so both Agents enter the building and begin looking around.

"What are we looking for?" John asks.

"Roman Bovanovski. He's the guy that told us where to find Dmitri. I left him here to dismantle the bomb when I came to find you."

"Where's the bomb?"

"In the basement. In a room adjacent to the one I was in."

"Then let's go get him."

CHAPTER 45

John enters the room where all the deceased bodies are, with Bryce right behind him. "You killed all these guys too?" He asks, seeing Dmitri and Victor along with the other DS members on the ground.

"Your blast did most of the work; I just took care of the rest."

"Where's your boy? I thought you said he'd be down here."

"He is, he's right in there." Bryce says, pointing to the door in the back of the room.

"That's where the bomb is too?"

"Yup, they built the room specifically to build bombs so they couldn't be detected."

Both men walk towards the door with their weapons drawn. They nod at each other, and then John opens the door so Bryce can peek his head in to make sure there won't be a sneak attack.

"We're good." He says, lowering his gun.

John follows Bryce into the room and is perplexed. "I thought you said he was in here." He says, holstering his gun.

"He was." Bryce responds, checking out the bomb and seeing that it's been worked on. "It looks like he disabled and dismantled the bomb like I asked. He took out the plutonium block and left it on the side. He was supposed to stay here until I got back."

"Maybe he had to use the bathroom." John says, examining a piece of the bomb.

"Yeah, maybe." Bryce says, distracted. "Something doesn't seem right though."

"Why do you say that?"

"Because he's not here."

"Maybe he went to get something to eat or to smoke. Maybe he finished doing what you asked him to do and then went home to see his family. Wouldn't you do that?"

"I probably would."

"There would be no reason for him to hang around once he was done. How would he even know that you would come back?"

"You're probably right, something just seems off and I can't put my finger on it."

"You want to look for him don't you." John says, already knowing the answer.

"I think we should." Bryce replies.

"Okay, let's do it. We can look for some intel too. Grab the plutonium."

Bryce and John leave the room with the plutonium and head out of the basement into the big room in the back of the building.

"What kind of intel are you looking for?" Bryce asks, leading John to the surveillance room.

"Anything with info about DS: their plans, who helped them, what intel they had. Basically anything that would help us figure out where Tiffany is heading or might be, and anyone else we would have to worry about in the future."

"Well, here is the surveillance room. There are six areas monitored around the building that you can see from here."

John walks in and heads straight for the monitors on the wall while Bryce stands guard by the door. "Where is this?" He asks, pointing to the monitor on the wall that shows four doors in a hallway. "It looks like it might be offices."

"That's upstairs." Bryce says, walking over to John. "How do you know they are offices?"

"I don't, but you don't put a camera on a closet door. You put it somewhere that is important. Somewhere you'd want to see if anyone is going in."

"We can't get there."

"Why not?"

"The only way up there is the staircases by the front door, and I put an urchin there. See, I put it right...." Bryce says before stopping mid sentence, when he sees the monitor that shows inside the front door. He turns and runs out of the room, down the hall, and towards the front of the building. John watches him on the monitor put his hands on his head in disgust and then leaves the room to join his fellow Agent.

"I'm guessing that's your guy?" John asks a visibly shaken Bryce.

"Roman Bovanovski, nuclear physicist. Husband and father." Bryce says, crouched over the body and looking through his wallet to show John a picture of Roman with his family." He warned Di9 about the attack on our safe house while I was there. I told him I would protect him and get him home safe to see his family and I failed him."

"His death is not on you. You never asked him to come here; he did that on his own." John says, trying to make Bryce feel better.

"Dmitri made him come here. He threatened his family if he didn't do what they asked. He was in my possession, and he died because I left him here."

"You didn't do anything wrong. You had a choice to make, and you made the right one. He had a choice to make and chose wrong. He put himself in this predicament by coming here. You didn't kill him."

"I set the urchin." Bryce reminds John.

"Look, man, things happen. You may think that you got him killed, but you came back to save him. Look at you, you were in a fight with one of the baddest men on the planet, and it shows. You got on a bike to save me and then came all the way back here to help a man who made a nuclear bomb for someone who wanted to use it on our country. That doesn't make you a bad guy. That makes you a hero." John pauses and puts his hand on Bryce's shoulder. "I'm glad you're on my side. If you will risk your life for a bad guy that you don't even know, then I know what you would do for me. And a man like that I would fight to the death for. I would go to battle with you any day of the week."

"Thanks, John." Bryce says, standing up. "He wasn't a bad guy though."

"What's that?" John asks, confused.

"He wasn't a bad guy."

"Didn't he make a weapon that would've killed millions of Americans and probably would've started a Third World War? Sounds like a bad guy to me."

"He didn't have a choice."

"I'm not saying that he wasn't in a tough situation, but everyone has a choice to either do what's right or what's wrong."

"What would you have done in his shoes?"

"I would've found a way to protect my family, and I would've done what was right."

Both men stay silent as Bryce thinks about what John is saying. He knows he is right about there always being an option to choose between right and wrong; it's just not always an easy choice. John pats his friend on the back and walks towards the stairs.

"Come on, lets head upstairs."

CHAPTER 46

4:59 P.M.

The two Agents reach the top of the stairs, see that it's clear, and holster their weapons. All four doors are shut, so they walk to the door on the left to start their search.

"It's locked." Bryce says, trying to open the door. "I can pick the lock though." He looks down to take a knife out of his pocket, and before he can look back up he hears a loud thud. John's size fourteen shoe strikes the door and swings it wide open.

"Lock picked." He says, looking inside the room. "There's nothing here that can help us. Let's check the next room."

Both men walk to the next door, and John grabs the handle, which is also locked. "You want to pick this one too?" He asks sarcastically.

"Go ahead, your way is faster."

John takes a step back and sends his foot towards the door with a front kick. The trim around the lock splinters and shatters as the door swings open. "Bingo." He says, looking at some computers in the room along with some filing cabinets. "Watch the door." He says before waking over to the computer, putting down his gun, and turning on the monitor.

"There's something I have to tell you." Bryce says from the door, facing the hallway.

"What is it?" John asks.

"This isn't going to be easy for me to say."

"Just say it." John says while typing on the keyboard.

"There was someone from Di9 working with DS."

Bryce can hear John stop typing and both men turn to face each other.

"You know that for a fact?" John asks.

Bryce stays silent but nods in disappointment.

"Who?"

"You were right, it wasn't Dakota."

"Who was it?" John asks again, more sternly.

"It was my brother." Bryce says, dropping his head and looking away.

"No, I don't believe that. He was killed in Philadelphia."

"They wanted us to believe he was dead."

"How do you know this?"

"His body is downstairs."

"You killed him?"

"No, Dmitri did. They told me everything though, I don't think they expected you to show up."

John stays silent not knowing what to say. He turns around and starts searching the computer again. "Are you going to tell Washington?" He asks without looking away from the screen.

"I think I have to." Bryce responds sadly.

"You don't have to do anything. We can tell Washington that we never found out. I'll go along with whatever you want to tell him."

"Thanks, John. I think I should tell him, it's the right thing to do." Bryce says, facing John again.

"You okay?"

"I hate that it was Travis, I would've never guessed that in a million years. Wasn't a big fan of seeing him shot right in front of me either, but I'll be okay."

"Good, I don't want to have to hug you or anything like that." John says, making Bryce chuckle. "I could tell Washington for you if you want. I'm sure it won't be easy for you to tell him."

"I appreciate that but I think I should tell him. As much as I don't want to." An awkward silence fills the room while John types away. "Did you find anything yet?" Bryce asks trying to break the tension and change the subject.

"Oh man, did I ever. Come check this out."

Bryce walks over to the computer and is stunned by what he sees. "Holy crap, that's a lot of files."

"Looks like they have info on everyone in their organization and everyone else they've ever dealt with." John says, scrolling through the files.

"Wait, did you see that? Scroll back up."

"What did you see?" John asks, slowly scrolling up the page.

"There." Bryce points to the screen. "They have a file labeled Di9."

John opens the folder and he and Bryce can't believe what they see. Their jaws drop and their eyes widen from what they are reading.

"Every Di9 Agent is in here. Their real names and code names, addresses, families, and their missions. They even have intel on other sectors of Di9." John states.

"My brother must have told them everything he knew. Look, they have Washington and the Professor in here. There's Amy and Mike too." Bryce shakes his head in disappointment. "What if DS shared this info?"

"We need to make a copy of it and run analysis to see if they did." John says, grabbing two flash drives to transfer the info over to both of them.

"What are we going to do when you're done making the copies?" Bryce asks.

"Destroy the originals." John says, pulling the second flash drive out.

"So you're just going to delete everything?"

"Kind of." John picks up his gun and fires

it into the computer where the hard drive is. The computer immediately shuts off as smoke starts to exit the bullet hole. He does that to every other computer in the room while Bryce looks on. "You said that bomb is disabled, right?"

"It looked like it to me, why do you ask?"

"We need to make sure nobody gets their hands on anything in here or sees what has happened."

"So what do we do?"

"Burn it down." John says, looking into Bryce's eyes. "Come on, lets go."

Bryce and John head downstairs to the kitchen and turn the knobs on the oven to high but don't ignite the burners. Gas pours out of the range as both men leave the kitchen and exit the building but not before John grabs a few things from the kitchen.

Now outside, Bryce watches John make a Molotov cocktail and place it on the window looking into the kitchen. They walk far enough away from the building to be out of range of what's about to happen and turn to face the building.

John aims his gun and begins to fire until he hits the cocktail. The bullet breaks the bottle and the glass window simultaneously causing the kitchen to be quickly engulfed by flames. It doesn't take long for the gas in the air to ignite.

KABOOM!

The back half of the building explodes

and is turned to rubble while the rest of the building begins to burn. "Let's go home." John says to Bryce. He stands alone for a few seconds in silence, watching the building burn before turning to follow John to the car.

CHAPTER 47

Bryce and Kaya's Home

Saturday, July 11th, 2026

8:00 A.M.

The sun has been up for a while and it is quiet and peaceful. Bryce lies in bed tired and worn out. His body is bruised and throbs from the pain of his battle with DS. Every breath he takes is a struggle and every time he rolls over he hurts. The light shines through the window onto his face as he reaches for the bottle of pills to relieve the pain. Even opening that tiny bottle makes his body wince. He pops a couple pills in his mouth and swallows them down without a drink before he lays his head back on the pillow.

Wanting to fall back asleep is every man's dream in the morning, but even more so when you're trying to escape the pain of a beating. As much as he would like to fall asleep he can't escape the sunlight on his face. He knows it's going to hurt, but he begins to roll over to get out of the light. Moaning and groaning with each movement he tries to get his swollen body to roll to its side.

Finally he gets to his side away from the window and faces his wife. Although not his intention, all the moaning and movement caused Kayla to wake up. "What are you smiling at? She asks still groggy from the sleep.

"I'm just happy to see you." Bryce says lovingly.

"How are you feeling?"

"Not so bad anymore."

"I guess the pills are working?"

"Not yet. You're just the first thing I saw when I woke up. That's better than any pill."

Kayla smiles and leans in to give Bryce a kiss. Just as their lips touch her phone rings and she starts to roll over to answer it. Bryce puts his hand on her hip and tries to pull her back over to him.

"Let me answer it." She's says as Bryce gives her another kiss.

"Just let it go to voicemail."

"Let me just make sure it's not my parents. They are watching Michael you know."

Bryce grunts in frustration and takes his hand away from Kayla's hip.

"It's Di9." Kayla says before she even answers.

"Put it on speaker." Bryce responds.

"Hello." She answers.

"Kayla, it's Washington. I wanted to check in on you and Bryce. How's he doing?" He asks.

"He's doing fine, it's nice to have my husband back. He's right here next to me. I have you on speaker but I can take you off if you want to speak to him in private?"

"No, it's okay, I want to talk to you both anyway. How are you doing, Bryce? I didn't call at a bad time, did I?"

"You have perfect timing as always, sir." Bryce says sarcastically. "I'm doing okay, I'm pretty banged up, but I'll survive."

"Glad to hear. John told me how beat up you are."

"You talked to John already?"

"He came in last night to drop off the flash drives for analysis. He told me everything that happened."

"He told you that Tiffany got away and about Travis?"

"Yes he did."

"I'm sorry that I let her get away."

"Don't worry about her. She'll slip up and we'll get her. You made the right call to save your fellow Agent."

"Thank you, sir."

"I did have to suspend John though."

"What? Why?" Bryce asks confused.

"He disobeyed a direct order. I told him not to go to Russia."

"Sir, if he didn't go to Russia then I

wouldn't be alive right now. There would also be a nuclear weapon going off right about now too."

"Just because it worked out doesn't make it right to disobey orders. If I let him slide then everyone will start disobeying orders. We wouldn't be Di9 then."

"Yes, sir, understood." Bryce pauses for a second, trying to regain his composure from being upset that John was suspended for saving him. "What did you want to talk to us both about?" He asks, changing the subject.

"When Kayla came in the other night we started talking......"

"They offered me a job!" Kayla interrupts excitedly.

"Really? That's awesome!" Bryce says ecstatically. "What will you be doing?"

"We thought we would put her in the intelligence division. With her background in mathematics and being a college professor that it would be right up her alley." Washington answers.

"When does she start?" Bryce asks.

"Monday. That's why I called so early. I wanted to tell you to take the weekend off to rest and spend some time with your family."

"Thank you, sir."

"We'll get Kayla situated and get you debriefed. Until then, enjoy your weekend. See you both Monday."

"Yes, sir." Bryce says before pausing. "Sir, I

have to ask you something."

"What is it?"

"When I called the other night, you said that you might've put me in the field too soon. Am I not going to be an Agent anymore?"

"That thought never crossed my mind."

"So why did you say what you said then?"

"I'm a manager. I have to manage every Agent and every single person that works for Di9. I need to know everything about them and what makes them tick. I never had any intention of taking you out of the field, I just said what you needed to hear to keep you focused and to get the job done."

"So you knew how I would respond by saying I shouldn't be in the field based on what you know about me."

"That's right. You're a man that wants to prove people wrong when they say you can't do something. You could've taken your Mother's name like Travis did when you were old enough but instead you worked hard for the approval of your Father. I felt that if I said you weren't ready that you would prove me wrong by getting the job done and seeking my approval, and I was right."

"Thank you, sir." Bryce says, not knowing what else to say.

"Now you kids enjoy your weekend. Well done, Bryce."

"Thank you, sir."

"Thank you, Washington." Kayla says, right after.

Washington hangs up the phone and Kayla does the same. She can't stop smiling about staring her job at Di9 and rolls over to face Bryce. "Do you think us working together will cause any problems? She asks nervously.

"Not at all. I think it will be good for us actually." Bryce responds.

"How so?"

"I hated having to lie to you about what I was doing or where I was going. Now I won't have to."

Kayla smiles and leans in to give Bryce a peck on the lips and then pulls away to stare into his eyes. He leans in aggressively and passionately kisses her while rubbing his hand through her hair before kissing her neck and behind her ear.

"Now, about that de-briefing." He whispers to Kayla.

Kayla looks at her husband and bites her lip before she rolls on top of him, takes her tank top off, and presses her lips against his. As she slides her hand down his chest she stops kissing him and puts her lips right next to his ear and whispers.

"Yes, sir, Agent Maine."

ACKNOWLEDGEMENT

To my Father: Thank you for all You do. I couldn't do this without You. Whether I sell one copy or a million, all honor and praise is Yours.

To my wife: Thank you so much for putting up with me. I could not have done this without your hard work and dedication. This book is just as much yours as it is mine.

To my son: Thank you for helping me push through when I wanted to take a break. Thank you for your ideas and support!

To my parents: Thank you for reading and re-reading this until you wree sick of it and still encouraging me and motivating me to finish.

To my cousins: Thank you for your help and being my trampoline when I needed to bounce ideas off of someone.

To my brother-in-law: Thank you for telling me what I needed to hear and for your support.

To everyone who bought this book: Thank you from the bottom of my heart.